EDITORIAL REVIEW

Dragoria: The Lost Dragon Realm
Book One

DRAGON MOON

"*Dragon Moon* sets high stakes, telling of one apprentice sorceress's struggle to prove herself amid a clash of kingdoms ruled by mysterious and powerful magic users. This fantasy novel will appeal to fans of *Harry Potter* and *Dungeons and Dragons* with its exuberant weaving together of old lore and modern tropes." Caroline E., Proofreader, Red Adept Editing

DRAGON MOON

DRAGORIA: THE LOST DRAGON REALM

KATRINA COPE

COSY BURROW BOOKS

DRAGORIA: THE LOST DRAGON
REALM BOOKS

DRAGON MOON

Dragon Moon
Ebook first published in USA in January 2023 by Cosy Burrow
Books
Ebook first published in Great Britain in January 2023 by Cosy
Burrow Books

www.katrinacopebooks.com

ISBN: 978-0-6455102-4-9

❀ Created with Vellum

Michael ~ your support means the world to me

Dragon Moon

Shadows hide our true friends as the light illuminates our enemies.

Recruited as a magical apprentice, Samara trains under a head sorceress with other apprentices. The Sacred Flame coterie is renowned for its reign and raises powerful magic wielders—each member bonds with a familiar to boost the strength of their power beyond any ordinary sorcerer's. It is an honor to be recruited by the coterie and fight the force rising against the kingdoms.

Samara's service means that she can help protect the kingdoms, and her family will be provided for and removed from slavery and poverty. Except Samara can't find a familiar. Having no familiar means she must overcome a formidable opponent that far outweighs her in size and outmatches her in fighting ability. If she fails, she will no longer be a coterie member and will end up either dead or enslaved, and the Sacred Flame coterie will no longer provide for her family.

In her darkest hour, she meets a sarcastic and grumpy dragon who curses himself for finding her companionship appealing. Together, they uncover the secrets of their world and find trouble that tests their skills.

CHAPTER ONE

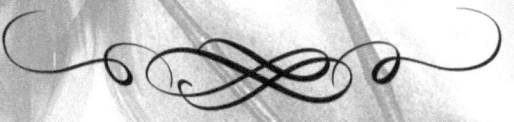

Samara's fingers lost their grip on the bowstring as magic suddenly pulsed through her veins, catching her off guard. The arrowhead sliced through leaves and twigs as it disappeared into the thicket, lost in the fog instead of the marked target on the tree trunk. She was familiar with the pulse, for it was the call of the great sorceress, Callista, requiring all the apprentices to return to the lodge. Not knowing where to search for her lost arrow, she pulled from her magic source and practiced her latest skill—calling items to her. With her palm outstretched, she waited as the arrow shot back through the shrubs. The shaft landed directly across her palm, and she wrapped her fingers around it.

A knife whistled softly past Samara's ear, slicing off strands of her pink hair before embedding in the tree trunk with a *thud*. Samara froze, her wide eyes fixated on the knife, before turning to the thrower. Though it was hard to see through the thick fog that had settled over their training ground, eventually, a shock of brilliant-blue hair appeared as the thrower approached, wearing a broad grin.

At the sight of his handsome face, Samara gasped. "Kaine, you nearly hit me." She tossed her arrow back into the quiver on her back, sucked in a deep breath, and let the smell of the forest wash its calmness over her.

"I didn't, though, did I?" Overconfident, as always, Kaine threaded the knife in his hand back into its holder behind his back and leaned past Samara to yank the wayward knife out of the tree trunk. His smugness washed away, replaced with a smidgen of remorse when he pulled back and took in Samara's irritated expression. "Sorry. That wasn't my intention. The fog is extremely thick. I didn't realize you were there. I would've called one of the healers if I'd hit you."

Samara crossed her arms, the leather of her fitted tunic groaning in protest. Kaine moved closer and clasped her upper arms gently as he looked deep into her eyes, concern marring their blueness.

Her heart melted slightly and her annoyance with it. Feeling uncomfortably sensitive within his grasp, she pulled away, taking in the surrounding area. "The fog is thick, and it accumulated quickly. Is this Mist's doing?"

Kaine observed the fog, and a breeze pushed a strand of his hair over his handsome face. The blue color was shocking, as was the deep pink in her hair, but for the Sacred Flame coterie apprentices, the teachers, and the head sorceress, brightly colored hair was a symbol of importance, a level of their magic's power, and an honored mark from the head of the coterie. Only magic bearers of great talent were bestowed with the initial marking from Callista. When Callista discovered the apprentices and teachers, she activated the color of their magic, and the color manifested in their hair. After the initial marking, the magic wielder was expected to upkeep the color as an expression of gratitude for being chosen by the sorceress.

Brushing the strand away from his eyes and briefly exposing his rounded human ear, Kaine winked at Samara. The move was tacky and over-confident, but Samara couldn't help the fluttering of her heart. A smirk grew across his face as though he could hear her heartbeat, and he brushed her chin with his hand. Her cheeks heated, and his grin widened. Having lived twenty summers, he was the oldest apprentice of the coterie and only two years her senior.

She pulled away and looped her bow over her quiver, unsure whether Kaine liked her, or if he was playing with her. He was the heartthrob of the coterie and was liked by many of the witches. He seemed to enjoy the attention, which confused Samara more when trying to decipher his intentions.

Hooking a strand of loose hair over her semi-pointed ear, she asked, "Well, do you know or not?"

Her sudden abruptness seemed to pull him back to her question. "It wouldn't surprise me if Mist created this fog."

"Is she upset?" Samara asked. Mist's real name was Kanara, but because of her ability to create fog and mist, the students had nicknamed her accordingly. The creation of fog was one of Mist's magic gifts. It wasn't elemental magic. Each student seemed to excel in creating magic others couldn't. Sometimes the student's gifts grew uncontrollable when their emotions were elevated.

"Didn't you hear? Mist has found her familiar."

Samara gaped at Kaine in shock. "What?" Although she was happy for Mist, she had only been at the academy for six months. "Where did she find it?"

"In the forest, of course." He indicated the vast

number of trees and the amount of vegetation surrounding them. "It's usually where we find animals out here."

She rolled her eyes. "I get that, but you and I have been here for a year, and we haven't found our familiars yet."

"Ouch! Way to make a guy feel good." Kaine screwed up his face but still managed to look striking.

Somehow, Samara felt that he didn't ever feel bad about himself, yet she replied, "I didn't mean it as a way to put you down. After all, none of the other students have bonded with a familiar yet, and Mist has been at the lodge for less time than many of us." She tugged at the back of her tunic, which rubbed against her neck, and huffed. "I feel like I'm not even close to finding mine."

He smiled, showing off his perfectly straight teeth. "I was only joking. I'm sure I'll find my familiar soon." He stretched, accentuating his tall height.

Samara resisted the urge to roll her eyes. He was always so confident. Then she chided herself for feeling nervous around him. She didn't want to be wooed like all the other females at the academy.

He placed a hand on her shoulder. "Come on. We've been called back to the institute. Didn't you feel Callista's call? I did, and I was deep in the forest."

"Yeah. I felt it. I was about to return to the lodge when your knife just missed me."

They made their way through the thick forest, finding it difficult to weave through the trees and foliage shrouded in fog. Eventually, they reached the dense clumps of pine trees that surrounded the building indicating it was near. Their boots crunched on the pine needles, releasing the smell of pine.

Samara loved that scent. Since she'd been invited to move to the coterie's apprentice housing, it gave her a sense of belonging. She had been chosen to live and be trained by the realm's most gifted magic wielders, and she hoped to live there for a long time, giving her a chance to learn the depths of her magic and serve under the head sorceress. Being chosen had improved her life and also her family's. They'd been homeless and living as servants, but Callista had been taking care of them by providing them with a profitable farm. For as long as Samara stayed at the coterie, abiding by its rules, and served the kingdoms under Callista, her family could continue to manage the property. Callista had proved to be a caring and compassionate leader. It made it easier for Samara to want to learn and work under her.

Each of the students' families had benefited somehow when Callista selected them. What each family needed in return varied, whether it be prestige, wealth, food, or something else. Samara's family had needed help to set them on a more stable path.

Kaine and Samara passed through several hundred feet of pine forest, the fog slowly clearing, before they reached an open plain with a large stone building only visible to the building's occupants. The wild grass whipped around their ankles as they crossed the field before climbing the stone stairs. Bare deciduous trees wrapped around the staircase and over parts of the stone railing, adding to the effect of a lack of building to the unseeing eye.

The large wooden doors were ajar, waiting for the students to return. As soon as Samara stepped past the boundary, the doors closed behind her and locked. They must be the last students to return. Many of them spent their time indoors during their free time, when Samara decided to practice her archery. Even though they were there to learn magic, mastering a weapon was also important.

Samara glanced over her shoulder at the doors— only to be met with the piercing yellow eyes of a black jaguar.

CHAPTER TWO

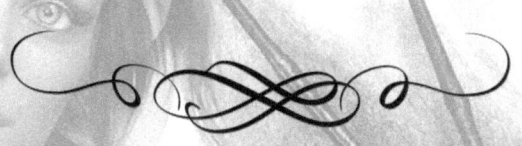

Samara swallowed her fear. The jaguar was only Mystique, Callista's familiar. Even so, she couldn't help feeling a sense of caution every time she saw her, despite the sorceress's assurance that they were safe.

Her arrows clattered together in her quiver as she spun to head toward the hall. Mystique sauntered behind her, and the apprentice's pace quickened over the stone floor of the foyer. She slung her quiver and bow onto a hook near the door and joined the gathering, leaving Kaine as the last to enter.

Gray stone walls encased the room. Windows broke the monotony on one side and had been opened to let in the forest's fresh air. A gust of wind blew in a few yellow leaves from a deciduous tree planted just outside, and they danced across the cold stone floor.

Callista sat on the far side of the room, framed by a display of fresh flowers lining the back of her over-sized chair made from intertwined branches. Every day, the array of flowers changed to whichever ones Callista decided to magically decorate the chair with for the day. The chair was large enough to be a small throne, and Callista leaned against the backrest, her legs crossed at the knees and covered with her long, flowing gown. Her long lilac hair's upper layers were tied back, revealing her pointed elven ears. An elegant golden diadem laced across her forehead and dipped toward her nose. Her striking blue eyes landed on Samara then Kaine, and her grip on the armrests tightened as a slight scowl creased her flawless skin. She looked to be in her thirties yet was more than five hundred years of age. Her gaze was intense, giving the impression of displeasure. "Nice of you to decide to join us."

All eyes trained on the late arrivals.

Samara hurried down the aisle between the rows of chairs and scurried to an empty seat. "Sorry, head sorceress. I was deep in the forest, practicing my archery."

Kaine's baritone voice followed Samara's as he scrambled to the last remaining seat on the opposite side of the room. "That goes for me, too, except I was practicing my knife skills."

The edges of Callista's mouth turned up, followed by a softening of her eyes. "Of course you were. I hope you found the practice beneficial."

"All practice is beneficial, head sorceress," Samara answered, nervously tucking her hands between her thighs.

Callista nodded, uncrossing her legs, and her gaze traveled to Mystique prowling down the aisle, her tail raised with confidence. The brown outlines of the cat's black spots shimmered over her lean muscles as they moved, her eyes surveying each student as she passed them.

Samara pulled her arms tight to her sides. Once, she had attempted to pet the familiar after Callista insisted that the jaguar was friendly. She'd quickly regretted that decision when the cat displayed a vast array of pointed teeth and hissed. Never again would Samara try to touch the cat.

Mystique climbed the two steps to Callista's chair and rubbed against the sorceress's outstretched hand before circling the chair and lying in front of her feet, her head resting on her large black front paws.

Callista fixed her gaze on the twenty apprentices, who were all in their late teens and surrounded by the five teachers. Although it was the coterie's place of learning, there weren't many students. The school was designed only for the select few Callista decided were worthy. Still, even though the building was invisible to outsiders, word had spread.

Samara's gaze wandered as she took in the magic students and the experienced sorceresses and sorcerers who had taken them under their wings. She had learned much magic and how to control it since she had been there. She was thankful for the teachers' guidance and knew she still had a lot more to learn. The instructors sat on the outside of the room, and the students gathered between them. Every individual had brightly colored hair, all in different colors that were determined by Callista and how she saw the individual's magic.

Seeing a shock of short, spiky white hair at the front row of the students, Samara craned her neck, determined to catch a glimpse of Mist's familiar. She studied every part of the thickset, muscular witch, only to give up in frustration when there didn't seem to be an animal in sight. She wondered if the familiar was a snake or a lizard and was hiding under Mist's clothes, or maybe it was a spider. Shivers ran down Samara's spine. She couldn't think of anything worse, but apparently, several witches and wizards were content with their creepy familiars. Mist wasn't exactly the most approachable apprentice in the coterie. Samara could easily picture her with one of the more unsettling animals.

Callista's soft voice cut through the air as if she were sitting next to each student. Every time she spoke to the group, her voice carried as though enhanced by magic. With a small crowd, it wasn't necessary, yet at the same time, it was an assurance that all within the room could hear what the head sorceress had to say. "Now that we are all here, let us begin." Her mouth pulled up at the edges into a reserved, welcoming smile. The sorceress often seemed restrained and controlled, even in the most excitable circumstance. "Today, we have thrilling news." She gazed at Mist. "We finally welcome our first familiar into this group of apprentices."

Everyone turned toward Mist, curious to find out what animal Mist had bonded with. Whispers of confusion rippled through the room when they couldn't find the animal.

The head sorceress's eyes softened, and she lifted a hand. "Rise, my dear Kanara. Let the students see your special bonded animal."

Fog crept through the windows, and Mist rose, closed her eyes in concentration, and took control of her magic, pushing the fog back outside. Her large muscles bulged as she raised her hands, and a caw echoed from outside before a streak of black careened through the open window. Spreading its wings to slow its momentum, a crow landed feet first on Mist's raised hand before furling its wings by its side. The crow's long, pointy beak angled in different directions as it surveyed those gathered in the room with its beady black eyes. Mist lowered the crow to her chest, and Rehan jumped as the crow jerked forward and cawed at him.

Mist chuckled. "Oh, Okak. You're hilarious."

The crow flapped his wings in response, and pride filled Mist's face.

Rehan's freckles pushed together as he scowled at Mist before running a hand through his short orange hair. Fifteen summers old, he was the newest and youngest in the institute and hadn't quite settled into the training center yet.

Mystique thumped her tail on the ground, her yellow eyes flickering with annoyance as Callista rose from her chair and descended the two steps, placing a reassuring hand on Rehan's shoulder. "Now, Kanara. That's not the way to treat your fellow students with your familiar, especially the newest one." Despite knowing Mist's nickname, the head sorceress kept to the witch's real name.

Mist inclined her head at Callista. "Yes, head sorceress. I apologize. The excitement of being the first to find her familiar is causing me to act foolishly."

Callista clasped her hands in front, her face blank as she planted her eyes on Mist. "That is understandable. But we must learn, even from the beginning, to respect our familiar and our fellow magic associates."

"Yes, head sorceress." Mist respectfully inclined her head again before casting a conceited gaze over her fellow students. She had every right to be proud. Having bonded with her familiar guaranteed her place at the Sacred Flame coterie. She could stay until her magic skills were honed, and she was ready to serve under Callista, bringing order upon the lands, a great honor for the witch and her family.

Her voice still projecting magically, Callista said, "Why don't you show your fellow students something useful you can do with your familiar?"

Panic flickered over Mist's face, which didn't escape the sorceress's attention.

"It only has to be something simple." Callista smiled at Mist. "After all, you haven't been together long and haven't had time to learn how to work together efficiently."

A frown creased Mist's forehead before her face relaxed. "All right. I've thought of something we can show them."

The edges of Callista's mouth rose slightly. "Wonderful. Give them a taste of what they're missing out on." She stood back, giving the couple room to maneuver.

Mist placed her forearm in front of her crow, and Okak hopped onto her wrist. Bringing the familiar close to her face, Mist whispered into his ear. He cawed once before launching into the air, circling high above the students. Every set of eyes watched him. Okak orbited a couple of students before swooping down and pulling one of Kaine's throwing knives out of their holster on his back. The crow dodged Kaine's attempts to retrieve his knife, flew back to Mist's raised wrist, and hovered to allow Mist to grab the knife before he landed.

Grinning, her eyes fixed on Kaine, Mist twirled the knife. "That was easier than I thought." Holding the blade still, she asked, "And what can you tell me?"

Okak looked deep into her eyes, and silence filled the room, as though everyone were expecting the crow to speak.

"Interesting," Mist said. "He has only five knives left, and Henriette's laces holding her tunic together have come undone." Her white eyebrow arched as her blue eyes landed on Henriette.

As all the students' attention turned to Henriette, her face turned red, and she glanced down to see the lace straps at the front of her tunic significantly loose and revealing her undergarments. Frantically, she tugged at the laces, quickly pulling the gap closed and tying them together.

Ripples of laughter filled the room, drowning out Mist's congratulating her familiar.

The crow hopped onto Mist's shoulder and comfortably preened himself as Mist beamed at the embarrassed-looking Kaine. It had only been a couple of days, but Mist was already working well with her familiar, which would make her stronger as a witch and defender of the realms.

A rush of jealousy and panic soared through Samara. Having been here longer than most, she knew her time to find her familiar was running out.

CHAPTER THREE

A rare sight of amusement passed over Callista's face. "Fantastic! That was a spectacular display of early bonding with a familiar like a crow."

Okak hopped onto Mist's shoulder, and the student returned to her seat.

As she passed, Callista beckoned for the knife, and Mist placed it hilt first into her hand. Taking slow, steady steps, the head sorceress returned it to a bashful Kaine. The normally overconfident apprentice slipped it back into its holster.

"Not only did Okak show that Kaine doesn't guard his weapons well enough, but he also has an eye for detail and can act as a scout or lookout for Kanara whenever she needs it." She paced to the front of the room, her golden gown embellished with black outlined leaves swaying around her long legs. "I hope you're starting to see the importance of a familiar, besides its role as a friend and an advisor to your actions." Callista squatted and petted Mystique's head, and a loud purr rumbled from the cat. After a couple of strokes, the jaguar began to clean her paws, and Callista stood to face the room's occupants. "A familiar is extremely important to those gifted with magic. You cannot be a sorcerer or sorceress strong enough to serve under me if you don't have a familiar. A familiar has an important role in making you stronger, wiser, and more assertive."

Okak squawked at Rehan, and the apprentice warlock glowered before clearing his throat.

Callista nodded at the teen.

"What happens if the familiar dies?" His voice cracked.

The head sorceress nodded. "Good question. The witch or wizard will not die but grow weak, as though they have lost a piece of their soul, until they find a suitable replacement. So it is important when you get a familiar that you guard and take care of them, just like they will take care of you as though you are their life."

As Callista turned in the other direction, a sly look crossed Rehan's face as he regarded the crow.

At the same time, Okak placed the teen under a watchful black eye.

"If you die, your familiar will wander around aimlessly, living a life without hope, unless they, too, are able to find another witch or warlock to bond to." Callista paced to the other side of the room, and Mystique's yellow eyes followed her movements, a low growl escaping her throat.

The head sorceress stopped pacing and faced the students. Her expression was blank and emotionless. "What I'm about to say never brings me joy, but it must be done. The addition of a familiar highlights a disadvantage this group holds. It is imperative that this is remedied as soon as possible. Some of you are new to the group and don't need to worry." Her eyes passed over the students that had been part of the coterie for more than a year, including Samara. "And some of you have been here for a while, long enough to have found your own familiar."

The head sorceress's voice was even and pleasant, yet Samara couldn't help feeling that the ground was caving underneath her when Callista's eyes fell on her.

"I took you all under my guidance because I could see your potential, hoping you would be bonded with your familiar by your second year as a member of the Sacred Flame coterie. In case you weren't as strong as I first believed, I have upheld a rule. By the end of your second year under my guidance, you must have bonded with your familiar. If you haven't bonded with a familiar, I will question my initial judgment of you, and you will have to prove your worth to me. Unfortunately, for the apprentices who have been here longer than Kanara, you have less time. You will be removed from the coterie if you cannot do this."

A stunned silence filled the room. Rumors that a familiar was important to the students to be able to stay had floated around, but there hadn't been any evidence of their truth. They were often told that their familiar would come when they were ready and not before.

Her head spinning, Samara felt giddy with panic and jealousy over Mist's early achievement. She should have bonded with her familiar already. Mist had been at the institute for half the time she had. Previously, the head sorceress hadn't been too forceful over her lack of familiar. It had only been a casual persuasion. She wished it had been made clearer earlier so that she would have had more time. The lack of having the expectations laid out early had cocooned her into a false sense of security. Instead of making Samara feel comforted, it seemed to extend the creeping tendrils of doom and wrap them around her heart. Her family needed her to stay in the coterie. If she didn't prove she was worthy one way or another, she and her family would both suffer.

"Head sorceress?" Kaine's face had paled stripping him of his usual confidence. He had been part of the coterie almost as long as Samara, and the pressure of limited time showed.

Callista faced him, her gaze intense.

"How do you expect the student witch or warlock to prove themselves if they don't find a familiar?"

"The second-year student witch or warlock will have to face a formidable enemy. They will need to use the magic skills they have learned up until that point combined with their weapons training." Even though Callista's face was usually hard to read, it made the news seem much more sinister. No emotion, compassion or otherwise, flowed through her voice.

Samara's blood turned cold. There would be no negotiation over the ruling. Although she had often found Callista approachable and understanding, there were times when she laid down the law.

Kaine's Adam's apple bobbed as he swallowed. "May I ask who the formidable enemy would be?"

Callista waved her hand dismissively. "Oh, it

could be many different groups who wish to take up the challenge. I send out an offer, and whoever accepts the challenge is the opponent. One group is the dwarves. They love to challenge the magically gifted. The centaurs love to see how our apprentices fend off many of their attacks at once. And of course, there are the ogres and trolls."

Samara's hands turned clammy, and she felt weak. "Um, that sounds like many opponents at once, not one against one."

Callista's gaze was stern and unflinching as her cool blue eyes landed on Samara. "Yes. That's correct. And if the student doesn't prove their magic worthy and defeat the attackers, they may face death, or the opponents may decide to keep the student as a slave, to use as they wish."

Gasps from the students filled the room.

The head sorceress coolly surveyed them. "You all knew it's a privilege to be taken under my wing. You must prove how much you appreciate this. There are consequences if you don't." She waved a hand over the students. "You all knew that. This isn't a free ride for you or your families."

Mystique yawned and stretched out on the floor as if taking a nap.

"What will happen to the families of the failed student?" Samara asked.

With her expression unchanging, the sorceress said, "They will be stripped of their benefits."

A murmur passed over the room. The only one unaffected was Mist.

Although Rehan still had a while to go, his already-pale face was whiter than usual accentuating his freckles. "What happens if the apprentice loses, is taken as a slave by the opponents, then escapes? Can they return to the Sacred Flame coterie? And if so, would the agreement be reinstated for their families?"

Clasping her hands behind her back, Callista paced slowly, deep in thought. "We have never experienced this. It would be a great feat, even if it were late." Her gaze dropped to Mystique, and the jaguar eyed her. The cat seemed to be consulting the head sorceress through the bond of their mind.

A few moments passed before Callista said, "I would have to consider my stance on this if it happened."

Though it wasn't much, it gave Samara a tiny sliver of hope. She didn't want to become enslaved, much less killed. She hated to think of what would happen to her family if Callista's benefits were ripped away from them because of her failure.

CHAPTER FOUR

The apprentices filed out of the hall, a flurry of shocked conversations filling the air. Several students crowded Mist, firing questions at her, only to be shooed away by Okak's wings and the crow moving to peck anyone who got too close. Glancing over her shoulder, Samara studied the head sorceress, who was sitting on her flower-backed chair, Mystique lying by her feet. Callista's face held her usual unreadable expression. She wasn't a smiley person or one who often scowled. Even so, typically, Callista was supportive of and friendly to the students, and it was hard to believe that she could be so final in her decision regarding the familiars. Samara understood that the students needed to prove themselves to the head sorceress, especially when she was also generous to the students' families.

Still, it was a harsh punishment if the students didn't live up to the expectations.

Callista's eyes met hers, and the head sorceress circled her hand and gave a flick in Samara's direction. Warmth and comfort washed over Samara, and she smiled at the sorceress before exiting the room. Samara didn't know what to make of the feeling. She was certain the wave of magic wasn't a pardon from the rule, but it felt as though Callista was telling her she had time, even though panic stirred deep.

Samara grabbed her quiver and bow off the wall hook, her thoughts filled with Mystique and Okak. She wondered what kind of familiar she would find and where she should go to look for it. The forest surrounding the institute was full of animals, including crows, but jaguars weren't common. Even the teachers' familiars weren't as exotic as Mystique. She loved the idea of having an exotic animal for a familiar, as it would make her life more interesting. Maybe it would even mean she would be more powerful, as Callista's power far outweighed the other instructors'. The more she pondered the different types of familiars, the more the realization sank in. The instructors' familiars weren't unusual animals for their location, but they still made their magic stronger. It didn't matter what animal she ended up with as long as she bonded with a familiar soon. As much as she cringed at the thought, she would even bond with a rat if, it meant remaining a member of the Sacred Flame coterie and helping her family.

A bell pealed outside, drawing her attention and that of many other students attempting unsuccessfully to siphon information off Mist. It was time for a few of the older students to go to weapons training.

She took the stairs two at a time to her room, her arrows knocking against one another in her quiver.

Tall stone walls surrounded her, leading down forked corridors. Some rooms looked over the forest, whereas others looked over the courtyard centered in the enormous square-shaped building. On the side without room, a balcony had been built on the second level to overlook the space. The construction was like an old castle, or so she had been told. Samara had never seen a castle. Prior to becoming a member of the Sacred Flame coterie, she hadn't traveled out of her village. Coming here had been quite a culture shock. Her village was constructed of small cottages on farms built within walking distance of one another, and the main meeting areas and markets were out in the open. At the learning place of the coterie, everyone was in the same building. Although there were fewer people than in her village, it had still taken a bit to get used to living under the same roof as everyone else.

As Samara passed down the large corridor to the right, it still amazed her that Callista had hidden the building from the eyes of those who weren't living within its walls. Surely keeping something like that hidden would take a lot of energy. Perhaps that was why Callista always looks so reserved. All her additional energy was being poured into the magical disguise.

Reaching the last room on the right, Samara flung open the large wooden door and entered her room. She grabbed her dark, hooded cloak hanging beside her door and looped it over her arm. Lately, Zofia, the weapons master, had upped the intensity of training for the four older students, and in return, they had started to wear hooded capes. Hiding in the forest with brightly colored hair had proved difficult, and after the first time, when she was completely exposed, she wouldn't risk it again.

She grabbed her canteen of water from beside her bed and closed the door before hurrying down the stairs, her boots tapping lightly on each step and echoing into the open room below. She zigzagged through the few students in the communal area, rushing to avoid being late.

After pushing back the large double wooden

doors, she hurried down the stone steps that veered right halfway down, before charging across the wild grass field to the edges of the pine forest. Mist, Kaine, and Paxton were already waiting by the weapons master. A grin was plastered on Kaine's face as he leaned against a pine tree trunk, his legs crossed. He seemed to be laying on the charm for Mist. Jealousy panged in Samara's stomach. She needed to remind herself that Kaine would pour on the appeal to any of the girls if he thought he would get something for his efforts. It made it difficult to tell whether he was seriously interested in any of them.

"It's about time you arrived," Zofia barked, uncrossing her arms and standing as tall as her five-foot frame could reach. "You were almost late, and I was starting to imagine ways to punish you." The weapons instructor yanked her double-sided axe out of its holder on her back and threw it into a tree trunk not far from where Samara stood.

"Sorry," Samara gasped out, her heart thumping wildly as she eyed the axe. "I was as quick as I could be."

A black figure sauntered by her. Samara's eyes widened as she watched Zofia's familiar pass. The bear moaned his protest. Technically, Jet was a small black sun bear, but it was still about half Samara's size.

Zofia indicated to the three students behind her. "Ha!" Sounding unconvinced, she grabbed the shaft of her axe, yanked it out of the trunk, and tossed it in her right hand. Her muscles rippled along her petite arms. The weapons master was tiny compared to many other adults, but the students had learned early on that that was never to be mistaken as a weakness. Zofia had moves that would put an average-sized warrior to shame. "Come on, then. Stand in line." She nodded toward the other students.

Kaine huffed a laugh and rested a hand on Mist's upper arm, gazing deep into her blue eyes. Seeing him openly flirting with any girl irked Samara. She wouldn't be surprised if he were laying on the charm to see if he could extract information from her about how she'd gained her familiar. He must be feeling the dread sinking in over not having a familiar yet. Paxton would be feeling it, too, and would undoubtedly want to know the secret, but he wasn't a charmer like Kaine. Adding to Samara's annoyance, Kaine had only arrived sooner than she had because his room was nearer the front entrance.

Samara stomped over to the other three students and stood beside Paxton, noting that his weapon of choice for the day was a flail with a morning star attached to a chain at the end. *Ouch!* She was determined to keep away from him, if the exercise was going to be as intense as it often was. Zofia loved to make their practice real, stating that the best way to learn was by having to avoid pain or feel the pain. If they were hit, the school healer would be called, but it still gave the students more than long enough to experience exactly what a real hit felt like. Only sometimes did Zofia allow them to protect themselves with a magic barrier.

As the weapons master approached, Kaine stood at attention. Zofia's assertive gaze passed over him. "In this class, Mr. Natas, charm isn't used as a weapon. If you wish to coax information out of someone, there are other methods." With a glint in her eye, she stroked her axe's blade. "Today, you are fighting each other to see who will be the first to retrieve the wanted information from Mist."

Mist's face paled, and Okak cawed disapprovingly. Her fighting skills were phenomenal for a student. Her shoulders were broad and her arms muscular from training with weapons. If anyone could withstand an attack from multiple assailants, Mist could.

Samara swallowed. She was glad she wasn't in Mist's shoes. It sounded like it would be a very dangerous lesson for her.

CHAPTER FIVE

Samara pulled an arrow out of her quiver and weaved her hand around the head, muttering an incantation. The arrowhead glowed briefly then returned to its normal appearance. She had been experimenting on her arrows lately because of something she'd learned about magic. The bow and arrow were her weapons of choice because she hated fighting hand to hand. It got too personal, and the view of the damage inflicted on the other person was too vivid. The teachers at the coterie had told her to toughen up. Not that the Sacred Flame coterie was a place for inflicting pain, but the students were encouraged to learn how to stomach combat up close. Samara had decided to perfect the archery she had learned from her father and her magic ability to avoid her empathy for others being noticed.

Enchanting her arrows seemed to be her unique magic ability. At least then she could control someone without actually hurting them.

The use of magic within the weapons class was mainly prohibited, unless it was to enhance the weapon somehow. Most of the students used their magic to guide the direction of the blade or arrow, but Samara had come up with something more original, just as Mist enjoyed using her fog as an inhibitor.

After covering her head with the hood of her cloak to hide her bright-pink hair and enchanting her arrows not to rattle against one another or fall from the quiver, she climbed a nearby tree. Her long leather cape draped on either side of the branch as she inched her way toward the leaves, her tall leather boots hugging each side of the branch. Movement caught her eye, and hardly shifting a muscle, she focused in that direction.

A figure moved among the trees, their face set within the shadow of their hood. Even so, Samara would know that overly confident gait anywhere. One day, it would be his downfall. *Possibly even today.* With slow movements, she enchanted another arrow and nocked it against her bow trained on Kaine. She kept the other tucked in her boot in case she came across Mist. Zofia had said everyone was against one another, and the first to get Mist to tell them how she'd found her familiar would win. No doubt, Mist had gone into hiding and could be anywhere, ready to protect herself. Samara pulled back her bowstring, prepared to release. Her chances of impeding Kaine were looking good.

A cry that sounded like Mist's came from behind Samara, and suddenly, Kaine spun in her direction. He spotted her, dodged to the side, and simultaneously threw a knife at her. Samara flipped, hanging sideways off the branch as a thud landed on the tree behind her previous position. A bead of sweat trickled off her forehead. That knife would have hit her leg or arm if she hadn't moved. She peeked around the branch, catching sight of Kaine as he bolted toward her. She tightened her knees around the branch, grabbed the bow with one hand, and attempted to nock the arrow again but found it impossible while hanging sideways from a branch. She gritted her teeth, waiting for Kaine to throw another knife at her, but when he charged underneath her, she realized he was more interested in heading straight for Mist.

Samara scrambled to right herself and followed Kaine with her eyes. She was no longer a hindrance for him, so she would have to fix that. After swinging over the side of the branch, she dangled from it for a moment then dropped more than twice her body height to the ground. Mist's cry indicated that Paxton had surprised her, possibly injuring her, which meant that Samara would be the last to find Mist.

Small branches and leaves crunched under her boots as she sought cover in the brush, winding her way toward the sound. Thinking of Paxton's weapon of choice for the day's lesson, Samara cringed. Being bludgeoned by a morning star seemed more terrifying than being stabbed by a knife or hit by an arrow. Paxton was a no-nonsense quiet type and didn't waste time getting what he wanted. He was only slower when he felt he needed to do research first and had no trouble diving into books to find the answer.

Fog made it hard to see farther than a few feet ahead. Samara pushed into its haziness, hoping it was a sign that Mist was near. A crow's caw sounded off to the right, drawing Samara in that direction. Surely, if that were Okak, he would stay close to Mist. Branches rustled as she pushed them aside, her ears attuned for any more telltale signs that the other three were near.

A whistle sounded before something collided with her head. Gazing up, she felt grateful that her hood was up, giving her some barrier from the crow's attack. She was sure her ear would have been sliced open by the crow's huge beak if it weren't for the hood's protection.

Okak cawed as he angled to land in the branch above, and she wasted no time grabbing another arrow, enchanting it, and sending it flying. It hit the tree next to the crow, who dropped from the branch and flopped onto the brush below, unmoving. If Samara hadn't cast the spell, she would've thought the crow was dead. She wouldn't dream of doing that to another student's familiar. Killing animals for her family to eat was hard enough. Instead, she'd only cast a stunning spell, which had exploded when the arrowhead collided with the tree, knocking out any living thing within a foot from the connection point.

Thinking she must be getting closer to Mist, Samara continued to the right, keeping her ears open. She hoped the other two were also lost in the fog. Otherwise, she would be the loser of the round. The thought stirred uneasiness in her stomach. Winning the mission was more important to her than any other task they had been given. She needed to prove her worth to Callista, not only to stay at the coterie but also so that her family of six siblings and parents had enough food and clothing to survive.

A scuffle sounded not far away, redirecting

Samara's path. She weaved her way around to investigate. Dry leaves crunched under her boots, sounding odd in the moist, foggy air, proof that the fog was unnatural for the surroundings. Branches cracked loudly ahead, followed by a thump and scuffling sounds.

Samara increased her speed. The two males must be fighting over getting to Mist first. Maybe she could sneak by them and attempt to get the information out of Mist—if she hadn't already escaped.

The scuffling grew louder, and Samara cautiously approached the edge of the bushes. She needed to get past the males unseen to be able to have full access to Mist. Grabbing the bow from her back, she retrieved the arrow she had made for Kaine from the side of her boot and nocked it. Bending her knees, she snuck closer and tried to stay away from the commotion, yet she needed to find Mist if she was near.

She edged forward, away from the protection of the last shrub. The scuffling sound had ceased for the moment, leaving her on edge and disrupting her sense of direction. Even though it was good practice for them to operate in any weather, Samara wished the fog would disappear. The only good thing about it was that it confirmed that Mist was feeling threatened by their closeness.

Trying not to disturb the eerie silence, Samara inched farther forward. Her effort was rewarded by a loud snap of a twig. She froze, her mind spinning for the ideal next move. Her muscles tensed as she readied to sprint, when a pointy black ball flew into her vision, and a chain wrapped around her calf. The ball's spikes ripped into her flesh.

CHAPTER SIX

P ain shot up Samara's leg, spine, and brain. She gritted her teeth until a scream charged up her throat, demanding to be released. The flapping of wings cascaded around her as the many birds she had spooked flew from the treetops. The spikes ripped through her flesh again as Paxton yanked the morning star back. Her knees crumpled and she landed on all fours, dropping her bow and arrow. Warm blood covered her calf and ran onto the ground.

Samara flung her head back, her eyes wide as she searched for Paxton through her pain-distorted vision. They were supposed to be training as friends or at least equals. She could go to the healer soon, but for the moment, she had to defend herself and continue with the mission. Sucking in a few shuddering breaths, she grabbed her bow, kneeled, and nocked her arrow, aiming in the direction from which the morning star had come. Her pulse roared in her ears, making it hard to listen for any sounds of danger nearby. Attempting to quiet it, she took another long, deep breath to calm her nerves.

She heard the rustling of the leaves before she saw the morning star swinging her way again, and she pushed through her pain and rolled backward, stopped on her backside, and released the arrow into the fog following the weapon. A thwack sounded, and a grunt followed. She didn't like hitting fellow students with her arrows, but she could make exceptions. Her calf roared with pain, but she only had to wait for a few heartbeats for the cries of fright. Samara smiled. Her enchantment was working perfectly. Judging by the noise, she knew Paxton was facing his worst fears.

The fog started to clear, as though Mist was regaining control of her emotions, and Paxton came into view several feet away, his back against a large tree trunk, his face white and his arms flailing. An arrow was sticking out of his upper arm. It must be killing him every time he swiped at whatever haunted him.

The fog cleared farther, and only a few feet away from Paxton, Kaine appeared. He spotted Samara at the same time as she spotted him, his mouth quirked with mischief, and he reached behind his back. Samara reached for another arrow. She didn't have time to nock it, let alone enchant it, before she pushed off with her uninjured leg and somersaulted. The knife whistled past and landed in the spot where her body had been only a few milliseconds ago. Samara waved her hand over her arrowhead, whispered the incantation, then nocked it right as the handle of a knife battered her in the head. Instantly, her mind went blank and her limbs limp as she flopped to the ground. Her eyes rolled back, and everything went black.

"Come on, Mist. Just tell me!" Kaine's voice cut through Samara's fuzzy thoughts.

She didn't know how long she had been unconscious, although it sounded like she'd woken to good news. She hadn't lost if Kaine was still trying to get information out of Mist. She still had a chance.

Rapid movements sounded from several feet in the opposite direction, and she cracked open an eye. Paxton carried on fighting his imaginary fears. His hands jerked around in defense, blood trickling down his arm.

Slowly, Samara tilted her head, still resting her cheek on the ground, to gaze toward Kaine. She was surprised to see Mist tied to a tree trunk and Kaine tracing her threateningly with a knife tip. They must've been there the whole time, only a few feet away.

Kaine moved closer to Mist, pointing the knife at her flesh. He traced it under her chin, and she flinched, her breathing rapid.

Kaine sneered. The corners of his mouth twitched. "You know I hate doing this to you, but you're withholding information I need to help me stay at the institute."

A coldness filled Kaine's face, making Samara hope he was only acting to scare Mist into releasing information. It painted Kaine in a completely different light.

When Mist didn't say anything, he huffed. "If only you had told me when I used my charm before the lesson. It would have been much easier for us both."

Mist raised her chin, defiance shining over her bruised face and swollen eye. She certainly had strength and guts. Her mission was to withstand any method used to extract the information. After watching Kaine, Samara felt sickened to think that the challenge had taken an awful direction. She would never have thought to inflict pain to extract information––even though she was aware that the enemy probably wouldn't hold back. The whole process was turning Samara's stomach. She had hoped that the males would have used different tactics. Maybe they did before Samara had come along, and after not getting anywhere, they resorted to more desperate measures. Taking in all the blood and injuries on Mist's body, Samara thought she had more strength than she could ever imagine holding.

Samara hoped she was wrong, and Mist had gotten the injuries while fighting the guys. Stealthily, she reached for an arrow in her quiver. She prepped the arrow with a whispered enchantment and nocked it, still lying on her side, and aimed at Kaine.

Kaine scraped the tip of his knife sideways down Mist's neck, leaving an ugly red scratch. She shivered then straightened when he removed the knife, her chin set.

Flinging himself back, he roared, "Come on, Mist! I don't want to hurt you! Just tell me!"

The outburst sent relief flooding through Samara's veins. They hadn't been torturing her. All her injuries were from her fighting back before being restrained. The males were, as she had thought, decent beings.

Instead of giving into his plea, Mist raised her jaw, defiance set in her eyes.

When Kaine turned to face her, his shoulders slumped. "If you don't tell me, I'm going to have to inflict pain. I really don't want to do that, but desperate times…"

He tossed a knife up and down in his right hand, catching it by the handle every time. His thin, muscular form showed hesitancy as he paced in front of her. He ran a hand through his blue hair, knocking off his hood, and cast one last pleading glance in Mist's direction. She didn't budge.

"All right, you leave me no choice." Displeasure on his face, he stomped away from the tree several feet before facing Mist again. "I'm going to throw this and aim for different parts of your body. You can either start talking or hope that I miss. And as you know, that's a rarity."

A bird whistled in the distance, cutting through the uncomfortable silence.

Kaine paused. "Where is your familiar? I thought they were supposed to help protect and advise you." He glanced over his shoulder and into the trees. When he didn't spot Okak, he shrugged, faced Mist, and lined up his throw. "Not that I think a crow could do that much."

A pang of guilt shot through Samara. She had

disabled Okak. He should be okay, only unconscious. Still, it was her fault that he wasn't around to help Mist.

Kaine released his knife, and dread filled Samara. He hadn't been exaggerating when he said he was a good shot. Mist flinched. She could do nothing to protect herself, especially when it was prohibited to use magic other than on weapons. Her face paled as the knife whizzed through the air, heading directly for her.

CHAPTER SEVEN

S amara released the bow's string, and the arrow hit the knife from Kaine's hand, exploding on impact. Kaine froze, disbelief plastered on his face as he spotted Samara lying on her side. He grinned, pointed at her, and laughed. With a hand over his stomach, he bent forward and gave a loud cackle. The change in his persona was astonishing and, within seconds, contagious. Even Mist found it hard not to laugh. Kaine's laughter didn't relent. Instead, he crumpled to his knees, eventually rolling onto the ground. That wasn't normal behavior for Kaine. Usually, every move was calculated, controlled, and filled with charm. Samara's spelled arrow had worked again.

Relief flooded Samara. She hadn't had to hurt Kaine to take him out of the competition. All that was left for her to do was extract the information from Mist. After watching Kaine's attempt, she knew it wouldn't be easy. She climbed to her feet, glanced at the laughter-stricken Kaine, and walked toward Mist. She had always admired Mist, and watching her refuse to cave to Kaine had made the admiration grow. At the same time, Mist was one of those people she would never connect with. They would never be best friends.

Trying to ignore the hysterical Kaine, Samara said, "I've just saved you a lot of pain. In return, would you mind telling me how you found your familiar?"

Mist grinned, exposing her blood-covered teeth. It looked worse in contrast with her pure white hair.

Samara grimaced, imagining her fighting off the two males.

"Tell you what. If you untie me, I'll tell you."

Samara frowned. She had hoped a little kindness shown by another female would help. Something silver caught her eye, and she glanced to the ground a few feet behind the tree. Mist's sword lay half-covered in leaves.

Samara looked Mist in the eyes. "If I untie you, you'll just fight me. I don't want to fight you in combat." Her gaze traveled over Mist's stocky form. She was pure muscle, whereas Samara was petite.

Mist's grin broadened. "Don't you think you'll have a chance?"

Shaking her head, Samara said, "No. Not really. Not without magic."

Kaine's laughter grew, and Samara glanced over her shoulder. Kaine had found Okak, and the crow lay motionless in his hands. "Wow. That must be the shortest bond between a witch and familiar ever."

A gasp escaped Mist.

Samara frowned, stomped over to Kaine, and took the crow from him. "He isn't dead," she chided. "He's only unconscious." Gently holding the crow, she placed him under a tree near Mist. When her eyes met Mist's death stare, she sighed. "I promise you. He's fine." She stood in front of her. "Now. Are you going to tell me and be reunited with your familiar, or do I have to hurt you?"

The girl grumbled, her eyes still trained on Okak. "Do what you want. Just know if Okak is hurt, I'll make you pay."

Samara nodded. "I have no doubt. If someone hurt an animal or familiar I was bonded to, I'd feel the same way. Now. Why don't you tell me how you found your familiar, and I'll let you go so you can be with him?"

Mist's eyes narrowed. "No."

Expelling a loud sigh, Samara said, "I was really

hoping I wouldn't need to do this. All I can say is that you brought it on yourself." She marched several feet away from the tree, retrieved the arrow she had prepared for Mist earlier attached to the side of her boot, and nocked it, aiming straight for Mist. "This may hurt."

As she released the arrow, Mist clenched her jaw, preparing for the pain about to be inflicted.

Archery wasn't new to Samara. She had helped her family by catching game, and her technique and accuracy had only improved under the guidance of Zofia. After Samara released the arrow, she waited for the scream of pain.

But it didn't come. Relief washed over Samara. She didn't want to hurt Mist, but for the spell in the arrowhead to work, it needed to cut the skin. Looking at the spot where she had aimed, she found her arrow sticking out of the trunk and a gash cut across Mist's leather pants, blood seeping through. *Perfect. Exactly the result I was looking for.* She took her time walking back to Mist. On the way, she stooped and collected the arrow she had shot at Kaine earlier. The tip was utterly obliterated. She would have to attach a new one. After another glance at the hysterical male still rolling around on the ground in fits of laughter, she knew it had been worth the effort. Stashing the shaft in her quiver, she approached Mist, yanked the arrow out of the trunk, added it to the quiver, and hung the bow over the top.

Samara leaned against a nearby tree. "So, Mist. Are you going to tell me how you found your familiar?"

Mist laughed. "It's really not all that special."

Relief washed through Samara. Her truth spell on the arrowhead had worked. "So tell me, then. If it's not that big of an achievement, there's no reason to keep it to yourself."

A bird chirped in the distance. Mist nodded toward the forest. "You're standing in the center of it."

Gazing around the area, Samara frowned. "The forest?"

Mist chuckled. "Of course. Where else can you find so many animals?"

Samara raised an eyebrow. "So you're telling me that the rumor is true. You found Okak in the forest, and there's nothing else to add?"

Mist nodded enthusiastically. "Yep. It's that simple."

"Are you trying to tell me you hung around the forest until an animal came up to you?"

Frowning, Mist said, "I'm not that lazy."

Samara shook her head, eyeing Mist's muscly

arms. "No. You are far from lazy. So what did you do, then?"

"Stars! Do I have to take you every step of the way?"

Samara quirked her mouth to one side. Her truth spell had taken Mist's usually direct manner to another level. "I just want to ensure I don't assume something and get it wrong."

Mist sighed loudly. "Every time an animal showed the slightest bit of interest in me, I talked to it. I would've thought that would be obvious."

"If it's that simple, why didn't you just tell us in the first place? Instead of going through all this pain?" Samara pointed at all the bloodstains and bruises on Mist's body as if to make a point.

The girl shrugged. "My mission for the lesson was to keep it from you." She glanced at a couple of the injuries and grinned. "Besides, you should have seen the other guy."

Samara shook her head in disbelief. It seemed ridiculous to put the older students through so much to find out an answer so simple. The effort they'd gone through made it seem as though it had been much trickier for Mist to connect with her familiar. Instead, it almost seemed like luck. Samara had spent time alone in the forest for different reasons, but she never felt as though the animals wanted to connect with her. Maybe they knew she used to kill animals to help feed her family.

After retrieving her sword, she set to work untying Mist from the tree and walked her toward Kaine. He had finally stopped chuckling, and beside him, Okak was stirring from his unconsciousness.

Mist hurried to her familiar, scooped him into her palms, and rubbed his belly, whispering into his ear. Okak stirred, and opened his eyes to look at Mist. She was surprisingly gentle with the creature.

Kaine rose to his feet and dusted his leather tunic and pants. "Well done, Samara. That was an innovative move. Since when have you charmed your arrows?"

Samara grinned. "It's the first time I've tried it. The class rules are that we can't use magic directly, but we can use it if it's on our weapons. I hate hurting people with weapons and would rather defeat them in a less violent manner. I'm just glad it worked."

Kaine searched the area. "Where's Paxton?"

Guilt washed over Samara. "Um. He received the worst treatment. I hope it's worn off by now."

"What did you do?" he asked.

"I shot above him with a fear spell. He was living his worst fears." She cringed. "It's not my favorite incantation, but it was the only one that passed through my head at the time."

They weaved through the bushes, the path much clearer since the fog had cleared. Not too far away, Paxton was sitting on the ground, and Zofia crouched next to him, her hand on his back. He was no longer thrashing and fighting off the invisible enemy.

The leaves crunched under their feet, and Zofia looked up, her eyes narrowing on Samara. "Did you use your magic on him?"

Samara's cheeks numbed, and she shook her head. "No. I promise. I used it on an arrow." She searched the tree trunks and spotted the white tail of her arrow sticking out of one behind Paxton. Hastily, she yanked it out of the trunk and showed the weapons master the smashed head. "See? I'm sure you know an arrow doesn't smash like this when it hits a tree trunk."

Zofia nodded, though her face still showed displeasure. "I believe you. But I must say the spell you used on him was rather brutal for you."

Riddled with guilt, Samara looked at Paxton. "I'm sorry. It's the first spell that came to my head in the heat of the moment."

The weapons master stood. "No. Don't apologize. What you did showed you have what it takes to fight the enemy. That is what this class is all about. It's also about learning how to use a weapon in case your magic leaves you or you're too drained to use it."

Zofia's praise didn't ease Samara's conscience. She still felt terrible that she'd made Paxton live through his worst fears.

The weapons master observed the students and Okak, who was starting to move more, and her eyes landed back on Samara. "To me, it looks like you've won today's challenge because of your inventive thinking. Is that correct?"

Despite Samara's disappointment in the simple solution of how to get a familiar and the guilt that still racked her, she nodded.

Zofia raised an eyebrow at Mist.

"Yes. That is correct. Despite being the most petite out of the group, Samara beat the boys and retrieved the information from me," Mist agreed.

CHAPTER EIGHT

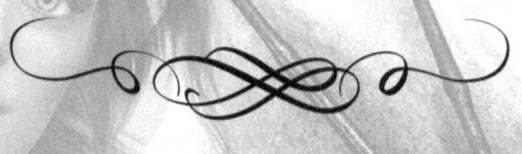

A bird chirped in the large tree near Samara's bedroom window. To those who couldn't see the building, the tree must look out of place in an open field in the middle of the forest. A cool breeze made the thin curtains billow, and Samara closed the window.

Dawn had barely broken, and the memories of the previous day swirled through her head. Samara was truly happy that Mist had found and connected with her familiar, despite the sudden pressure for her, Kaine, and Paxton to connect with theirs also.

Her stomach growled, and she changed out of her pajamas into leather pants and a fitted tunic with long sleeves, as the mornings were still cool. After pulling her long pink hair into a ponytail, she made her bed with a quick incantation and watched the sheets and blanket cover the mattress neatly and tuck in at the sides.

Images ran through her head from the previous day's weapons lesson. She had seen a different side of the institute. She'd initially thought it was a friendly place, but since Callista's speech, the atmosphere had turned competitive, especially for the older students. Each one was desperate to stay at the institute for their and their family's sake. Samara was disappointed that the students had turned against one another to find out simple information.

Opening the wooden door, she headed down the carpeted corridor, doors to rooms on either side, and descended the stairs to the common room. Large stone pillars held up part of the upper floor among an open rock floor. Two cauldron water features framed by stone chairs decorated the open area. The common room was quiet, as not many students were up yet, but breakfast would have started.

Samara passed the large glass doors that faced the courtyard, which had chair-framed gardens lining the open stone-pathed area. In the center stood a water feature with a statue that, if colored, would be an exact image of Callista with her hands raised as if she were conducting a spell. Mystique sat by her side, her long tail wrapped around her.

Mist was sitting on one of the garden bed chairs with Okak perched on her hand. It looked like they were talking, probably getting to know each other better. All their wounds had been healed after weapons class, and they looked refreshed after a night of sleep. Samara wished she could say the same about herself. Instead, she had spent the night tossing and turning, wondering if she would ever meet her animal familiar.

She hurried to the dining hall, her stomach rumbling harder when the smells of freshly baked bread and honey biscuits wafted into the corridor. She quickened her step, grabbed a plate from the stack, loaded it with biscuits and berry syrup, and topped it with a couple of pieces of bacon and an apple. Every morning, the selection far outweighed what her family had eaten before she met Callista.

Samara turned to decide where to sit and spotted Kaine and Paxton seated at the same table, their eyes on her. She swallowed the lump in her throat, feeling terrible for what had happened the previous day, even though she hadn't done anything wrong, according to the rules. It still made her feel uncomfortable.

Weaving her way through the tables, she made her way over to them. The hall wasn't big, as they didn't need it to be because there were so few students.

Her plate clunked when she placed it on the table next to Kaine.

He grinned up at her. "Here she is. The most stunning archer!"

Samara balked. That wasn't the reception she'd been expecting. "Ah. I thought you two would be mad at me."

Kaine's blue eyes fixed on her, and she couldn't read any malice or spite running through them. "How could I be mad at someone as beautiful as you?" He flashed his straight white teeth.

Samara's cheeks heated, and she looked at Paxton, trying to hide her embarrassment. Kaine's compliments would be much easier to take if he didn't say them to all the girls. Paxton's face was unreadable. His lack of a smile helped ground Samara. Keeping half an eye on Paxton, she took a bite of a biscuit covered in berry syrup. She had always loved the taste of berries.

When she finished her mouthful, she noticed that Paxton still didn't look happy. Paxton was the only apprentice the same age as her and she hated to lose his friendship. "I'm sorry about yesterday. I should have thought of a better enchantment to place on the arrow I sent you. I didn't think you'd have a fear that would make you act like that."

Paxton's eyes narrowed, and the signs of aggression on the normally reserved apprentice put Samara on edge. "Oh. Are you trying to tell me you don't have any fears?"

Samara fiddled with her knife and dug the tip into her apple, twisting it until a tiny circular piece cut away. "I'd probably be more scared than you." She put down the knife. "Honestly, I'm sorry I put you through that."

Paxton sat back. "I'm okay. Really. I didn't like it at the time." He gave her a solemn look. "But it's not what's getting to me."

Feeling the pressure lift off her chest, Samara asked, "What is it, then?"

"I'm worried about finding my familiar. I can't have my family losing Callista's protection." A strand of emerald-green hair had fallen out of his ponytail, and he hooked it behind his semipointed ear. "I don't know what it was like for your family, but mine was shunned because of our mixed race. My father is a human and my mother an elf. Without the school's protection, they would fear for their lives."

Samara chewed the tiny circle of apple. "I'm sorry to hear that. Mine weren't in danger from the villagers. I guess our village is more open-minded.

They only discriminated against us because we were poor. My family needs food and supplies to survive. I have six siblings. That's a lot of mouths to feed, clothe, and provide accommodation for." She ate some more of her berry-covered biscuit.

"That is a lot to care for." Paxton huffed. "Aren't you worried about finding a familiar to ensure your family gets what they need?"

"More than you can imagine. Especially since I only found out yesterday that we can't take all the time we want to find one." Samara finished her mouthful and sat back. "I won the challenge yesterday and still feel like I don't have the proper answers. Mist said she just tried to talk to any animals that seemed interested in her. It makes me feel like I have to go and live in the forest until I find a familiar, or else they'll never warm to me."

Kaine shook his head. "After all they made us go through to find out, you would think the answer would be better than that. It sounds too good to be true." He tilted his head to one side. "If you guys are panicking, what about me? I'm two years older than you. I should have found a familiar first."

"How's your family benefiting by you being here?" Samara took a sip of her orange juice.

Sheepish, he replied, "I'm an only child. Because of that, my parents have had an easier time providing for me, and my father has an excellent job in the city. But they always wanted more."

Samara rubbed his back between his shoulder blades. "I'm sure you'll work out how to charm a familiar into falling for you. Just like you have with all the females in the institute."

Kaine grinned, his blue eyes shining. "You're right. Surely I can charm them into loving me." His eyebrows rose. "Just like *all* the females at this institute?" He nudged her with his elbow. "That would mean you too."

Samara took another bite of her biscuit, hoping Kaine couldn't see her embarrassment. He was alluring but also confusing. She couldn't stand not knowing whether he meant his compliments or he was only playing her like all the other girls.

They finished their breakfast in silence, each deep in thought. Under the watchful eyes of the males, she cut her apple into sections and ate them before they headed off to class.

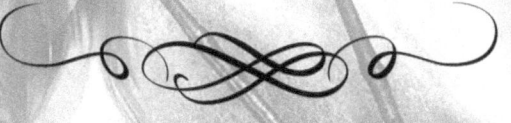

CHAPTER NINE

Samara, Kaine, and Paxton walked through the classroom door, their shoes clopping on the stone floor, cutting through the silence of the student-less room. The room lacked furniture, and intertwined sheepskins covered the stone floor. Samara's heart skipped a beat when their teacher spun from facing the wall and flicked her wrist in their direction. Quickly, Samara flicked her wrist in a circular motion and constructed an invisible barrier in front of them. A force connected with her ward, sending her sliding backward into Kaine's solid chest. Firmly, he grasped her waist and held her, buying her time to stabilize her stance. Paxton twirled his wrists, ready to attack the teacher, but Samara caught his eye and shook her head. As soon as he dropped his plan, she shoved her barrier forward, sending the teacher's thin elf form off balance, then pushed. She relented her force about a foot before shoving back at her teacher harder. The move made the teacher slam into the wall, her ankle-length beige gown pressed against the stones.

The teacher's brown eyes connected with theirs, and her face broke into a smile.

Samara exchanged looks with Kaine and Paxton and dropped the attack.

"Good morning, students," Devi Tempest called across the room. Her pale cheeks were flushed with exertion. She ran her hands through her short, spiky salmon-colored hair.

"Good morning, Devi." Samara's mouth twitched with amusement. The institute's teachers insisted on the students' calling them by their first names. Though the school was a place of learning, the formalities of a school environment weren't expected from them, which was why they were called the apprentices of the coterie.

"Fantastic defense for an unexpected attack," Devi said to Samara.

Samara smirked. "I came mentally prepared. After all, you never quite know when you'll be attacked in this class, even if it hasn't started yet."

Devi nodded. "True." Zion, her familiar, a light-copper-colored wolf, padded to her and pressed against her leg as she assessed the three students. She ran her hand through the flecks of gray fur on his back. "You three are here early. All the other students are probably just getting out of bed and heading to breakfast."

"Didn't you hear the news?" Paxton plonked down on one side of the sheepskins. "Mist has her familiar."

"Yes, I did hear that. That's great!" Devi said.

"It is for her." Samara sat not far from Paxton. "But we only learned yesterday that this means we have to find a familiar soon or face a formidable opponent. We need all the practice we can get."

Kaine sat on the other side of Samara. "The three of us are threatened by death or entrapment, and somehow, I don't think my charm will help me with that."

Devi moved to sit in the middle of the mat, and Zion lay behind her. She draped the long fabric of her gown over her knees and faced them. "Didn't you know you had to find a familiar soon?"

Samara shook her head. "We knew we had to find a familiar, but we didn't know it had to be within a certain time frame or that if someone younger found one first, we would have to find it very soon afterward."

"Is that what you all thought?" Devi asked, and Paxton nodded.

Kaine shrugged. "Callista kind of threw that at us yesterday. She made it clear that we had to find a familiar very soon. Within the year, maybe even sooner."

"And now we're all worried that our skills to fight off these potential opponents aren't enough."

"Why do you think that?" Devi's brow creased.

"It sounds like she's talking about trolls or something like that," Paxton said.

"But you all have incredibly strong magic powers. Surely you can learn some more and enhance those further to help defeat any opponent. How are your weapons skills going?"

Samara rubbed her upper arm as worry sent chills through her body. "Our weapons skills are also improving, but we still don't feel it's enough. Callista has repeatedly said how much stronger we will be once we have a familiar." Her goose bumps reduced, and she sat on her hands, warming her fingertips. "I fear we won't be strong enough to fight off anybody."

Devi's kind face filled with compassion. "We will continue to train you and build up your defenses. But don't worry about a familiar. I'm sure they will come shortly." She reached behind her and rubbed

Zion's head. "Did you ask Mist how she found hers?"

A deep frown passed over Paxton's face. "Mist just said that she found the animal in the forest. Nothing special."

Devi cupped her hands in her lap. "That can't be that hard."

Samara huffed. "Yeah, but we had to use questionable techniques, thanks to weapons class. It was horrible! We were almost forced to do something we didn't want to against a fellow student because we were desperate to get the information."

"But you *didn't* do something nasty to the student. Did you?"

Everyone turned to the door to see Callista standing there, her yellow-eyed familiar following closely behind. She entered the room with smooth, graceful movements. Her long, pale-golden gown was embossed with a continuous pattern of leaves and swished around her legs. Her lilac hair cascaded over her shoulders and down her back, the sides and top secured at the back of her head, exposing her pointed elfish ears.

The students stared at Callista in stunned silence as Mystique sauntered past Zion with her head high and her tail lashing before she sat in the opposite corner.

The head sorceress paced around them individually in slow and steady movements. "You should not be ashamed of fighting for what you need, whether for survival or for information to help others. It's important that you learn what you need to fight for and what you do not. In this case, you needed to fight for the information for your families." She studied each of them. "And you also needed to fight for yourselves to make sure you had what you needed to stay at this institute. That was the only way you could continue to learn from these rare individuals you call your teachers. These special sorcerers serve our realm, Wraeyanor, under my leadership and will help you do the same to make this a better realm, stronger than any other, and protect it from our surrounding enemies." She paced some more, her soft moccasins padding lightly on the stone floor.

Paxton cleared his throat, and when Callista focused on him, he asked, "Head sorceress, what are these enemies you always talk about?"

The sorceress's steps halted. "Ah. Yes. I forget that most of you are from small villages and are naive to the devastation wrought by the other realms." She smiled at them. "I should take your lack of knowledge of the hostile surrounding territories to be a compliment of my work. Under my leadership, our kingdom has been safe from their threats. My head sorcerers, with their armies, camp just outside our boundaries, eliminating any threat rumored to be surfacing." Her face returned to her usual blank expression. "Two kingdoms surround us. One is Clialarion, the kingdom of the elves."

The apprentices instantly looked at Callista's pointed ears with confusion.

"Yes. My ancestry is elven. Even so, some of the inhabitants of Clialarion wish to cause us harm. They conspire against us and harbor individuals who wish to destroy our kingdom."

Samara felt the tips of her ears. They weren't as pointy as Callista's because she was also part human. "What individuals?"

Callista clasped her hands behind her back. "There are elves who shapeshift into hideous creatures."

Kaine kicked his legs out in front of him and leaned back. "What kind of creatures?"

The head sorceress paced. "Creatures like none you have seen before. Enormous, with horns on their heads and large membranous wings. Long, thick tails trail their large, scaly bodies, and to top it all off, they have a vast array of teeth."

His face paler than normal, Paxton asked, "Are there really creatures that look like that?"

All the apprentices' eyes turned to Devi as she wrapped her arm around Zion, but the teacher only looked at Callista.

The head sorceress nodded. "When these shapeshifters were many, they used to cause all kinds of trouble. They controlled all the kingdoms, reigning over the lands under the banner of oppression. They controlled us with fire, imprisoning us within the kingdom of Wraeyanor. We weren't allowed to leave, forcing us to live off the products we grew on our land."

She threaded her fingers together in front of her and paused her pacing. "When they were in their elf form, they were also strong and trained like soldiers. On the outside, they looked like any other elf unless they were unable to control their emotions, and their skin turned scaly, like the hideous creature they could turn into." She fiddled with her headdress. "Much bloodshed was brought upon us as the sorcerers of Wraeyanor fought against their unfair treatment. Against being trapped in our kingdom and not having control over our borders. They took bribes from people desperate to pass through, but no matter what we offered from our kingdom, the inhabitants of Wraeyanor were never allowed to travel."

"What happened to these elves?" Samara asked.

"To stop this unfair ruling and to keep all the realms safe, the strong magic wielders, including me, joined forces and took down these elves. They have been banished from our kingdom. And any rumors of them in either Clialarion or Slosiaran are dealt with before the elves become a problem. Now the citizens of Wraeyanor are free to travel as they wish. The borders are governed by the magic wielders who are keeping the peace." She clasped her hands behind her back and resumed pacing. "But the threat remains. There are still some of these elves who are trying to bring back their return. This is why we must train and rid our lands of them and their human and elf supporters."

"How big are the creatures they turn into?" Kaine sat forward, pulling his knees to his chest.

Callista's mouth pressed into a thin line. "These hideous creatures come in all shapes and sizes. Some are small enough to sit on your shoulders, and others are larger than a cottage. Large enough to carry several of you on their backs."

Paxton straightened his spine, sitting tall. "What is the threat to the human kingdom?"

"Some of the elves moved to the kingdom of Slosiaran. There are rumors that some humans have taken a liking to these shapeshifting elves. This fondness must be stopped if we are to continue living with the freedom we have today." Stopping in front of the students, she stood at attention. "Has this enlightened you over your importance here and why you must bond with your familiar to grow into a stronger sorcerer or sorceress?"

The students nodded.

Her piercing blue eyes hardened as if to emphasize the point. "Then this should have also explained that if you wish to serve under me, I need people who can make tough decisions and do what is best to get to the final result, even if it means hurting a fellow student." She pulled back her shoulders, straightening her back. "I cannot have soft people who fail to make hard decisions or prefer to take the easiest route and give up if things get tough." Her expression softened as she gazed at Samara, and a sense of pride filled her eyes. "Besides, as you showed yesterday, if you are resourceful, there are other ways to achieve your goals. Instead of using torture or any other disgusting, horrible means to get to your result, you came up with a way that inflicted the minimum amount of pain and still got the information you needed. You should be very proud of that."

The apprentices stared at her in disbelief as silence filled the room.

Samara finally plucked up the courage to say

what needed to be said. "But the information wasn't that helpful." She cringed as soon as the words left her mouth.

The head sorceress inclined her head at Samara. "That may be how you see it. But the goal for yesterday was small, working toward maturing you enough to make bigger decisions. You worked through the difficulty and pushed past the comfort barrier to get what you needed." Sauntering, she circled the students again before stopping in front of them and fixed each one with a scrutinizing stare. Her blue irises seemed to cut like ice. "You may have seen the information as fairly unhelpful, but have any of you gone to the forest and attempted to speak to animals?"

Samara looked at the ground. "No, we haven't."

Callista's eyes narrowed, and she exhaled loudly. "So you're telling me that after you found out something as important as this, you still haven't put it into practice?"

Paxton ran a hand through his emerald-green strands. The gesture indicated he wanted to raise his hand but was too hesitant to do so. "I went." He put his hand quickly into his lap. "I went last night."

"That's wonderful!" Her face beaming, pride streaked through Callista's voice, and she turned her full attention to Paxton. "And how did it go?"

Paxton suddenly found a loose thread on his jerkin interesting and in need of twisting. He tucked his chin and muttered, "I wasn't successful." He sighed and brushed at the thread before looking at Callista, disappointment etched on his face. "Although I did try. A couple of animals came close to me, like an owl and a possum. And I thought maybe they were interested in communicating with me. But not long afterward, they ran away."

Samara looked at Paxton in shock. She'd had no idea Paxton had gone to the forest, and Kaine's expression showed he hadn't either. He hadn't even told them during breakfast.

The head sorceress bent over and placed a hand on his shoulder. "That is a start, though. Night creatures are wonderful familiars. They are often very wise and sit and watch while you sleep and work under the cover of darkness at night when others least expect it."

Guilt washed through Samara's body. Her gut had told her to go to the forest and attempt to talk to animals, but her head had talked her out of it. After all, she hadn't had any luck before. "With all due respect, Callista, I have tried to talk to the animals in the forest in the past. I've had hardly any animals want to communicate with me. And I fear that I will not be successful in finding a familiar.

And that put me off going into the forest last night."

"It's good of you to admit that, Samara." The sorceress stood in front of her. "I understand your fears, but that doesn't mean you won't connect with a familiar. You just need to be in the right place at the right time for your familiar to be able to talk and connect with you. Unless you pick up a house mouse, a spider, or an insect, you're best to leave the building and head toward an area that's more likely to hold animals."

The head sorceress strolled over to Mystique, who was sitting in the corner, and rubbed her around the ears. A satisfied purr rumbled across the room as the black jaguar pressed into Callista's hand. "And to be honest, we don't have many mice or tiny animals inside this building. Mystique catches a lot of them."

The jaguar yawned, her yellow eyes surveying each student with an air of superiority, making Samara feel uneasy. Although Callista was often hard to read, Samara held a deep respect for her and felt safe under her protection. She swallowed her apprehension. Callista was right, as usual. She needed to expose herself to animals outside the building. "Then I shall try again later after our classes."

"Me too." Kaine smiled at Samara. "Perhaps we should go together."

A hint of something lay in his voice, and butterflies flitted in Samara's stomach. She couldn't help entertaining the idea that he was trying to get her alone. Whether it was true or not, her emotions rioted.

Callista steepled her fingertips. "It'll be good for you to try to find your familiar soon. The sooner you find one, the less pressure is on you. But in the meantime, you must also practice every other talent and magic you can." Her usually expressionless face twitched into a semi-smile as she looked at each student warmly. "After all, I wouldn't like my students falling into the hands of formidable opponents. And I would hate to take away the reward your families received when you decided to come and serve under me in order to uphold a better kingdom."

Callista looked at Devi. "I think I've taken up enough of your time. I'll let you continue to teach. If these older students are here early to learn additional techniques before your class begins, I'll let you do so." She turned to the students again. "Good luck! I hope you learn lots." Without waiting for a response, the sorceress quickly stepped out of the room with Mystique in tow.

CHAPTER TEN

Paxton whispered something and flicked his wrist in Samara's direction. With a swift swirl of her wrist, Samara constructed an invisible barrier, blocking whatever spell he had sent her way. Devi flicked her hand at Samara right as she was distracted by Paxton's attack. The teacher often attacked the apprentices right after they had attacked or defended, stinging them with a magical rash or a mini lightning shot, to keep them on their toes.

Samara constructed another barrier just in time to catch the force of the blow on her invisible shield. Immediately after, Devi shot Paxton with an attack, and he moved to block it, but he was too late. His invisible shield caught half of the bolt of electricity, while the rest shot into his hand. He let out a cry of pain and shook the struck arm, muttering a healing spell through clenched teeth.

The attacking attempts were meant to be fun as well as practice. Still, a somber mood hung in the air like an ominous cloud over the sitting apprentices. Callista's reassurance hadn't helped lighten their spirits. The need to find a familiar pressed hard on Samara's mind, and the downturned expressions on Kaine's and Paxton's faces showed they felt much the same.

Something orange caught Samara's eye. She turned, but she was too late. Rehan's hand flicked in her direction.

Samara quickly constructed a barrier, kicking herself for not being on guard. She wouldn't be able to block the spell in time and should've been more careful. Throwing random spells as they entered the room was common practice. She clenched her teeth, bracing for the pain. Instead, a small pop sounded as the spell hit a barrier in front of her. She blinked. Someone else had built the barrier. Hers wasn't finished. She turned to see Kaine's hand holding it. He had saved her from an attack. Breathless with gratitude, she gazed up at his face and was met with a grin. Kaine winked, his blue eyes sparkling as her cheeks heated.

"Thanks," she muttered. She'd intended to offer a

more sincere response, but it fell flat because of her bashfulness. He'd always had a way of sending her nerves into a flurry.

Kaine muttered something and flicked a hand in Rehan's direction. Rehan dropped to the floor and rolled on the ground as if to quench a fire.

Samara cringed. She was thankful for Kaine's intervention, but whatever spell he had placed on Rehan looked painful, and she couldn't help but feel sorry for him.

Devi jumped to her feet and placed a hand on the roiling teen, whispering incantations. It took a few moments before his writhing settled, and his face calmed as he rested on his back, gasping. Silence filled the air as the students waited for him to move.

Wide-eyed, Rehan pushed himself into a sitting position and faced Kaine. "That was horrible. I never want to feel that spell again." He huffed a laugh and shook his head. "It felt like my whole body was burning with an itch. I didn't know where to start scratching."

Samara breathed a sigh of relief. After what she had witnessed in the weapons class the previous day, she'd been worried that Kaine had made the boy's blood boil or made him feel like he'd been set on fire. She shivered. Either of those would be torture.

Rehan rose to his feet and entered the room. Just

as he did, a flash of turquoise hair appeared within the door frame then disappeared behind the wall.

Kaine muttered something and twirled his wrist before pushing his hand toward the room's entrance. Rehan's face paled, and he dived to the side of the room, knocking into Devi. Kaine's spell skimmed past him and hit an ashen hand protruding from the doorway. Instantly, the hand went limp and flopped as though made of rubber.

"Stars above!" Henriette moved into the room's entrance with an enormous smile. She held out her ghostly white arm, which hung limply from her elbow as if her forearm were absent of bones. As she tossed her hand around, her fingers caught in the straight strands of her waist-length turquoise hair. Grimacing, she stilled her hand with the other and slowly drew it out. She smirked at Kaine. "And I thought you liked me."

Kaine grinned. "I do. That was me being nice."

A pang of uncertainty made Samara's stomach clench. Again, he was flirting with other girls, although Henriette was four years his junior.

With a toss of her head, Henriette flicked her hair over her shoulder then sauntered over to Kaine, her hips swaying in her tight leather pants. The sixteen-year-old was average-looking, but her fluid hip movements added sensuality to her features. She held out her arm to him, her pale-blue eyes shining. "Since you're being nice, can you please heal it for me?"

He rocked back, stretching his legs in front of him, and placed his weight on his arms. As he shook his head, a strange satisfaction danced in his eyes. "Sorry. My healing ability isn't that adept yet. I can only heal superficial wounds." Shifting forward, he gently clasped her floppy hand and lifted it so that it aligned with her arm. "But if I could, I would certainly heal it for you."

The girl pushed his forehead with her normal hand, rocking him backward. "Pfft! You're such a flirt."

Kaine's smirk deepened. "I aim to please."

Grinning, she shook her head and held her arm out to Devi. "Oh, lovely magic teacher, can you please heal this for me?"

The absence of bones didn't appear to be hurting Henriette, just rendering her arm useless. Without waiting a moment, Devi firmly clasped the girl's arm and muttered incantations. Henriette gritted her teeth as the arm slowly started straightening, the bones pushing against the floppy flesh.

"Well, I can't say that was pleasant. The regrowth was more painful than the removal." Henriette faced Kaine, something flashing in her eyes only a second before she uttered a soft incantation and flicked her hand in Kaine's direction, striking him with magic.

He involuntarily sprang to his feet, tucked his hands under his armpits, and clucked like a chicken. Maneuvering through the room, he shifted his head in jerky movements and scratched the toe of his boot across the stone floor as though digging it through the dirt.

Raucous laughter burst from Henriette, and she said to Samara, "It looks like you've found your familiar after all."

Rehan keeled over laughing, clutching his stomach, while Paxton smiled slyly.

Struggling to keep her composure, Devi undid the spell. "You lot still need a lot of practice in defending yourselves, and you especially need to practice being on your guard more."

Kaine stopped imitating a chicken and sat on the ground next to Paxton, his face red.

Devi shook her head. "This is the defense class. The name tells you that you need your defenses up before entering. It's almost shameful that you aren't on your highest alert."

Rehan sat on the floor opposite Kaine. "But isn't this also about learning different attacking spells?"

The sorceress paced the room, her long brown gown rippling with each step. Her hair glimmered against the sconce lights as she nodded. "Yes, you're right. However, the main goal is to learn how to defend. It is much easier to attack an unprepared being than defend against a rapidly concocted spell."

Peadar, an extremely tall male with short yellow hair, peeked around the entrance. He shifted quickly, but Devi blocked his spell before it hit anyone in the room then indicated for him to sit, and he stumbled on the uneven rock floor until he reached Rehan and sat.

"Nice try with the spell," Devi said. "But I think it's time to properly concentrate on the class."

Mist sprang into the doorway and aimed a spell at Paxton, but Devi blocked that one as well and indicated for her to sit.

Disappointment filled Mist's face as she ran a hand through her spiky hair, but it changed to happiness when Okak flew through the entrance and onto her arm.

Eventually, the rest of the students trickled into the room, and class began.

CHAPTER ELEVEN

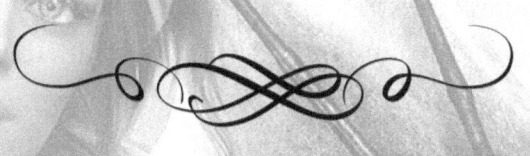

E liphas Heliot straightened his back, his head rising from between the plants. A dark-green ponytail trailed halfway down his back, where Phobae, the master gardener's extremely long stick-insect familiar, rode on top, his stick-like limbs clinging to the strands. The plant-eating insect seemed fitting because of the teacher's obsession with all kinds of plants, and he would have a constant supply of food for her.

The coterie's twenty students were crowded into the greenhouse, surrounding the master gardener, watching his every move, and waiting for his next instruction. The elderly human had proved to be a strange man and was often awkward around people, making his lessons interesting.

Standing in the middle of the group, flanked by

Kaine and Paxton, Samara observed the stick insect, unable to help ogling over the creature's strangeness, which edged toward creepy. Eliphas had said it was a Phobaeticus kirbyi, even though there are far worse crawlies, like spiders and cockroaches. This particular stick insect was one of the largest of its kind, almost thirteen inches long, plus the length of its legs. The creature was aptly named, as each piece of it looked exactly like sticks joined together.

As the insect clung to the herbology teacher's hair, its whole body executed a strange rocking maneuver backward and forward.

Eliphas pulled out a plant by the base of its stems, removing the roots from the snugly fitted pot. The wrinkles on his face deepened as he smiled at the plant with more affection than he had shown most humans. He muttered to his familiar, "You're correct, Phobae. This one is ripe for picking." Phobae climbed to the top of his shoulder and peered at the plant.

Eliphas nodded as though agreeing with something the insect had said and as though the class weren't even there. He brushed away the dirt, exposing the lumpy roots. Round white bulbs hung from the plant, and the teacher looked satisfied with his collection. It was often the way it went in Eliphas's class. He was an extreme introvert and shied away from interacting with people—a strange personality trait for a teacher. Still, a passion for plants shone, especially magical ones.

For that, the students learned to work with his awkwardness, ready to encourage him to talk about his specialty. They were used to standing around and watching him work, asking questions when they could.

The gardener placed his hands on his hips and leaned back, exposing a large belly that poked from under his cardigan and over his rustic leather pants.

"What is it, Eliphas?" Rehan asked, his face distorted with confusion as he tried to catch up on his studies to be at the level of the other students. He had only been in the coterie a little more than a month.

"Hmm?" The teacher looked up. At first, his face was distorted with confusion before he nodded when he made eye contact with Rehan and sucked in a loud breath. "Ah, yes, that's right. You lot are here." He gazed at the plant in his hand then held it out for the students to see, showing off the white bulbs. "This is a kohlunous plant."

Rehan raised an eyebrow. "It looks like turnips."

Eliphas frowned down at the roots. "I guess it does." He twisted them around on his palm. "But kohlunous roots don't have any purple on them, as turnips do." He screwed up his nose. "And I wouldn't recommend eating them. They can give you a very upset tummy." A grin spread across his face. "Actually, I recommend you offer these as food to someone you don't like. They will spend most of the day visiting the toilet—one way or the other."

"Here. Why don't you all have a closer look?" He handed the plant to Rehan, the first student in line. "Make sure you pass it around."

Each witch and wizard fiddled with the plant's roots and leaves then passed it along the line.

The plant reached Paxton, and he, too, studied the different features of the plant, taking in its textures, breaking some skin with his fingernail, and sniffing for a distinctive smell. "It smells bland, almost starchy. I imagine that would make it easy to hide in food." He looked questioningly at the teacher.

Eliphas nodded. "It would be difficult to tell if it was mixed in your food."

Paxton seemed in his element among the plants, although he was often found with his nose stuck in a book. "Is there anything that will counteract the effects?"

Eliphas twisted his mouth to the side and glanced at Phobae as the stick insect rubbed her front legs together then shook his head. "Not really." The teacher held out his hand, and Paxton placed the plant in it. "You could try some peppermint. It's always good for the stomach, but it's unlikely to work well for this particular digestive issue."

"What else is it used for?" Mist asked. Okak was perched on a small branch beside her, preening his black feathers with his long, pointy beak, his beady eyes constantly surveying the room.

"Upsetting the stomach of your enemy is pretty much it. That way, they're too distracted going to the toilet, so you may do whatever you need to do." His hazel eyes danced with amusement as his crow's-feet deepened. "It's quite ingenious, really." He chuckled, cut away the green stalks and leaves, and put the bulbs in a glass bottle. "The person will be on the toilet for a good half day." As he moved along the row of plants, Phobae sat close to his ear, as though constantly whispering. He pushed through the students, working among them as though they weren't there. The students cleared the way then circled him, ready to catch the next accidental part of the lesson.

Several minutes passed without Eliphas saying anything, until Peadar cocked a hip, putting most of his weight on one leg, and crossed his arms, his face filled with impatience. "Are there any other plants that could cause anybody discomfort?" He seemed to be struggling to keep the annoyance out of his voice.

He had only been at the coterie for a little more than a month and was still learning to deal with the different teachers and their odd ways.

The teacher fumbled through more of the pots on a bench as though he didn't hear him, making Peadar's irritation grow.

Eventually, Eliphas reached through several plants, grabbed a potted one, and put it aside on another bench before turning his back on the students again. He fiddled with the other plants, lining them up in neat rows. It was as if he hadn't heard Peadar's question.

Henriette picked up the discarded plant and studied it. "Here." She shoved the potted plant at Peadar. "It's not harmful, but it certainly has the potential to cause mischief." She smirked. "I think you'll find this to your satisfaction."

Peadar stumbled back slightly from the force of the pass, almost tripping over a student behind him. When he regained his balance, he studied the leaves. "What does it do?"

"It tastes delicious. That's what it does."

Eliphas ignored the exchange and continued fiddling with the plants lined up in neat rows on the bench.

"That's not exciting!" Peadar moaned.

Henriette grabbed a small knife from a nearby

bench and cut some foliage from the plant. She lifted his hand, pried open his fingers, and shoved the leaves into his palm. "Here. Why don't you try some?"

His face somber, he said, "It had better not taste like salad." His nose scrunched. "I hate salad."

She shoved his hand toward him. "I guarantee it doesn't."

His face bore distrust as he chewed, the crunching sound filling the room. Eliphas slowly shook his head as he pretended to ignore the students and continued to work among his plants.

After a while, a peculiar look passed over Peadar's face. He swallowed and looked at Henriette. "It tastes like aniseed. This *is* delicious." He threw the rest of the leaves into his mouth, chewing gleefully.

"Would you like some more?" Henrietta offered when he swallowed his mouthful.

The older teen nodded enthusiastically, and Henriette cut off another piece and handed it to him. In his enthusiastic state, he opened his fingers too wide, and the cuttings fell through the gaps between his fingers. He grunted at his lack of coordination, squeezed his fingers tightly together, and moved his open palm closer to Henriette.

"I'll give you some of the stalk. I think you'll enjoy that more," she said.

He shrugged, gladly accepting the stems offered to him. They looked like celery. He bit down, tearing off a large chunk.

"Was that nice?" Henriette tilted her head to one side.

He swallowed and smiled broadly. "That was delicious!"

Laughter rippled through the group.

His smile faded when he glanced around. "What?"

Eliphas rose from studying the plants, gazed at him, and shook his head. A slight smile grew on his face.

"What?" Peadar asked again, sounding more desperate.

Mist lifted a hand to Okak, resting on a branch above her. "If only you could see yourself."

Eliphas rummaged around the greenhouse, muttering, "I had one here somewhere." He fumbled through the plants, knocking aside different tools. "Ah, here it is." He pulled out a small piece of mirror and abruptly held it out to Peadar.

Peadar took it and peered into it. Instantly, his face turned bright red. His teeth, gums, and lips were all purple. "Henriette!" He darted toward her, only to be stopped by her blocking spell.

Henriette smiled smugly. "I think the purple goes

well with your beet-red face and yellow hair." She assessed him. "Maybe you should grow your hair longer to benefit from the color combination."

Eliphas reached high to tap Paxton's tall shoulder. "I feel your pain. I hate being the center of attention too." The herbology teacher took a good look at the stains. "Don't worry. It'll wash off in a couple of days."

"*A couple of days?*" Peadar looked horrified. "How can something that tastes like aniseed do this to me... and for that long?" He surveyed the other students and stopped on Luna Iliac, a beautiful elf. He ran a hand through his hair, exposing his half-elf, half-human ears.

Eliphas rubbed between his shoulder blades in calming circular movements. "Now you have a prank you can do to the next new student. It's been a tradition here for as long as I can remember." He leaned down and whispered loudly into Peadar's ear. "Even Henriette had the same thing happen to her." He nudged him softly with his elbow and grinned. "I hope that makes you feel better." He turned. "Even the pretty Luna had this done to her. You're definitely not the only one."

A smile spread across Peadar's face, the stress about what had happened to him in front of his fellow students seeming to wash away. "That does make me feel better."

Once the giggling had settled, Paxton asked, "Is there anything that will attract animals in the forest? Any sort of food or smell?"

A frown deepened the lines on Eliphas's forehead. "That's a strange kind of request."

"I need a familiar. I want to attract one to come to me when I go into the forest. I hope it will give me an advantage in meeting animals."

The deep lines of Eliphas's face deepened even more making him seem older than his sixty summers. "I don't think you need to attract animals." He placed his hand under Phobae, and the stick insect slowly crawled onto it, seemingly in deep conversation with him. "Like Phobae here. She came when she was ready and not a moment sooner." Phobae slowly transferred between his hands as he circulated them. "Perhaps you'll attract a stick insect as I have."

"At this stage, I'll take anything," Paxton said, "but I would like to try everything within my power to ensure I stay at the institute. I have my family to worry about as well."

Eliphas's stare at Paxton was intense under the raised bushy eyebrow, then he shrugged. "If you really want to attract animals, then take some of this." He lifted a potted plant from their straight rows and handed it to Paxton.

"What is it?" Kaine asked.

A stained-teeth smile spread across the teacher's face. "It's a sweet potato plant. The animals love the leaves." He shoved another pot at Kaine. "Why don't you go grow some outside and watch the animals come to eat it." He spun back around to his potted plants on the bench. "Either that or a mulberry tree."

Looking perplexed, Paxton said hesitantly, "Thanks. Its growth will take a little longer than I'd hoped, but at least it's a start." He clung to the pot, his muscles straining as though his life depended on the hope the plant provided.

Samara grabbed the mulberry plant pot that sat not far from them. "Do you mind if I take this? I'll quite happily plant it in the forest."

Remaining hunched over other pots, Eliphas waved a hand. "Of course, of course. Take it." He straightened and glanced around at the eager faces of the class once again. The realization that they were here to learn from him passed over his face. "I'm pretty sure it's time for the lesson to close, so I'll finish. Before you go, is there anything you wanted to learn from this lesson?"

Most students shook their heads, expressions of bewilderment showing on their faces. Eliphas's lessons were the most disorganized ones they had. Only the brilliance of Eliphas's mind made it worth coming to the lessons.

"What about a healing plant?" Kaine asked.

The wrinkles on the teacher's face deepened. "Well, it depends on what you want to heal. I could easily recommend aloe vera for any type of burns or open wounds." He picked up a plant that looked similar to a cactus but without as many spikes and broke off the tip. "The thick juice inside, or the pulp, has soothing qualities with a minimal smell." He picked up a small tree with long, thin needles protruding from its branches. "But then you also have things like ground-up pine needles, which make a nice antiseptic." He broke off some thin dark-green needles and crushed them in his fingers, and the faint smell of pine wafted through the room. "You could also try comfrey, which will help heal an upset stomach and can also be gargled for gum disease or sore throat. It's not the best-tasting plant." He picked up a large-leafed green plant and handed it to Kaine for him to pass along so that they could feel its furry leaves. "Or it can also stop inflammation, if you apply it to the skin as a compress, to name a few healing purposes." He raised an eyebrow at Kaine. "Is that what you mean?"

"That is a start. Thank you." Kaine said. "I'll make

sure I put some of this into practice. It's nice to know our options if our magic fails or is not up to the standard for the type of wound."

Eliphas nodded slowly. "Absolutely."

The comfrey plant had done the rounds of the students and landed back in Kaine's hands.

Eliphas indicated the plant with his head. "The comfrey plant also attracts animals, like deer."

Kaine's eyes lit up, and he placed the sweet potato plant on the bench. "Can I take this, then? I really need a familiar as well."

"Of course. I don't think you will need them. Still, I wish you all luck in finding your familiars. Your magic will be much stronger with them." Eliphas looked at Phobae on his shoulder. "Insect or animal."

CHAPTER TWELVE

Eliphas's class was the last of the day, so Samara, Kaine, and Paxton grabbed their weapons from their rooms and headed toward the forest with their plants.

Kaine's short blue hair shone in the afternoon sun as he gazed back at the greenhouse. "That has to be the worst teaching I have ever seen. I'm always amazed by how badly organized the class is."

Samara pushed her mouth to one side. "I don't know about it being the worst teaching. Although I agree that he's pretty bad at giving the class some structure. Otherwise, he's very knowledgeable."

"That's yet to be seen," Paxton said. "It's not that I don't trust his judgment or knowledge. But before I agree, I want to see if this really does attract animals." He held up his sweet potato plant.

Samara held her mulberry tree in line with her face. "Then I guess we'll soon find out. We're taking the first step." She turned to Kaine. "Do you like your choice?"

Kaine broke off a small piece of leaf and placed it in his mouth. His nose scrunched, distorting his handsome looks. "I hope Eliphas is correct, and the animals like it. As far as I'm concerned, it tastes disgusting, and the furry leaves feel weird on my tongue." He held up the pot and studied the ample foliage. "It's quite a strange plant. I have heard that pigs like it, too, so we'll see if the deer or other forest animals do as well. Maybe I'll get a boar or a strong stag." A grin lit his face. "They are two animals that would be a suitable match for my strong personality and rugged good looks."

"Perhaps a boar is more suited to your humbleness," Paxton chided him.

Samara smiled. His words were few and often accurate.

As the three headed into the forest, the birds chirped around them. The afternoon showed signs of retiring, and the sun slowly disappeared behind the trees. Dinner wouldn't be far away, and they didn't have much time. Although if they bonded with their familiars, giving up their nighttime meal wouldn't be a problem. The somber mood had cast a cloud of silence over the small group.

"Do you ever feel that we're trying too hard?" Kaine asked.

"I don't see it as trying too hard if it's going to allow us to stay here." Determination washed over Paxton's face. "I, for one, really hope this works. I don't want to be kicked out of here, and my family can't afford it. And I certainly don't want to be taken hostage or killed."

"Join the club." Samara nodded. "My family needs food and shelter to live." She glanced at Kaine. "And we don't want the horrible outcomes either."

Kaine nodded.

"We're going to have to separate," Paxton said. "I believe it's the only way we will see any animals. If we stay together, I think we'll only manage to scare them off."

Despite the forest being full of dangerous creatures, they separated. Each student should be able to defend themselves with their magic.

The wind whispered through the trees as Samara veered to the right, passing through the pine trees and thinking about what Eliphas had taught them about the pine's healing ability.

The pine needles crushed under her boots. Her bow rested over her shoulder, and her quiver hung on her back, the arrows rattling softly with each step. She always grabbed her weapon when she went to the forest, in case she needed to defend herself against anything if her magic failed. It was always good to have a backup plan. She had learned that the hard way as a novice student. Magic was not always there to use, especially when learning.

Birds chirped in the distance, and a caw sounded above her. She searched for the crow and wondered if Mist was following her. She spun around, unable to see any sign of her, and trekked on. Even if Mist followed her, it wouldn't matter—although she would prefer to find her familiar without being watched.

She stumbled deep into the forest before she sat with her back against a tree. Waiting, she eyed every squirrel, bird, or anything that moved, remaining hopeful that something would approach her. It felt ridiculous, although Paxton was correct in saying they were willing to try anything to stay at the coterie. None of them wanted to be kicked out or made to battle a formidable opponent. Despite being under Callista's wing for a year, Samara wasn't ready to fight a strong opponent yet, even though she had tried to learn every bit of magic she could from the teachers.

The night began to creep in, the temperature

dropping and sucking away the sky's light. Still, no animals had come close to her. She got up from the tree and walked to the plain about thirty yards away. Crushing a narrow path through the wildflowers, she grabbed a stick and churned the dirt before digging a small hole with her hands, then she planted the mulberry tree in the center. The plant was small and didn't need much digging to bury the roots. As she covered them with the loose dirt, a wild wind whipped her pink hair across her face, and she gazed up at the sky to see dark clouds looming. Satisfaction settled over her. *Perfect timing.* The rain would water the plant and aid its growth, and maybe the plant would be an attraction for animals of all sizes.

Her stomach growled, and she looked around the forest again, longing for a sign of any animal. Not even a mouse wandered her way. She would have to give up and try again later. If things went well, she might find an animal eating the plant and be thankful for what she had offered and, because of it, want to pair with her as a familiar.

Wandering back through the forest, she listened out for every animal noise. When an owl hooted in the twilight, she couldn't squash the hope that maybe it would be her familiar. She stopped to give the owl a chance to come down and even held out her elbow for a more accessible landing place, yet it didn't come. Unsuccessfully trying to squash her desperation, she called to the owl, "I'll be your friend, if you come and be my familiar."

The owl hooted and tilted its head to one side.

"Is that what you're trying to tell me? That you want to be my familiar? I promise I'll look after you." She stared at the owl's big, wide eyes, hoping the eye contact would reinforce her promise.

The owl remained on the branch, spinning its head one-hundred eighty degrees before pushing off the branch and sweeping down to collect a mouse not far away. Samara cringed, hoping the mouse wasn't her familiar coming to be with her. The way she felt, that would be her luck.

Having been abandoned by the owl, she pushed through the twilight, heading back toward the building, and climbed the stairs, which turned sharply to the left to the front door. With heavy steps, she passed through the large common foyer and into the dining hall, following a smell that caused her stomach to protest its hunger. Kaine was sitting by himself at a table in the distance with his back to the door. She grabbed a plate and filled it with roasted potatoes, sweet potatoes, roasted deer, and a splash of gravy with boiled greens and charred carrots.

Eliphas had grown all the vegetables, and Zofia had caught the deer.

She headed over to sit by Kaine. "Is Paxton back yet?"

Kaine shook his head. "I assume he's staying out for the night and skipping a meal just to get a familiar."

"Then I hope he's successful. Because I certainly wasn't. Were you?"

He shook his head sadly. "Nope. Not a single animal came near me. What did you do with your mulberry tree?"

"I planted it in the middle of an open field. It looks like it's going to rain, so I hope that will help it."

"I did the same with the comfrey. I've planted it in a spot with enough light. I'll revisit it daily to see if I can attract any animals," he said.

As he spoke, thunder clapped loudly, and rain poured down the windowpane not far from them. The volume of water that flowed down the glass unsettled Samara when she thought of Paxton getting drenched, but the emotion was mixed with joy when she thought about the water nourishing her mulberry tree.

Kaine swallowed his mouthful of food, surveying the wild weather. "It's been quite a while now. If

Paxton is still out there, I hope he'll get his familiar. If he's putting up with this, he's definitely determined and deserves it."

They ate in silence, listening to the thunderstorm, and were considering a bit of dessert when a sodden plop sounded on the bench opposite Kaine. Looking up, they found Paxton with a massive grin on his face.

In his hand, still wet from the rain, was a tree frog. "I finally got my familiar."

"Congratulations!" Samara and Kaine said simultaneously then briefly exchanged worried glances.

"Well, I can't imagine that the sweet potato plant would have attracted that," Samara said.

"No, it didn't." Paxton shook his head and laughed. "It most certainly didn't, but I don't care because I got my familiar." He shrugged. "It's not what I expected. But I'm so glad I stayed in the rain for it. He's quite a beautiful creature." Paxton studied the tree frog. "It's going to be difficult, though. He's already told me I can't touch him unless my hands are wet, because I'll burn his flesh. So either he'll have to hop on me, or somehow I'll have to keep water by my side so that I can handle him."

"That is going to be interesting," Samara said. "Did you want me to get you some dinner before they put the main course away?"

"That would be fantastic. I'm famished." Paxton's brown eyes filled with appreciation. Before Samara rose, he added, "But let me tell you. What they say is true. I already feel much stronger. Just from his talking to me and advising me during our short time together. I can feel my magic growing."

CHAPTER THIRTEEN

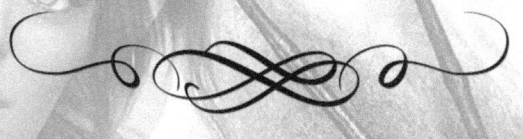

The next day, Samara made her way to potions class. She moved through the corridors and down a flight of stairs. At the back of the large building, she pushed through double wooden doors into a tiny room. It felt like entering another universe. Hanging from the ceiling were all kinds of items clustered in different areas, from strange, twisted roots to chicken feet, dried herbs, and other things she couldn't quite make out in the dim light. Bottles of different sizes containing all kinds of strange things sat on several shelves along the walls, from pig's heart to rabbit's foot to claws from a large creature Samara hoped she would never face. Farther along, several small, thin-necked bottles filled with potions, dried herbs, and spices clustered in a corner. The light of two sconces mounted on a wall flickered eerily on the glass items.

Standing in the middle of the room, preparing for the day's lesson, was their teacher, Artemise Snow. Her bright-orange hair billowed around her head and fell to her shoulders like a big puffy bowl as she bent over the cauldron on the fireplace. A tabby cat sat curled up on the edge of a bench, watching her witch with one eye. Artemise used a big spoon to stir the cauldron's contents, then she measured a few ingredients, pinched some powders, and tossed them into the cauldron, listening to them bubble and pop.

A strange smell filled the air. Though it wasn't potent, it wasn't exactly pleasant. Although it didn't seem to disturb Artemise. It appeared to comfort her as she swayed slowly in time with her stirring.

A crow cawed, and Mist swung open the large doors to let Okak fly in. Pride filled her face, and Samara couldn't blame her, but the expression managed to stir her insecurities, bringing sickness to her stomach. She only found solace in reminding herself that Paxton had found a familiar the previous night. Therefore, there must be hope for her and Kaine to find theirs before their time was up.

More apprentices piled in, and the teacher looked up from her cauldron, squinting as though she needed glasses. "Ah. Good, good. You lot are finally arriving." Her eyes widened with excitement before she picked up the long-handled spoon and began stirring again. "We have a potion that is almost ready for the most important ingredients."

Most students had filed into the room, including Kaine, who moved to the front and stood beside Samara. Dark circles rimmed his eyes, which seemed sunken, marring his handsome looks.

Shifting closer, she whispered into his ear, "You look tired. Didn't you get any sleep?"

His somber eyes slowly lifted to hers. "No, I was too worried about getting a familiar. How about you? You looked just as tired."

After expelling a sigh, Samara straightened her mouth into a thin line. "Indeed. I'm happy for Paxton, but I wish this were all over." She searched the room. "Have you seen him this morning?"

Kaine shook his head. "I imagine he's bonding with his familiar and has lost track of time."

All the other apprentices had filed into the room, ready for the teaching to begin. Paxton wasn't usually late. Surely he shouldn't need more than the whole night to get acquainted with his familiar.

Artemise Snow surveyed the students before her eyes narrowed, and she pointed her gnarled finger at an empty spot. "Where's that quiet boy?"

The students were silent as they glanced at one another, working out who she was referring to.

She waggled her finger harder. "You know. The clever one." She waved a hand over her hair while she explained. "The one with the emerald-green hair often tied in a ponytail. The half-breed."

Scowls grew on the students' faces. Many students were half-humans, half-elves, including Samara, and the comment seemed uncalled for, especially as it had often been used against the students as an insult in their villages.

Kaine cleared his throat, disapproval plastered on his face. "Do you mean Paxton, our fellow student and friend who is the same breed as many students?" he asked through clenched teeth.

"Yes. That's the one." The witch wagged a finger at him.

"Then perhaps you should've stopped your description at the emerald-green hair and quiet persona."

When Artemise's face remained unchanged and lacking any remorse, Kaine continued, "We're not sure where he is. Perhaps he is getting acquainted with his familiar."

The potions instructor squinted, the lines around her eyes deepening. "I guess we shall begin. Maybe the one missing will turn up soon, but we can't wait."

She shuffled back to the cauldron, her hips stiff with age. She had just grabbed the handle of the large wooden spoon, ready to stir, and opened her mouth to speak when Paxton charged into the room.

"Sorry, miss, I didn't mean to be late." His cheeks were bright red.

The fire burning under the cauldron cast strange shadows over the instructor's face, deepening her wrinkles as she nodded her acknowledgment.

Paxton weaved his way through the other students and stood between Kaine and Samara.

Kaine whispered, "Why are you late?"

Paxton replied worriedly, "I can't find Jojo."

"Who?" Samara asked.

"My familiar, the frog. I named him Jojo. I can't find him anywhere." He scratched his cheek, his eyes darting in all different directions, as though he was still looking for him. "He's just disappeared." His hand clenched and unclenched. "I haven't even had the welcoming ceremony for him yet."

Kaine placed a hand on Paxton's shoulder. "I'm sure he'll turn up. Maybe he just went and had a swim in a lake."

"Or maybe he's swimming in an overwatered flowerpot or something," Samara added.

Paxton shook his head. "I don't think so. I've looked in all the flowerpots and every puddle I've seen. I can't find him." He wrung his hands. "I don't know where he's gone. I thought familiars were supposed to hang around the one they're bonded with. I feel like a failure. I'm so worried. He was next to me on my nightstand when I went to sleep last night. I didn't expect him to be gone when I woke up."

Seeing the distress on Paxton's face wiped away all the envy Samara had felt earlier. He needed his familiar to remain with him to stay at the coterie. She wouldn't let him lose his familiar so soon, especially when it wasn't his fault. "I'll help you look after class."

"I appreciate it." He ran a hand over his hair.

Squinting, Artemise gazed up from her brew at the three senior students before fixing her eyes on Paxton. "Are you finished talking? First, you arrive late, and now you disrupt my class by talking."

"Sorry," the three of them said.

"I'll be quiet now." Paxton lowered his eyes to the ground.

Artemise nodded, stirring the cauldron a few more times. Her long black witch's gown swayed around her ankles as her hips moved. She reached up to a bunch of dried herbs hanging from the ceiling and broke off clumps, making them shower around her. "Now we need to add dried rosemary, oregano, and thyme." She tossed them into the pot before reaching for the bottles lying on the bench. "A small handful of ground dried pig's foot, tree blood, and scotch thistle." She tossed them in and stirred the pot again. A delicious smell wafted through the air, and if Samara didn't know any better, she would think the teacher was making a delicious meal, not a potion.

When Artemise glanced at Paxton, a glint came to her eyes. "You have arrived just in time for the most important ingredient."

The students stood fixated as the instructor reached down, grabbed a box from under her bench, and placed it on the wooden counter. After dipping her hand into a bowl of water, she slightly lifted the lid and pulled out a green tree frog.

A cry of despair escaped Paxton, sending tingles down Samara's spine. "No!" He dived forward, attempting to grab the frog. "That's Jojo, my familiar!"

Artemise swiveled, pulling her hand out of his reach. "It can't be a familiar. I found it in the corridors. Besides, I've never heard of anyone having a frog for a familiar."

Paxton lifted his chin. "Well, I have one."

"Pfft! Where's the proof?" She waved the frog over the mixture. "This is an animal critical to this potion. If you don't like what I do with the creatures needed for my potions, then you can leave this class."

"But Jojo is my familiar. We were only bonded last night. We haven't even had the welcoming ceremony yet."

Mischief danced through Artemise's eyes. "And there you have it. If what you say is true, you aren't officially bonded yet, so it doesn't count."

"But, Artemise, you can't use the frog if someone's claiming it as their familiar," Rehan called.

The potions master squinted at him and frowned. "Too bad."

Pouting, Luna put in, "But then poor Paxton won't have his familiar."

"That doesn't matter. This recipe needs the final ingredient." She lowered the frog over the cauldron.

CHAPTER FOURTEEN

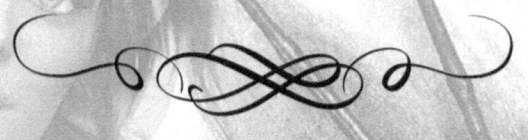

Samara's breath caught in her throat as Artemise held the frog over the cauldron. The teacher's fingers twitched, ready to release the amphibian.

Desperation filled Paxton's voice as he protested. It would be a shame if he lost his familiar the first day after they'd bonded. All his hope and potential would be lost, not to mention the bond would be severed, crippling his heart.

Henriette screamed as Artemise's fingers opened, releasing the frog. Something flashed in the corner of Samara's eye, and the frog levitated as if held by something invisible. Mutters of confusion filled the room as the frog drifted higher, away from the boiling mixture.

"Now, now, Artemise" came a stern, authoritative voice.

The entire class turned to find Callista at the back of the room, her arm outstretched and her hand twirling, beckoning the frog to float toward her. Jojo slowly drifted across the room before landing in her open palm. Her disapproving look landed on Artemise. "You know that's not the way to treat familiars, and I'm certain you know after all this time that we hold them in the utmost respect." She inclined her head to the curled-up tabby. "I'm sure you wouldn't like it if someone treated Tabatha that way."

Artemise shifted as if to block her familiar from harm.

Raising her hand, Callista stared into the eyes of the frog. A slight smile passed over her face when he croaked.

"You're welcome." Callista brushed her long lilac hair over her shoulder as she slowly weaved through the room, the leaf patterns on her beige dress swaying softly with her hips as she headed toward Paxton. "A certain familiar I know informed me that an apprentice's familiar had been taken." Pride crossed her face as Mystique strolled into the room, her tail held high.

When the head sorceress transferred the frog to Paxton, he breathed, "Thank you. I've been looking for him all morning."

Callista nodded. "I'm sure you were." She watched as Paxton crooned over the frog. "Familiars don't always sit by our sides and don't have to. They are their own beings." She glanced at the potions master. "And sometimes they are kidnapped by certain people. So you must always look after your familiar and ensure you know where they feel safe."

"When I went to sleep, he was in my room. I just thought he would be there when I woke up."

Callista inclined her head in acknowledgment. "A rookie mistake." Slowly, she made her way through the room and stood by the potion master's side, towering over her. Though Callista was five hundred summers old, her elven heritage made her look less than half Artemise's age. The potion master's seventy-plus summers made her human form look weathered.

The head sorceress faced the apprentices. "I was coming to introduce Paxton's familiar, Jojo, and make a big deal, but it looks like that moment has been tainted." She faced Paxton. "Still, you should be proud. It's a spectacular achievement that you have found your familiar, Paxton. Congratulations. You are now safe to stay here and learn from your teachers of the coterie. However, you must ensure you keep your familiar alive and well." She lowered her gaze to the potion master, her blue eyes hardening to stone.

Paxton nodded enthusiastically. "I'll do my best."

"I'm sure you will." Callista turned to address the apprentices. "Make sure you congratulate Paxton. He has achieved much." She looked back at Artemise. "Now, as for your potion, you needed a frog, although one that isn't someone's familiar." Callista held out her hand. Within it was a frog, as if it had magically appeared. She offered it to the potions master.

Her eyes wild with excitement, Artemise grabbed the frog and plopped it into the cauldron. The apprentices gasped. It seemed cruel to put a live frog into the potion, even if it was a necessary ingredient. It seemed contradictory to search and bond with an animal to enhance their magic while throwing animals into potions, especially when the animal was the same creature as one of the familiars.

Callista faced them. "I guarantee that this was not anyone's familiar. This one was found in the forest this morning. After last night's rain, it was still hanging around."

Despite Callista's reassurance, Paxton hid his frog underneath his tunic, and Jojo curled against his neck. Samara's nose crinkled. Frogs had strange skin that often felt slimy. Having one pressed against her bare neck would be an odd sensation.

The potion popped and squeaked, and the potion master's eyes widened in excited pleasure. She rocked back and forth, rubbing her hands together, her enthusiasm almost launching her into a jig. "It's working. It's definitely working." Eventually, she seemed to remember that she was instructing a class, and she pulled her gaze away from the potion. "Who can tell me what I'm making?"

Paxton cleared his throat. "A potion," he said with sarcasm.

Artemise pointed at him and responded with equal derision. "I like this one. He has potential."

"Nearly killing my familiar is a strange way of showing it," Paxton muttered.

"He does have a point," Callista added. "There should be loyalty among the witches and their kind. We should look after what is ours, especially the animals who have given up their lives as they know them to help us by becoming our familiars." She studied the students. "Once you have all found your familiars, you will understand how valuable they are to us, more than just being an animal that should be loved. We must treat them with respect and look after them."

As her scrutinizing gaze fell on Artemise, the potions master had the decency to look slightly guilty before nodding.

"I apologize. I needed a frog for the ingredients. I guess I had my heart too set on completing the potion." She scooped a ladle into the cauldron and pulled it out then poured some liquid into a glass. She offered it to Paxton. "Would you like some as a peace offering?"

With a wan face, Paxton backed away and pulled his collar up to cover Jojo. "That's an immobilization potion. If someone drinks it, they won't be able to move for quite some time."

Artemise rubbed her hands together. "Ah. I see someone has been reading their potions book."

Paxton nodded.

Artemise arched an eyebrow. "So. You have been doing some advanced reading."

When Paxton nodded again, Samara gaped at him. She knew he read a lot but was surprised at how advanced his learning was compared to the rest of the apprentices.

The potions teacher offered the potion to Peadar, who ran a hand through his hair and shuffled back a couple of steps while shaking his head.

Callista tutted. "Now, now, Artemise. Be nice to the students."

"I *am* being nice." Placing a hand over her heart, Artemise feigned hurt. "If I weren't, I'd be offering poison." She smiled, showing off her crooked, browned teeth. "It'll wear off in a few hours."

CHAPTER FIFTEEN

Samara finished her lunch, pushed back from the table, and took her plate back to the area to be washed. Piles of dirty dishes were stacked high on the bench. A dwarf with a hooked nose appeared, his boots clopping on the floor. A bushy beard framed his jaw, cut in a straight line giving him the look of a squared lower face. He grabbed a small stack of plates from the bench and stepped down, making only a tuft of dark-brown hair on the crown of his head visible over the counter as he shuffled to the sink. He then climbed onto a chair to wash them by hand and stack them on a dish drainer. Once he'd done that, he got off the chair, waddled back over, and climbed another chair, grunting as he grabbed some dirty pots. As he went about his work, a deep scowl creased his forehead, making him seem disgruntled or angry. The job looked like a massive ordeal and seemed odd to give someone so short. Samara had seen the dwarf in the distance as he did small chores around the building and outdoors, but she had never seen him so close or doing the dishes. In fact, she hadn't seen anyone do the dishes before and hadn't even thought about how they were cleaned. The dwarf seemed exceptionally grumpy, and watching how much effort it took for him to do the dishes, she didn't blame him.

When she set her plate on the benchtop, guilt wracked her. "Hello!" She tried to sound cheerful, hoping that having someone talk to him would lift his spirits.

The dwarf ignored her as he jumped onto a stool to grab a few more plates before descending the chair and carrying them to the other bench, lifting them over his head and sliding them onto the bench. He then climbed the stool with a grunt and picked up a plate to wash it in the soapy water.

Samara tried again. "Hello!" When he didn't respond, Samara pressed further. "I just want to thank you for your wonderful work here." She maneuvered to try to catch his eye, only for the dwarf to shift so that his back was toward her. "I see you occasionally, working hard around the castle. We appreciate your work."

The compliment seemed to startle the dwarf, and he stopped, eyeing her suspiciously. "What do you want?"

Affronted, Samara pulled back and held a hand to her heart. "I don't want anything. I just wanted to thank you for all your hard work."

Still skeptical, the dwarf jumped off the chair next to the nickel-silver sink and climbed onto the one at the bench in front of Samara. "I've been here for eighteen years, and not one person has said anything to me."

"I'm sorry to hear that." Samara was genuinely shocked. "I thought more people would talk to you."

His scowl deepened. "Why? I'm the help. Nobody cares about me." He tugged at the shoulder straps of his beige overalls and rocked onto his toes.

"I do. I just haven't been close enough to talk to you before." She extended a hand. "I'm Samara. What's your name?"

The dwarf suspiciously eyed her delicate hand for a few moments before cupping her fingers in his stocky ones and giving her hand one shake. "I'm Forgrac."

Samara smiled. "It's lovely to finally meet you."

Forgrac grunted and grabbed a few more plates before jumping off the chair and sliding them onto the opposite benchtop near the sink.

"Where are you from?"

The dwarf's skepticism deepened, and his answer was hesitant. "The Perpetual Vale in Slosiaran."

"The human realm?" Samara asked.

With one eyebrow raised, he nodded. "My caves are in there."

"Is that far from here?"

Forgrac's hands paused as he dropped a dish into the water and faced her. "You lot are definitely sheltered, aren't you?"

Samara frowned. "We all used to live in small villages. Why? What did I say wrong?"

The dwarf wiped his hands on a tea towel then flicked it over his shoulder. "You didn't say anything wrong. It's just what you said shows you are extremely naive, like the rest of the apprentices here." He pulled a cloth out of the dishwater and squeezed it before wiping a spot on the bench. "Yes, the human realm is quite far, especially for someone my size. But it's farther to the Hidden Yonder in Clialarion."

"The land of the elves?"

He nodded.

Samara's eyes widened. "What are you doing here, then?" She held up her hand when annoyance flashed over the dwarf's face. "Not that I don't appreciate your work."

Forgrac sighed, and his shoulders sagged. "I used to act in a traveling stage show. We were in Wraeyanor when trouble brewed in the human and elven realms. All the borders were slammed shut by magic. Now they're guarded by minions serving under the head sorceress, and no one can travel between the kingdoms unless granted permission by the sorceress. I can't travel to Slosiaran, nor can I stay with my cousins in Clialarion. I can't go home."

"That's horrible!" A deep sadness passed through her as she imagined never being able to see her family again. At the same time, she was confused. Callista had said that the people were freer while she oversaw the borders. She held her tongue, knowing she didn't know the full story. "Can't you ever go home?"

Forgrac grabbed a few more plates from the bench in front of Samara, jumped to the ground, and slid them onto the other bench. Noticing again how difficult it was for him, Samara darted around the bench and stacked a pile of dirty plates next to the sink.

The dwarf eyed her appreciatively then scrubbed the plates one at a time with a brush made from pine needles before stacking them on the dish drainer. "I couldn't. I had no hope of crossing until I finally found Callista. She promised she would help me cross after I proved myself after many years of servitude."

"She didn't help you cross straightaway?"

"Pfft! Of course not! You have to earn your way in this world. Getting favors from the head sorceress requires some kind of payment. She doesn't do anything from the good of her heart." He scratched his nose and shrugged. "I can't say I blame her. Otherwise, everyone would simply take and take."

Frowning, Samara stacked more dirty dishes next to the sink. "How many more years do you have to serve?"

"I'm almost there. Only another two years out of twenty." He piled more clean dishes on the drainer.

"You've served Callista for eighteen years?"

The dwarf nodded. "That's nothing, love, compared to the eighty it took for me to find her."

Pausing, Samara eyed the dwarf's face to see if he was telling the truth. "It took you eighty years to find Callista?"

He huffed. "It's a long time, I know. About half the life of a dwarf. But do you know how hard it is to find someone who mostly lives in an invisible building?"

Samara frowned. "True. It would be difficult. It's sad you have to wait longer."

As he loaded more clean dishes onto the drainer,

he shrugged. "What can I do? I'm doing the best I can."

Deep sadness washed over Samara. "You must miss your family."

He exhaled loudly. "You have no idea. And my wife probably thinks I'm dead and has married someone else."

After grabbing the tea towel from his shoulder, Samara wiped some plates. "I'm sorry. That would be horrible to think about."

He shrugged one shoulder. "It saddens me. But I couldn't blame her if she married someone else."

"Maybe you're wrong, and you can reunite with her when you leave. I wonder who will do the coterie's dishes when you're gone."

"I don't care, love, as long as it's not me. I want to go back to my family."

Apprentices plunked more dishes on the bench, and Samara grabbed them and placed them on the other side, closer to the sink, earning an appreciative glance from Forgrac.

She dried a few more dishes and stacked them on a clean bench. "It was nice talking to you, but I'd better hurry to my next lesson with Callista, or I'll be late."

"Is she back?" Forgrac's eyebrows rose. "Hasn't

she been away all week, checking on the other kingdoms and helping control any uprisings?"

"I believe so. Apparently, there were reports that there was trouble in Clialarion." Pride filled Samara's chest. There were people under Callista willing to sacrifice everything to keep the peace. She longed to be part of her leading defenders.

Scrunching his nose, Forgrac replied, "Love, there're always things for her to check over, especially reported uprisings in either Clialarion or Slosiaran. Some of these rumors are disturbing, and some aren't. I guess it all depends on what you believe."

Samara picked up another dish and wiped it, her interest piqued. "What do you mean?"

Suddenly sheepish, the dwarf busied himself with investigating every spot on the dirty dishes. After scrubbing a few, he said, "If you're an apprentice here, you must have a family that needs supporting."

She stacked another dried plate on the clean pile. "Very much so. I have six siblings and two parents. They need help providing for that many people. We were pretty much starving slaves before Callista chose me to come and learn under her." She placed her tea towel on the clean bench. "Which reminds me, I can't miss this next lesson. I need all the training I can get, or I may be kicked out. It means too much to me and my family."

"Isn't your place here secure? You're only learning."

Samara rubbed her upper arm. "Unfortunately, another apprentice and I need to find a familiar very soon, or we must improve our skills enough to fight an enemy to hold our place and the charity for our families."

Forgrac stopped washing and looked at her. "Oh, love! That's terrible. I've seen it happen to others in the past."

The look on the dwarf's face, even hidden under his bushy beard, almost crushed Samara's hopes. "That bad, is it?"

Forgrac tugged at the ends of his rugged beard. "No, no!" His gruff voice suddenly rose in pitch.

Samara raised an eyebrow.

He grunted. "All right. It didn't go well for the others. But you still have some time to get your familiar and keep practicing your magic and weaponry, don't you?"

Samara sighed and crossed her arms. "I don't know how long we have, but it's not much time." Her fingers dug into her upper arm. "Seeing how the other two students' magic was enhanced after they bonded with their familiars, I understand the reasoning behind requiring us to have one. It's just worrying. I have so much more to learn." She bit her bottom lip. "It's not only Paxton's and Mist's magic that improved after they bonded with their familiars. Mist's crow, Okak, flies above, screaming his warnings to her during weapons class. While Paxton's frog, Jojo, seems absent, Paxton always knows what is being planned. It's as though the frog is hidden away in branches, warning Paxton every time a plot against him is near. Even their reaction times in the magical defense class improved. They've also advanced in potions class. It's only been a week since Paxton and Jojo bonded, but Paxton's knowledge and ability to mix exceptional potions rapidly has improved his top-of-the-class status. And Okak is doing the same for Mist in weapons class. She has grown stronger and faster at wielding her sword."

With a somber face, Forgrac climbed off his chair and directed her out of the kitchen. "I appreciate your help, love. But you have enough to worry about. You need to be on your way to learn some more from the head sorceress and find that familiar of yours so that you can stay here for yourself and your family. Now, scoot!" Gently, he shoved her out of the kitchen.

CHAPTER SIXTEEN

Mystique sat by the door, guarding the room where Callista liked to teach. The black jaguar's tail flicked from side to side with annoyance.

Feigning confidence, Samara smiled at the cat, though the gesture didn't reach her eyes. "It's nice to see you again, Mystique."

The cat squinted, eyeing Samara with a look of distaste. Apprehensive, Samara passed through the door, remaining as far away from the cat as possible. The cat hadn't struck her before or any other student she knew of. Yet she often held an air of irritability, keeping the students on edge.

When Samara entered the room, she saw she was the last one to arrive and felt Mystique tracking her movements.

The head teacher sat at the front of the room, her back straight, making sure she didn't crush the new flower display she had concocted for the back of her chair. The sorceress's eyes met Samara's as she moved out of Mystique's reach, and embarrassment heated Samara's cheeks. She couldn't imagine it was wise to be late to class when trying to prove her worth to the coterie.

"I'm sorry I'm late."

"Nonsense! You're right on time." Callista waved a hand.

Still feeling the heat of Mystique's scrutiny, Samara gazed over her shoulder, her nerves tingling.

"Oh. Don't mind Mystique. That's just her normal face." The sorceress stood and paced to the back of the room to pet Mystique's head. A purr vibrated through the room as the jaguar pressed into Callista's hand. "She often likes to act like she's the ruler of everyone. You know, like the queen of all."

Giving Callista a small smile, Samara remained apprehensive and moved a couple more steps away from Mystique into the room.

Callista returned to the head of the hall and indicated a chair in the front row. "Come in and sit."

Samara scooted down the tiny aisle, passing the sea of students. Paxton sat in an aisle seat, and she spotted Kaine sitting next to the beautiful elf, Luna, his arm draped over the back of her chair. The chair's wooden legs moaned under Samara's weight as she sat in the indicated chair next to Peadar, whose yellow hair was bright even among the other colors. Kicking her feet under her chair, she crossed her ankles.

Callista faced her apprentices, her expression remaining unreadable. "It's nice to see you all again. It's always good to come back to this pleasant little community and see potential magic users who will help us protect our realm, and it is an honor to guide their way." She glanced around the room, making sure she looked at everyone. "There is so much potential in this room, and it makes me proud."

Peadar beamed from ear to ear at Callista's praise, his teeth almost as bright as his yellow hair.

"The magic in most of you has grown tremendously since you came here. And others who have found your familiars have grown even stronger in that short time." She paced in front of them, her long, beige leaf-patterned dress swaying around her ankles. She worked something in her hand, making it clack. "Today, we will learn about crystals and the power they can bring to accentuate your magical gifts. As you have learned, magic stems from different substances for different people. Crystals will enhance anyone's magic, especially if the person's magic is based on crystals, like mine. If you're a crystal witch or wizard, having contact with crystals will enhance your power with the power of the particular crystal."

The head sorceress paused to let the words sink in before taking a few more steps. "Those who have connected with your familiars and trained well, the crystals will make you almost unstoppable." After twirling the contents of her hand a few more times, she opened it and exposed two small stones, one red and one blue. "These are crystals." She held them up for the class to see. "Who can tell me what they do?"

Silence filled the room until Paxton cleared his throat. When all eyes turned to him, his gaze lowered for a moment, and his frog leaped from one shoulder to the other then slowly crept down his arm.

"Yes, Paxton."

Self-consciously, he raised his gaze to Callista. "The red one gives you strength, courage, action, and assertiveness. The blue one helps with peace, leadership, justice, authority, and collaboration."

"Very good. So the red one will give me a lot of power. And the blue one should give me the peace and assertiveness to better control it and put up with any stupidity."

Laughter rippled through the class.

Rehan raised his hand, and Callista nodded to him. "Yes?"

"Does that mean you need the blue to help give you the patience to teach us because we're annoying?"

Everyone laughed again.

"Surely not!" Kaine folded his hands behind his head and stretched his legs in front of him. "We're perfect angels." He gave Callista an endearing grin.

The edges of Callista's mouth twitched with amusement. "Sometimes we need patience even to deal with angels."

Another chuckle followed.

"The answer is no. I don't need patience to be with you. I only need it when you require a little extra help to learn or take longer than usual to understand something. Do any of you know if you are a crystal-based witch?"

The students shook their heads in unison.

"Okay, then perhaps we should try an example a different way. Let's have the two older females come up to the front. One who has a familiar." Callista indicated Mist.

Okak flew from the windowsill to her shoulder as she rose to her feet.

"And one who has not yet gotten her familiar." Callista indicated Samara, causing her stomach to twist into knots as she stood.

Callista spotted the uneasiness on Samara's face. "This is not to embarrass anybody. It is merely to prove a point. I reinforce this is definitely not to bring out your flaws. Each of the students in this room is strong in their own way and at an exceptional level for how long they have been with us."

The sorceress wriggled her way between Samara and Mist and placed a hand on each of their shoulders. "We have a student who has been here for a year and has powerful magic that has grown greatly in her time here. But she doesn't have a familiar." She squeezed Samara's shoulder before doing the same to Mist. "On this side, we have a student who has been here half the time but has bonded with a familiar. I'm going to get you both to do a special spell and see who is the strongest. I want you both to try as hard as you can. Perhaps you will prove me wrong. Perhaps Samara will be stronger than Mist and her familiar. But we will see."

The head sorceress went to the corner of the room and picked up a red crystal and a blue crystal from a small table laden with crystals before returning to the front of the room. She held up the crystals. "As you can see, these crystals are the same size, color, and shade. This is to make sure that this competition is fair. If you wish to double-check the results, we can even have the ladies swap the crystals after their experiment." She handed one set of crystals to each of them, and the warmth from being in Callista's hand radiated from the crystals.

After a brief inspection, Samara clenched them tightly in her fist.

"So the winner of this competition will light a strong fire quickly. We shall judge who is the fastest to light it and how strong the flame is after it's lit. I have already prepared two firepits." After she'd muttered something, the two firepits floated from the side of the room and clunked when they landed on the floor not far from them. "All right! Prepare yourselves, because it'll be a race, of sorts."

Samara took a deep breath and focused on the pile of kindling and firewood, preparing the word in her head, ready to say it. From the corner of her eye, she could also see Mist preparing. She wondered how a fog and mist maker would be able to light a fire as quickly as her, even if she had a familiar. Samara had lit a fire before, just not as part of a race. Her hands by her side, she waited for instruction.

"Ready... go!" Callista commanded.

Instantly, Samara twisted and lifted her hand, pointing at the fire. *"Ignito!"* The kindling burst into flame, slowly burned, then the fire devoured the more solid sticks and wood. After seeing the flame burning strongly in her pit, she turned to observe Mist's progress. The flame in her competitor's firepit was double the size of hers.

Callista stood behind the two flames. "Perfect! You both did it on the first go and within a very short time. Even so, there is still a clear winner. Kanara was as quick as Samara, and her flame was stronger." She gave Samara an almost-apologetic look then flicked a hand at each of the fires. *"Douso!"* The command quenched the flames with water from the nearby jugs. "Excellent! Now we should try it again. But this time, we shall swap the crystals." She held her hands out, and they handed their crystals to Callista. The sorceress swapped them and gave them back. She then waved her hand, and the two pits disappeared. After a second flick, two more pits centered themselves on the stone floor in front of them.

"Okay, get ready. We're going to do this again." Her blue eyes shone with excitement as Samara and Mist waited tensely. "Go!"

Instantly, Samara flicked her hand at the firepit in time with the enchantment while she clutched the crystal in her other hand. The kindle ignited with a flame the same size as before, and the hope she'd felt at getting a second chance to prove herself died as she glanced at Mist's flame. Once again, the flame was double the size of Samara's. Her mouth felt dry, and her tongue stuck to the roof of it. The little exercise was proof that she needed to find a familiar.

CHAPTER SEVENTEEN

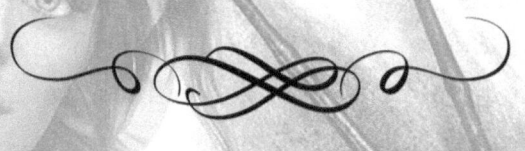

The lesson with Callista had left a massive hole in Samara's heart, adding more pressure to her finding a familiar. Her desperation was already mounting every day, and her state of mind was probably not helping her find a familiar. She wouldn't be surprised if the familiars ran in the opposite direction. And the last thing she needed was a familiar to look at her with pity. But still, she had to try.

She slid on her dark leather pants and fitted, thigh-length sleeveless jerkin and pulled on her long black boots. Then she grabbed her quiver from the wall and threaded the straps over her shoulders. The arrows rattled as she hooked her bow over her body. She always took her arrows when she left the coterie building in case of an attack by a vicious animal.

The latch clicked as she pulled the wooden door shut and entered the vacated corridor. Her boots clacked down the stone steps before she passed through the main room. The younger apprentices were playing with their magic by trying to fling buckets of smelly liquid over the other apprentices or cause their limbs to fly bizarrely in different directions. Those tricks normally amused Samara and were a good way for the younger students to practice. But that day, she was in too much of a bad mood to even stop and look as she stomped past once again to spend her free time in the forest.

Even trying to push down the annoyance was making her mood worse. She clomped down the outside stairs that veered off to the right, past the small deciduous trees that looked worn and almost as though they were embracing the side of the stone steps.

A fresh breeze brushed her face, and the coolness and the smell of nature slightly lifted her spirits. Perhaps being outside was what she needed, even if she wasn't successful. The twilight sky was clear and striped with pink and orange as the day made way for another night. As she trudged through the pine forest, the smell of freshly stomped pine needles lifted her mood further. In a concealed pocket was the stone she had borrowed from Callista, and she squeezed it. She hoped the blue crystal would bring her peace and patience to help her connect with a familiar. She pulled out the crystal and fingered it, already feeling more calmness washing over her and pushing away some desperation and worry.

She had planted the mulberry tree far away from the weapons class and any disturbance the coterie might bring. Aided by her magic spell, the bush had grown well, bearing lots of fruit and healthy green leaves to feed the animals. A slight breeze brushed her deep-pink strands of hair across her face as she left the pine forest and entered the one consisting of a mixture of trees and shrubs.

Birds called to one another from the treetops, and she paused and gazed behind her. Her quiver brushed against a tree, making some small branches snap from its trunk. She stroked the tree's bark as though trying to fix her destruction. "Sorry," she muttered before moving farther into the forest.

A bird flew down near her, and she called to it, "Hello!" The blue wren flittered then flapped its wings before it flew in the other direction. Samara exhaled, hoping to clear her annoyance so that she wouldn't scare away any more animals. Again, the bird wasn't interested in staying near her. Her fingers stroked the blue crystal, and she leached the peace out of it.

A rabbit scurried in front of her, pausing momentarily to gape at her. Its twitching nose could barely be seen under the trees in the twilight. Samara slowly reached a hand toward it, but its eyes widened, and it hurried off.

Shoving aside her disappointment, she pressed through the long grass and shrubs to find the small path she had already worn away, leading to the open plain. After weaving around a few more trees and shrubs, she stood at the edge of the clearing and peered at the large tree she had planted. Not daring to move a muscle, she watched as a doe stood underneath the mulberry tree, eating the leaves on the underside. Birds flapped above and jumped from branch to branch, pinching the fruit before flittering onto other trees, eating what they had snatched. The sound of cicadas grew louder as the light dimmed, egging Samara on to take slow steps onto the plain toward the deer. She remained on the outskirts, determined not to scare the deer away. The creature was beautiful, muscular, robust, and a peaceful character. She looked at it with longing as the deer munched away at her offering. She would be proud to have the animal as her familiar. The doe seemed oblivious to Samara's presence until suddenly, the wind blew from behind her, pushing her scent toward the deer. Her nose twitched, and her eyes landed on her, widening.

"It's okay." Samara held out a hand and slowly progressed forward. "I'm just watching you eat the plant I grew. Please help yourself to the leaves. It's all for you."

The deer stamped her front foot but stood her ground. After finishing her mouthful, she craned her neck and ripped off more leaves from the bottom of the tree. Another round of birds flew in, grabbed some mulberries from the tree, and took off. Other birds bounced from branch to branch, knocking a couple of mulberries that got in their way onto the ground.

The deer didn't seem threatened by Samara, so she took another step. With her ears twitching, the deer's head shot up, and she focused straight on Samara. She stomped her hoof but stood her ground, refusing to leave the tasty tree. Samara took another slow step forward.

"You can stay there. I won't harm you. I just want to talk." She advanced a few more steps, and her heart thumped rapidly against her ribcage. Her hopes started to rise that she had finally found her familiar. Tentatively, she moved another step toward the deer. When the creature stood her ground, Samara paused and drew a deep breath. The last thing she wanted to do was seem desperate and harass the deer to come near her.

She clasped the crystal tightly, rubbing it roughly with her fingers, determined to calm herself. It seemed to work. The deer didn't start when she shifted closer to her. The doe's deep-brown eyes constantly watched her, since she was only a few paces away. Samara was close enough to touch the outside leaves of the tree. The deer snorted and moved to the other side of the tree.

Samara refused to let that upset her. She steeled her nerves and waited. "Aren't you beautiful?" In case the doe was her familiar, she wanted to shower her with compliments, sweetening the creature's mood. "You look very peaceful and assertive and wise for your young years." She inched farther forward, and the deer still stood her ground. "Would you consider being my familiar?" She gritted her teeth, tamping her nerves. She wanted it so badly.

The deer watched her as she chewed, and her ears twitched as Samara moved closer. The doe wasn't moving, but her legs stood ready for flight.

"I'd be so proud to have you as my familiar." Samara smiled, trying to seem friendly, but felt awkward. "Although I'm not quite sure where I'd put you. I think you would make my tiny room quite crowded. Still, I'm sure I could make room for you somewhere there."

The deer shook her head.

Samara nodded. "Of course. You'd like to sleep outside instead. I don't blame you." Her longing for the deer to be connected with her grew almost unbearable. "If only you would become my familiar."

Slowly, she moved another step forward and extended her hand. The deer stomped again. When she didn't move, Samara shifted closer. Stretching her long neck, the deer touched her soft brown nose against the back of her hand and sniffed.

Samara's heart thumped wildly. *This must be it.* She glanced at the almost-dark sky. *Please, let this be my familiar. Then everything will get so much easier and better.* She remained still with her hand extended for the deer to investigate for quite some time before she shifted forward a tiny bit more.

The deer sprang to life and charged away, leaving Samara alone in the dark with a broken heart.

CHAPTER EIGHTEEN

Sick to the stomach with disappointment and worry, Samara skipped dinner. The thought of nearly having a familiar then losing it at the last second was too much to bear. She'd never come closer to securing a familiar. After the deer had left her, she stomped back to the building and sat on the front steps to pull her thoughts together. Two sconces burned on each side of the main door, casting a dull light over the top level of the stairs.

Perched on the top step with her elbows on her knees, she rested her chin on her hands and gazed wistfully into the dark forest. An owl hooted in the distance, and she instinctively looked toward the sound, irritated. The annoyance was directed toward the lack of finding a familiar rather than the actual owl, because she truly loved animals. Acquiring a familiar would be one of her dreams even if it didn't give her extra magic. She would feel complete if it only meant she could save her family from starvation again. Although obtaining stronger magic and having an animal friend to offer guidance were also big drawing cards. Lost deep in thought, she stared between the pine trees.

A baritone voice cut through her thoughts, echoing from the bottom of the steps. "Well, look who it is."

Samara turned to see Kaine below at the diverted section of the steps holding his weapon and wearing his large black boots that went to his midcalf. Unable to drum up any enthusiasm, Samara stared at him blankly.

His handsome face twisted with amusement as he climbed the steps two at a time. The leather in his pants squeaked its protest when he sat by her then nudged her with his elbow. "Why so glum?"

Samara exhaled loudly as she dropped her hands from her face. "I was so close to getting a familiar this afternoon, but it just didn't happen. And it was a deer too. That would have been a fantastic familiar."

Kaine wrapped an arm around her shoulders and leaned playfully into her. "Well, you did a lot better than me. The pigs have been eating my comfrey leaves, but nothing has stayed around. I've also checked up on Paxton's sweet potato plant. I'm lucky to see an animal. Even the birds seem to disappear." Kaine pulled his arm off her shoulder and clasped his hands between his knees, his side pressing against her.

"Then how are you so cheerful? Aren't you worried about your future here and for your family?"

His blue eyes seemed to sink into the shadows as his face twisted in concentration. "Yes, I'm worried about my future. But surely we have more time. It's only been a couple of weeks since we were warned."

Samara rocked sideways, sliding lightly into Kaine. She tucked her hands under her backside. "I don't know. I just feel the deadline for obtaining a familiar is approaching soon. Maybe I'm just stressing too much." She gave Kaine a small smile. "I just thought that if I behaved and did everything I'm supposed to, I'd be able to stay here. Suddenly, that was ripped out from under me. I knew we'd have to bond with one eventually but not this soon."

Something landed on her back, causing her to jump up. She spun, trying to find what had landed on her shoulder, and found Paxton closing the front door, a look of amusement on his face.

"Sorry. Jojo got a little bit jumpy," he said.

Samara peered over her shoulder and spotted the

green head and legs of the frog. His throat bobbed up and down as he breathed. The frog was probably the size of her palm.

She smiled, her stress easing slightly. "That's okay. I don't mind. He's completely harmless."

The frog watched her with his beady black eyes.

Paxton shoved his hands into the pockets of his loose brown leather pants. "He said he wanted to stretch his legs and get some fresh air outside the building." He moved closer to Samara and Kaine, holding his hand out to the frog, and Jojo slowly climbed on top.

An owl swooped down and landed on the balustrade of the stairs. Quickly, Paxton whipped his arm back, hiding Jojo under his top. The owl eyed where the frog had disappeared.

"Go away!" Paxton cried as he shooed the owl.

Samara gently restrained his arm. "Jojo is safe. Let's leave the owl alone. Perhaps it's wanting to bond with one of us."

"Sorry. I forgot you two still need a familiar." He held his other arm over where he had hidden his frog as an added precaution.

"What are you lot doing?" A voice called from the top of the stairs.

A crow swooped over the predator, and the owl took off, returning to the forest.

Suddenly, the front door slammed shut, and heavy footsteps clopped along the stone entrance.

Mist brushed past Paxton and stopped a few steps lower than where Samara and Kaine sat. She leaned against the railing and crossed her arms. Her large biceps bulged under the sleeves of her brown leather jerkin as she studied the others. "You lot look somber. What's going on?"

"I was trying to protect Jojo from an owl, and these two were trying to see if the owl wanted to be their familiar," Paxton said, still covering his frog to protect him.

Mist chuckled. "Well, none of you got what you want. Okak made sure of that. Your frog's still in danger from Okak, and he chased the owl away."

"Yeah, thanks, Mist," Samara replied dryly.

Mist huffed. "Oh, cheer up. You're making it too hard. It should be an easy process."

Samara crossed her arms, and her arrows rattled in her quiver. "Easy for you to say."

"I'd have to agree with Samara." Paxton kept his hand over Jojo, especially when Okak sat on the railing next to him, eyeing the movement under his jerkin. "After you got your familiar, it put a lot of pressure on the three of us. I'm all right now, if Okak doesn't eat Jojo." He glowered at the crow. "But I understand their worries. It's quite stressful. I honestly feel that luck has a lot to do with the timing of the bonding."

Mist shrugged. "I guess you're right. I'm glad I'm not in your shoes." Her eyes met Kaine's then Samara's. "If it's luck, then I hope it's on your side."

The owl returned to the railing, chasing Okak from his spot. Paxton flinched and covered Jojo's hiding spot with his other arm.

"Who would've thought four skinny young folks would hog the whole stairs," a gruff voice called, followed by the click of the front door.

Samara turned to find Forgrac the dwarf making his way to the top step. She moved aside, allowing him room to go past. "Sorry, Forgrac."

The owl flew off suddenly, and Samara groaned. "Oh. I hoped he wanted to be either Kaine's or my familiar."

"Don't worry, love. He wasn't here for that. That one only had eyes for the frog. He was simply looking for dinner." Forgrac slid between the students and went down a couple of steps before staring up at them. Mischief crossed his face as he turned toward Paxton and eyed the spot he was protecting. "I wouldn't mind a few frogs' legs myself."

Paxton protected his frog under his shirt with more intensity.

The dwarf laughed. "Relax. T'was a joke. I'm not gonna eat your familiar." He screwed up his nose in distaste. "I don't like frogs' legs anyway."

Paxton's shoulders relaxed, allowing Jojo a little more freedom to breathe.

"Who are you?" Paxton asked.

Samara indicated the dwarf. "This is Forgrac."

"I didn't know we had dwarves in the castle." Kaine stood and leaned against the balustrade, making Forgrac seem even smaller against his six-foot frame.

"That'd be right!" Forgrac ran a hand over his bushy beard. "The handsome one doesn't see anybody but himself."

Kaine straightened his jerkin and tugged at his collar before running a hand through his short blue hair. "Actually, I see plenty of females." His eyes passed over Mist then Samara. "There are plenty of pretty females around here."

Samara stiffened. She didn't know how to react, especially when his gaze lingered longer over her. She thought that he showed other females too much attention, and she didn't know what to do with any of it passed her way. Besides, just because he'd looked at her didn't mean he was complimenting her.

The dwarf rolled his eyes and grumbled, "Well,

you wouldn't see me coz I'm the one doin' the dishes and other menial chores 'round the place."

"Oh!" Kaine frowned. "I didn't realize someone physically did them."

Samara gaped at Kaine. "All you had to do was glance over the bench when you put your plate in the kitchen. He's within view, doing the dishes."

Kaine shrugged. "I guess he was too short for me to see."

Paxton inclined his head. "Nice to meet you. Thanks for doing the dishes. It's not a job I would want."

Forgrac pointed his stubby finger at Paxton. "Look at that. He's appreciative and level-headed." He faced Samara and nodded toward Kaine. "Even though he's not as handsome as this one, he'd make a loyal companion."

Paxton gaped and chuckled bashfully. "I'm not looking for anybody."

"And I'm more worried about completing our tasks and ensuring we stay at the coterie," Samara said.

"Fair enough." Forgrac stepped down a couple more steps.

"Wait!" Samara held up a hand. "You said before that you saw students who didn't get their familiars in time. What happened to them?"

"You're seriously at that stage, are you?" Depression washed over Forgrac's face. "I'm sorry to hear that. No wonder you hoped to bond with that owl." He rubbed the sleeve over his upper arm. The movement made him look apprehensive, all the playful confidence from before washed away. "Yes, I've seen what happens to those who don't get familiars. The outcome has never been good."

The blood drained from Samara's face, and her cheeks turned numb as the worry flooded back into her bones.

Forgrac eyed her, an unreadable expression on his face. "Just make sure your magic is up to scratch. Don't waste any practice time. Get it as refined as possible. If you don't find a familiar by the deadline, what you will face will be pretty much impossible to overcome."

"Jeez! Don't sugarcoat it!" Kaine retorted.

The dwarf slowly shook his head. "There's no sugarcoating it. You need to be at the top level with your magic, or you need a familiar. If you don't have one, you will face an opponent you never thought you would face before." He gazed down at the steps. "And it's never been pretty. I haven't seen one student who has been able to stay without a familiar."

Paxton whistled and tightened his protection

over his frog. "That sounds nasty." He looked down at Jojo, and their eyes met. "I'm glad I found you."

"Do you have a familiar?" Mist asked.

Forgrac shook his head. "I'm not a magic wielder. I'm merely a servant. Only the strong magic wielders, mostly from this coterie, have familiars. It's like an emblem, like your brightly colored hair. You ain't a formal part of this coterie if you don't have those two things."

Samara's heart sank.

Forgrac squeezed her arm, his eyes filled with understanding and concern. "Well, I've gotta go, love. I need to get outta here for a bit."

CHAPTER NINETEEN

Samara sat backward on a wooden chair in front of her open window, her arms resting on the chair's back. A breeze brushed against her face. Her mood was wistful as she watched all the tiny critters scurry around the edge of the trees. The afternoon glow had settled in the sky, framing the top of the trees with brilliant hues of orange, blue, purple, and red. She was contemplating another trip to the woods to attempt to bond with an animal, but her continued failure only gnawed at her confidence.

A knock sounded on the door, pulling her attention back to her room, large enough to hold a single bed and a writing desk with a chair.

"Come in!" Samara turned to face the door in time to see Mist swing it open, Okak on her shoulder, preening his black feathers.

"Callista wants to see you in her office."

Samara studied her, but her face was void of emotion, not giving away the reasoning behind the summoning. Not being close to Mist made it harder to read her emotions.

Weeks had passed, and Callista had come and gone several times to check on the progress of the kingdoms' safety–sorting out any trouble that was too strong for her commanders to handle alone.

"Did she say why?"

Mist shrugged. "Not my business. Just passing on the message." She backed out of the room and closed the door behind her.

Samara's heart thundered. She could only suspect one thing, but there was still a tiny thread of hope that she was wrong.

Quickly, she pulled herself together, exited her room, and made her way through the stone passages and up the stone stairs to Callista's office. As her stomach twisted in knots, her eyes fell on some insects hovering near a sconce on the wall in a corner. She was tempted to grab one and pretend it was her familiar. She scoffed at how ridiculous she was being. Callista would see past that. She could test the strength of her magic and know it was just an ordinary insect. Crossing her fingers behind her back, she hoped the meeting wasn't about her lack of a familiar. It would be lovely to find out she was stressing for nothing.

Despite never going to Callista's office, Samara knew where it was. Callista didn't invite many people in there, which meant their meeting would be important.

Mystique sat in front of the double wooden doors, almost as though standing guard, her tail whipping wildly, and an aggravated noise rose from her throat as she watched Samara approach. The black jaguar's piercing yellow eyes fixed on her.

"Hello, Mystique."

The cat yawned then ran her long tongue over her sharp, pointy teeth.

Unimpressed, Samara pointed at the door and asked the jaguar, "Should I just go in?"

Mystique rose and stood in the middle of the doorway, blocking Samara's path.

A few moments later, the door opened, and a pale-faced Kaine exited, moving quickly past the familiar.

Samara approached him, keeping away from the scowling cat. "What happened?"

He appeared frail as he looked at Mystique then back at Samara and shook his head in slight jerky movements as if to avoid being seen. "I can't discuss it," he whispered.

Before Samara could ask more, he took off down the stairs.

A level voice sounded behind her. "Samara."

She spun and found Callista standing in the entry wearing her usual leafed dress, only the color was green. Samara's thoughts vanished as she gaped at the head sorceress. As much as Samara enjoyed having the head sorceress at the coterie base, lately, her returns made her nervous. She knew that one day, Callista would tell her that her time was up. And from the look on Kaine's face, the day must have come.

"Come in." The sorceress stood aside.

Samara struggled to find something charming to say, but her words faltered. The sorceress seemed to love her dresses. The leaves appeared to be her way of saying she was an elf and in touch with all nature. "N-Nice dress," she finally managed to get out.

Callista smiled and spread the skirt of her gown wide. "Thank you. The green seems to make the leaves more like their natural self. Don't you think?"

When her words caught in her throat, all she could do was nod in jerky, unnatural movements.

With a broad sweep of her arm, Callista indicated for Samara to enter.

Apprehensive, Samara scooted past Mystique. The hinges squeaked as Callista closed the door behind her, giving Samara the feeling that her fate was sealed. It was an effort for her to shake off the feeling of doom and take in the room.

The first part of the room housed a thick wooden desk that faced the doors and had a large wooden chair behind it. In each of the four corners stood a pillar. All except one had a large glowing crystal sitting on top: one red, one blue, and one purple. Samara struggled not to gasp. The crystals were the size of someone's head. A faint vibration filled the air, as though the crystals were thrumming and talking to one another. Callista stood in the middle of them, her face peaceful and her head tilted back, her hair draping toward the floor as if she was sucking in the energy they emitted. Her arms spread wide, and she looked to be in a state of praise as she absorbed their energy.

After several awkward moments, she faced Samara and caught her gazing at the empty pillar. "Yes. That's one I'm still looking for. I believe that once I have this final crystal, I will be able to control the lands and bring peace to the kingdoms with a much stronger force."

Taking in the room, Samara felt she shouldn't ask any more questions about the crystals. However, she knew from the lessons with Callista that crystals gave off much energy, accentuating witches' and wizards' magic and making them stronger. With the size of the ones on the pillars, there must be some serious power in those. As she watched the head sorceress interact with the crystals, Samara wondered if it was because of the large crystals that she had the power to take over the realms and keep control over them.

Callista eyed the empty pillar, a rare flash of sorrow on her face. "Clialarion has caused great trouble over the years. This convinced me that the elves are hiding it within their kingdom, and the crystal is giving them strength." She clenched her fist by her side. "I must stop this riffraff and find the last crystal. It's imperative for the safety of all of us."

"What can I do to help?"

Callista's face softened slightly, and she shook her head. "That's what I have my head commanders for—ones who have familiars and are trained in the art of the different magics so that we may be strong enough to uphold the peace." She indicated a chair in front of the desk, and Samara sat, the lump of worry blocking her throat again. After she'd seen Kaine's face, her stomach was churning.

Callista moved to the other side of the desk, her dress swaying softly. She looked revitalized from all the energy she'd taken from the crystals. She clasped her hands together on the desk and leaned toward

Samara, her face returning to its unreadable expression. "I have heard you haven't yet found a familiar."

Samara gulped, trying to swallow the lump in her throat but without success. Giving up on words, she nodded. The room remained silent, and she steeled her emotions enough to answer. "I have tried. I try with trees and leaves, and I've tried hanging around the forest. I've even thought of insects within the building, but nothing has bonded with me." Her gaze dropped to the ground.

Callista sat back, her face still unreadable and her eyes hard like the crystals. "I was afraid this would be so. As you haven't found one yet, I'm afraid the time has come. No longer will the higher power be happy for you to stay here."

Samara found it unnerving not to see any emotion from someone who had practically replaced her family. She tried to place herself in Callista's shoes. Maybe it was easier for the head sorceress to act emotionless especially when she had to do unpleasant work.

"You will have to face a formidable opponent, and the same goes for Kaine. It saddens me, as you are both strong in your magic and have been good apprentices. But I simply cannot keep people here who do not have a familiar to accentuate their gifts." Samara thought she saw a flash of regret or sadness soften the intensity in Callista's eyes. "It isn't allowed. Especially ones as old as you two."

Samara couldn't bring herself to say anything, instead staring at the sorceress, her hands clasped tightly in her lap. She was about to face her greatest fear, and she could feel it deep within her.

When Samara didn't answer, Callista continued, "I can only hope you and Kaine have learned enough to protect yourselves against your opponent. I have talked to my board of commanders, and they will organize the battle. You must fight and succeed, or you will die or be taken captive."

Samara finally found her voice. "What about our families?"

"Per the agreement, if you fail, they will lose all our protection and help. We cannot afford people who do not give us anything in return. Their payments are their siblings' or children's service."

Hearing that delivered without emotion or care for the ones she loved was hard. It broke her heart to think of what her family would go through if she failed. "When is this going to happen?" Samara asked, hoping she had enough time to prepare.

"The day after tomorrow, after an early breakfast. You and Kaine will fight them together. That is how strong these opponents will be."

Samara choked back a sob. It sounded as though

Callista thought she and Kaine combined still wouldn't win against whatever was coming. That scared her. Whatever the opponent was, it must be huge or evil.

"Now, as I told Kaine, you need to go and rest to prepare yourself mentally for this fight. It will be the fight of your life." Callista leaned forward, her palms facing up. "Remember, this isn't personal. It's what must happen. This is ruled by the authority above, who blesses our powers if we stick to their requirements."

CHAPTER TWENTY

The following morning Samara dragged herself out of bed, her mind restless after a pitiful night's sleep. Slowly, she pulled on her black leather pants then her sleeveless fitted jerkin and long black boots. Both she and Kaine had tried again the previous night to bond with a familiar, but she seemed to have less luck every time she went to the forest.

After closing the door behind her, she clopped through the corridor and around to the other side of the building.

Finding Kaine's room, she knocked rapidly. By the time he opened the door, her mind had raced faster over what would happen that day. As agreed, he had dressed in his combat training clothes, consisting of large boots and brown leather pants, with a black leather jerkin strapped tightly to his muscular chest. His handsome face was paler than usual and marred by a slight dark shadow under his eyes. When she looked closer, he almost looked depressed, and his confidence seemed to have wavered.

As though sensing her thoughts, he winked and grinned, appearing not to have a care in the world. "Ready, gorgeous?" He stepped through the door, giving Samara a glimpse into his room. The bed was covered in silk sheets and a thick blanket, and his pillow seemed much fluffier than Samara's. The table was topped with ornaments, his quill pen had a fine feather, and his beautiful ink pot was edged with gold. They were items Samara could only dream of owning.

The door clicked shut, blocking her view into his room. Mortified, she realized he was still watching her. Her cheeks would've flushed with embarrassment if she weren't so nervous about their future. He had a way of making her feel special until she reminded herself of all the other females he had made feel the same way.

She steeled her nerves, raised her chin, and looked him in the eye. "Still plastering on the charm, even though we're facing the biggest battle of our lives tomorrow. Anyway, I'm sure you'd say that to any girl."

Feigning offense, he replied, "I only save it for the special ones like you."

Samara raised an eyebrow. "Uh-huh. I'm sure you say that to all the girls too."

They walked down the corridor and descended the steps, moving through a group of students hurrying to herbology class.

"Looking at all our fellow apprentices rushing off to a different class makes me think we're missing out. Surely we should be learning more about plants to protect ourselves from whatever opponent we're about to face." Kaine turned to Samara and grinned, amused by his own joke. "Don't you think?"

Samara's stomach did a backflip at the reminder that they were about to embark on the fight of their lives and definitely not because Kaine's smile always made her insides flutter. She scowled at him. He didn't seem the slightest bit nervous, yet her insides were turning inside out. "How can you possibly be making light of our situation? My heart is pounding so rapidly with apprehension that I feel like it will explode."

Their steps synced, and he threaded his arm through hers. "I'm trying to lift our spirits, not make you upset." He squeezed her hand. "We're in this together. At least we have that, even though our situation is bordering on hopelessness."

They turned in the opposite direction to the rest of the students and headed down to the lower-level corridor.

Kaine continued, "We both have a lot to lose. As for our families, mine have less to lose than yours. Mine will lose their newfound prestige and social positioning in their city. They will think that's just as bad as your family's problems, but now that I'm removed from them, I can see it's nothing compared to fighting every day to put enough food on the table."

"I don't want either of us or our families to lose anything. We have to get through this."

They turned a corner and unhooked their arms. Kaine entered the protective arts room, preparing for an attack, and Samara followed. The hairs on the back of Samara's neck stood on end as she surveyed the room. Devi sat alone, cross-legged in the middle of the floor, her eyes closed as if she were meditating. Her brown gown draped over her knees and was tucked under her. Her behavior was unusual. Not only was her familiar not with her, but she also hadn't attacked them when they entered, which made Samara even more on edge.

On full alert, they approached the center of the

room and sat not far from their teacher. Samara's head swirled as she searched for Devi's copper wolf to make sure he wasn't about to pounce on them.

Devi opened one eye and squinted at them with amusement. "It's all right. You can relax. I'm not going to attack you."

Nothing seemed out of place in the room, and it wasn't entirely uncommon for a familiar to be absent for a brief time. Samara's shoulders and neck relaxed, and she crossed her legs, her leather pants squeaking. Kaine's did the same.

Lavender from a scented oil burning in the corner wafted through the room, leaving Samara to think that the defense teacher had opted to spend their limited time left teaching them how to meditate. The thought filled Samara with despair. They needed to practice defending themselves, not relaxing and finding their peace.

Despite her apprehension, Samara trusted Devi's ability and knowledge. After a glance at Kaine to see him obliging, she closed her eyes, took a deep breath, and focused on centering her thoughts. Perhaps meditation was what she needed.

A sound came from behind her just as she hit the edge of peace, though it was brief and extremely soft, which tempted her to think she'd imagined it. Lazily, she cracked open one eye and peered over her shoulder just in time to see Zion, Devi's wolf, baring his teeth, ready to pounce on her.

Her eyes widening, she threw up her hands to protect herself. She only had enough time to put up a small barrier. As disappointing as it was, it was enough to block the attack and deflect the wolf toward Kaine. The wolf knocked him over into a fetal position. Teeth exposed, Zion towered over him, and all Kaine could do was tighten his position and attempt to shoot magic or reach for one of the blades sheathed on his lower back, but he was unsuccessful.

Samara recovered quickly, shooting a stunning spell at the wolf before he or Kaine could get hurt. Zion froze, his two front paws weighing Kaine down. The second Kaine realized Zion was incapacitated, he sprang into action, grabbing the wolf's front paws and rolling his stiff body to his side before scrambling backward on all fours.

Wide-eyed, Kaine glanced from Zion to Devi. It took a few moments for the color to return to Kaine's skin. "Did you plan for that to happen?"

Devi remained cross-legged on the floor, her kind face showing no remorse. "It was part of your training. I wanted to see how quickly you would react while in a state of relaxation and how far you would let your guard down. Don't get me wrong.

Meditating and centering your focus is good, but you must still be on your guard."

"Isn't that kind of going against the whole idea of relaxing?" he asked.

Devi nodded. "It is, but at the same time, you still need to be ready to defend yourself even when you think you're among friends. It sounds cynical, yet it's true. You never know what someone else is thinking, especially when it comes to either your life or theirs."

"That sounds a bit much. Are you saying we shouldn't trust anyone? I mean, I thought this was a safe place. A place of learning and bonding so that we can help defeat this great evil lurking in the lands." Samara released her spell on Zion, and the wolf slowly rose to his feet, unfazed.

Devi took a deep breath. "Yes. That is true. I'm not saying you can't trust anyone, only that you should always be wary. The lesson today is to be on guard, as I have always taught you. This is slightly different, as it's bringing to light to be on guard when you think you're in friendly company. It's unlikely that the opponent you're about to face will act trustworthy. Although if they keep you alive and take you as a slave, you will need to know this so that you'll know how to deal with any other slaves you come in contact with."

Samara and Kaine glanced at each other. Although Samara didn't know where Kaine's interests lay, she didn't think he would be a backstabber. She felt the same about Devi. Out of all the teachers, she seemed the most trustworthy and genuinely friendly.

CHAPTER TWENTY-ONE

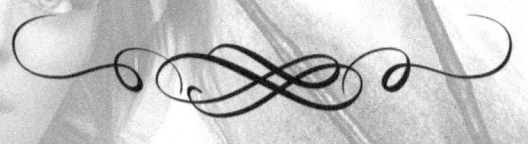

Both Samara and Kaine left their lesson with Devi in confusion. After grabbing their weapons from their rooms, they took apples and some nuts from the food hall then headed through the common room, weaving through the students as they arrived after their herbology class.

"There you are!" A feminine voice barely carried over the din of the room.

Samara turned to look for the voice's owner, only to be brushed aside as the tall, golden-haired Luna made her way to Kaine. The slender elf threw her arms around him, almost squashing his head into her ample cleavage exposed by her low-cut dress. Samara looked away after she caught the dreamy look on Kaine's face, and a strange feeling burned in her abdomen. Luna was three years his junior, a year younger than Samara, yet she didn't hesitate to almost throw herself at him.

"I'm so sorry. I was looking for you in class and heard you have to go against the enemy, and that's why you weren't with us." She squeezed his head tighter against her chest. "That's horrible! And all because you haven't been lucky enough to bond with a familiar yet." She was extremely tall, almost half a head taller than Kaine, making him seem short. She kissed him on the crown of his head. "I need you to win and come back to me." She released the pressure on his head a little.

Kaine winked at her. "Don't worry. I'm not done fighting yet. You know how good I am with my blades."

Samara fought the urge to roll her eyes. His corniness and overconfidence were getting ridiculous. She almost pointed out that she'd had to save his backside back in defense class but decided to leave everyone with some hope that their favorite male would return and be able to stay at the coterie.

She grabbed Kaine by his elbow. "I'm sorry, Luna. But I need to take this fantastic warrior to train with me so that I can learn from his expertise. I want to return here as well."

Luna released him, her mouth agape. "Oh. I'm sorry. I didn't realize you also have to prove yourself." She placed an elegant hand on Samara's shoulder, each finger adorned with elven rings, some jeweled. That alone made it clear she came from an affluent family. What her family was getting in return for their daughter's apprenticeship was a mystery.

Samara shrugged it off. She had more significant problems to deal with at the moment. Of course Luna wouldn't have realized she was missing from class, despite there only being twenty students. Even though Luna had always been friendly to her, their friendship had never really blossomed. "That's all right. Although surely you understand I need him all the time he has to spare at the moment."

Luna wrapped an arm around Samara's shoulders and squeezed. "Of course. We want you both to come back."

A strand of Samara's hair brushed across her face, and she pulled it away. She held back the accusation tickling the tip of her tongue and smiled. "Thanks. That's good to hear." Pulling harder on Kaine's elbow, she turned and led him out the front door.

When they were out of the large building they called their home, Samara pulled out her apple and took a bite, savoring the juices. She hoped that if captured, they would still have an abundance of fresh food, especially fruit. Their pace was more casual than normal, giving them time to eat as they walked through the pine forest surrounding their complex.

"Thanks for saving me back there."

Shocked, Samara replied, "Saving you? Please! You looked like you were in your element." She took another bite of her apple.

He grinned. "I play my part well. Don't you agree?"

Samara swallowed. "I don't know about playing a part. But you're certainly lapping up all the females' attention."

Kaine eyed through the forest. "As I've said before, only your attention matters."

Samara rolled her eyes. "And as I've said, I'm sure you say that to all the females."

"Believe what you want. I know the truth."

"And I'm pretty sure I do too." Samara threw some almonds into her mouth and tugged on the string of her bow slung across her chest. They were supposed to meet Zofia for weapons practice, but there was no sign of her. "Do you think Zofia will use Devi's method on us?"

"Do you mean surprise attack us?" Kaine's blue eyes suddenly clouded, and his fingers edged toward his back, where he sheathed his throwing knives.

"Something like that." Samara threw her apple core under a tree, unhooked her bow, and grabbed an arrow from her quiver. Calming her nerves, she listened but heard no strange sounds. The birds were still chirping. That usually meant everything was normal for the forest animals. She relaxed slightly yet still kept her eyes peeled. "What did you think about what Devi said?"

"Which part?" Kaine also remained on high alert, which wasn't surprising after what happened in the defense class.

"About basically not trusting anyone."

He pulled a face. "I think it was a little over the top. If you can't trust anyone, what's the point of living? Life's to be shared with people."

"Exactly!" Samara lowered her bow.

"Although there are always some you should always keep an eye on and never let your guard down. I don't think there are any at Sacred Flame that we need to worry about." He let his hands fall to his sides. There hadn't been any sign of anyone in the woods.

"That was my thought also. I guess she was only being overcautious in case we're captured."

Kaine shivered. "I still don't know what's worse, being captured or being killed."

"I guess it depends on how the captors treat you."

She paused at the edge of the pine forest before the change in trees. "Let's hope we'll be able to work together and defeat whoever we have to fight." She gazed at Kaine, trying to find doubt or apprehension in his expression.

Something whistled behind Samara, and before she could turn to look, Kaine slammed into her, knocking her to the ground. At the same time, he threw one of his knives in the direction of the sound. The wind rushed from her lungs. A thud sounded above them, and Samara glanced up to see the rounded blade of a chakram embedded in the tree trunk behind where Samara had stood only moments before.

It took a second for her to be able to breathe. Then the reality hit her hard. She had nearly been sliced by that weapon, but Kaine had saved her.

Kaine crouched, reaching for the knives tucked behind his back. Still struggling for breath, Samara pounced to her feet and nocked an arrow. The way things were progressing, their next lesson was going to be much like defense class. It made sense. After all, they were about to face an enemy that could either kill them or capture them.

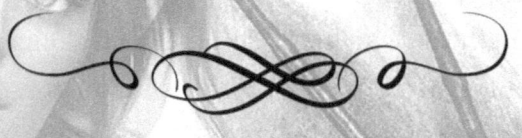

CHAPTER TWENTY-TWO

Keeping her eyes peeled, Samara followed Kaine through the forest. Zofia was somewhere in the trees. Or she hoped it was Zofia. Or else the enemy had already arrived. At least Zofia shouldn't be trying to kill them, only injure them to a point that they could be healed.

The sound of a chakram cutting through the leaves progressed toward them. Samara ducked to the side, pulling Kaine with her. Leaves were sliced in half, and more thumping headed their way.

Samara caught a glimpse of a shuriken just as it flew past, the silver flashing in a small ray of sunlight through the trees. His eyes wide, Kaine grabbed the knives from his back, one on each hand, and they progressed forward, stepping cautiously, trying not to make a sound. The last thing they needed was a large branch to crack under their footsteps. At the same time, they scanned the forest for any sign of Zofia's bright-purple hair. That color would show through the trees. At least Samara hoped they would find the weapon master's hair instead of facing their formidable opponent early. Even if they spotted her familiar, Jet, it would be a welcome sight.

They'd progressed several more feet when the soft whistling of a flying weapon headed their way. They squatted, shifting to the side. That time, an axe hit a tree not far behind them at their former head height.

Wide-eyed, Kaine said, "I've never known Zofia to throw weapons at our heads before. Maybe our fight against the outside opponent has started."

Samara followed his gaze. The axe wiggled, the handle shifting up and down slightly before it flew out of the trunk and back in the direction it had come.

"Unless our opponent has magic, I would say that is a telltale sign that we're being attacked by Zofia or someone from this coterie as practice."

Working quickly, she pulled her quiver off her back and unpacked her cloak, shrugged it on, and pulled up the hood to hide her bright-pink hair. Kaine did the same. They should probably have done it earlier. But the robes blocked some of their vision.

Kaine's shoulders relaxed, although the tension lines around his eyes remained. "That's kind of good news. Except someone we can't see is attacking us."

Remaining low, the two followed the direction the axe had taken—until an attack came from the right, causing them to question their direction. They were about to turn to follow the origin of the last weapon when Samara spotted a moving shadow.

She tugged at Kaine's arm and pointed at the movement obscured by the bushes. "Is that Jet?" she whispered.

Kaine squinted then shrugged.

They didn't follow the shadow because the familiar might attack them, too, and they would rather not fight a large bear, even if he was small for his breed. The shadow seemed to be moving in another direction. Using signs, they decided to continue after the last weapon. Another black shadow appeared on the right, and they froze. Either Jet had somehow scrambled ahead of them and circled back in a short time, or that was another familiar or animal. When a weapon flew over their heads from another direction, Kaine indicated that he thought there were two attackers. Samara nodded before suggesting they separate.

They dropped to the ground and progressed closer, sticking to the cover of the foliage. As they moved farther apart, Samara glanced one last time at Kaine. His hood had fallen, though his blue hair wasn't too evident in the shadows of the forest. Eventually, he disappeared through the bushes.

Pulling her hood farther over her hair, she dropped further, almost crawling on all fours. Pausing, she took a deep breath. If the attacker was someone from the coterie, then she didn't want to harm them too much, and she definitely didn't want to kill them. She had to prepare for either option. After fishing a few arrows from her quiver, she muttered incantations over individual arrows and strapped the charmed arrows on her thighs. One side was for friendly fire. The other was for potential outside opponents.

When she felt prepared, she spelled another arrow to find the person attacking her. Her knees cracked as she crouched low, then she nocked her arrow and released it into the sky. The arrow rose above the highest treetops, abruptly turned, then dived toward the last spot that the shuriken had come from. Seconds later came a small explosion of bright-red dust, which settled in the leaves and branches.

Samara picked up her pace, determined to take down that attacker. That time she didn't worry as much about the noise she was making.

When she had sprinted a hundred yards, she shot another charmed arrow into the sky to determine whether the person had moved. The arrow shot up and deviated slightly from its original target before exploding with a shower of a bright-yellow powder several yards away. The lack of a thud convinced Samara that the arrow hadn't landed in a tree.

She increased her pace again. When she thought she was almost there, she crouched behind some bracken to scope out the area. A sound came from her right, and she spun quickly. Either Kaine was lost, or the two opponents were coming together. Worried, she tried to organize her thoughts and started toward the yellow explosion while keeping an eye on her right. Another movement came from there, and she spotted Kaine's blue hair through the leaves. He had seen her, too, and edged toward her until another weapon attacked him from his right, and he set off in that direction. The yellow explosion must have caught his attention, dragging him away from his attacker. He probably didn't know Samara had been the one behind it.

Samara continued forward, catching sight of another movement not far away. She crouched behind a tree, carefully checking around the side. A hooded figure stood poised and ready. The face wasn't visible, but Samara suspected it was Zofia because of the figure's size.

She let another arrow fly at the hooded figure, aiming for the legs. It hit. The figure reached for the arrow sticking out of their leg and flung their other arm in Samara's direction before crumpling to the ground.

Distracted by her success, Samara didn't hear the soft whistle of a shuriken until it hit her in the upper arm, slicing off a piece of skin. She gritted her teeth as pain shot through her. It was only a flesh wound, something she could heal later.

Zofia's blue eyes found Samara behind the tree trunk, and she bared her teeth. Samara nocked another arrow, tears forming in her eyes.

"Don't move!" Samara moved to a ready stance. "If you move one muscle like you're going to throw something, I will shoot."

Zofia grinned slyly and her eyebrow twitched, putting Samara on edge. Zofia was planning something. She must be about to send another shuriken her way. Samara kept her eyes trained on her teacher.

Something solid and heavy rammed into her side, knocking her to the ground and pinning her there. Turning her head, she was met with the big black face of Jet. His vast array of pointed teeth was exposed, and drool dripped from his mouth.

Samara curled into a ball, chastising herself. Of course Jet would be there, protecting his bonded. Zofia might be small and feisty, but her bear seemed scarier. As far as she knew, he had never killed an apprentice. Still, she wouldn't take any chances. As Jet pawed Samara, she could see Zofia rising to her feet. She had to move. Struggling, she worked her hand up through her compacted limbs. Finally feeling a breeze on her fingers, she opened her hand and shot a bolt of magic at him. "Petra!" she whispered.

The bear froze, one paw raised. Samara shuffled from underneath him, rolled onto her back, and pushed him over with her feet before standing.

The whistle of a shuriken was barely audible in her ears, and she quickly spun to the side, grabbed her bow and another non-lethal arrow, and shot Zofia in the arm. The force of the arrow knocked her to the side. The shuriken scraped Samara's thigh right as Zofia hit the ground and her feet buried underneath the soil.

Despite Zofia's obvious pain, she chuckled. "Well played." The teacher waved her hands, her palms open. "I'm not going to attack you."

Samara inched forward, her body still poised for attack.

"I promise. I'm not going to attack you," Zofia insisted.

Since Zofia hadn't made any sudden moves, her battle seemed to be over, and she allowed her body to relax slightly. "Is it just you out here, or is someone helping you?" She edged toward her teacher, ready to help her, when a dull whistle sounded from the right. Samara shifted and watched the weapon fly by, astounded to see another axe. That confirmed it. Zofia had help. But how much help, she didn't know.

She searched the area where the weapon had come from to find Kaine charging out of the bushes, knives raised. He threw himself at a slim figure, knocking them to the ground.

Then he forced the hooded figure onto their back, his knife poised at their throat. Their hood fell off, exposing Callista's long lilac hair.

CHAPTER TWENTY-THREE

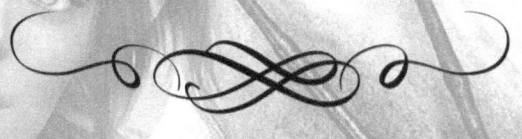

K aine gasped as the head sorceress scrambled to her feet. "I'm so sorry!"

Callista swept her leg behind Kaine's, making him flip. He landed on all fours, his knife still in hand. Pulling his knees to his chest, he jumped to his feet and swung his fist. Callista lurched backward and struggled to remain standing. Kaine shifted forward, only to be blocked by Mystique, her claws out and her teeth bared. When Samara moved to help him, Zofia held her back by her arm.

Kaine lunged toward Mystique with his knife, only to have his arm blocked by Callista. Quickly, he spun backward and kicked Mystique in the backside, sending the jaguar flying. The cat howled and cowered, lowering to the ground as Kaine prepared for another attack.

Coldness entered Callista's eyes, turning them into blue stones. She shot out a hand palm first. It connected with Kaine's chest and knocked him backward. "No one touches my familiar!"

The iciness in her tone sent shivers down Samara's spine.

When Kaine landed, his body fell limp, almost as though he didn't have bones. "Sorry!" he gasped, sounding winded.

Callista strolled forward and calmed Mystique, instantly healing the bruise on her backside. "Don't be sorry. You fought well." With Mystique safe, she turned her attention back to Kaine. "You both should be proud of what you've done."

Panic passed through Kaine's eyes as she neared.

"I won't attack you now." Callista lifted her hands palms forward, in a similar move to releasing a spell, and Kaine's eyes widened. A moment later, his body relaxed, and he pushed himself into a sitting position. "Now heal your wounds. I have come out today to help fight you both because I want to see if you can handle yourself. It seems the answer is yes, and I hope you will both be able to stay in our little community and learn under us. It is a shame that you haven't found familiars. But it is a requirement from the higher power. As I have clarified, you are stronger if you have a familiar. Without them, you both still have weaknesses."

The sorceress placed a hand on each of their shoulders. "Even so, I hope you'll be able to put these aside to win tomorrow. Because if you don't win, tonight will be your last night with us. You will be either deceased or enslaved."

"What happens if we're captured and manage to escape?" Kaine asked.

"If you do and find your way back, you will be given another chance. But still, you will need a familiar to be able to stay. Because I guarantee there are enemies out there that you will not be able to stand against, even with your strong magic, unless you have the added strength of a familiar by your side." She shifted forward and spun to face them. It felt strange to see her out of her leaf-patterned gown. "Now, I'm going to leave you in Zofia's hands to teach you as much as she can in one afternoon. After today's lesson, I want you to eat, rest, clear your heads, and be ready for tomorrow, because your enemy will be great."

THE FOLLOWING DAY, Samara met Kaine, and they had an early breakfast. Though it was hard for her to eat anything, she forced herself, knowing she would need strength. They still didn't know who they would be facing. Callista either didn't know or wasn't going to tell them, probably so that they wouldn't be even more scared.

When they were about to leave the dining hall, all the students filed in and crowded around.

"Good luck!" Paxton said. Jojo sat on his forearm, his black eyes observing Kaine and Samara.

Mist moved next to him. Okak stood on her broad shoulders, instantly causing Paxton to protect Jojo. "I wish I could be there to help you fight, but it's against the rules."

Samara clasped her hands tightly in front of her. "If only we could have you there. Your fighting skills would certainly be useful."

"Thanks, beautiful." Kaine winked. "I'm sure we'll be spectacular and defeat them."

A flash of gold charged at Kaine, and Luna wrapped her arms around him, hugging him close to her ample cleavage. "I hope you come back." She wiped the corner of her eye. "I'm going to miss you." She held him at arm's length, her thin frame towering over his. "It's so not fair. I really hope you defeat them." She looked at the apprentices circling them. "And I hope all of us get familiars and don't have to go through what you're about to go through."

The noise in the dining hall grew as the worried students broke into animated chatter. Then suddenly, all fell silent. After a quick search, Samara spotted Callista standing outside the door. She grabbed Kaine's arm and nodded toward the head sorceress.

Her golden diadem sat across her forehead. She often wore the trinket when she was about to conduct serious business. "Are you ready?"

Kaine and Samara locked eyes. Worry flashed through his then disappeared, and he winked at Samara.

"We're ready. Aren't we, Samara?"

His confidence was a lie, but she didn't blame him. She nodded, trying to force down the large lump in her throat.

Callista addressed the apprentices crowding around. "Now, everyone. You are to stay indoors and out of the way. You are not to come down to be with them." When she had finished scrutinizing the other students, she turned back to Samara and Kaine, her blue eyes seeming to gaze straight through them. "Now, come. I will lead you there."

CHAPTER TWENTY-FOUR

Callista led them out of the food hall, her leaf-patterned beige dress swaying in time with her hips. The jaguar followed closely behind them, and Samara could feel the cat's eyes on her, making her nerves jangle. A melancholy blanketed her and Kaine.

"Where are we going?" he asked when they reached the edge of the pine forest.

"I'm taking you through the forest to a spot where we agreed to meet. It's out of the way, where the other students cannot see you. It won't do their morale any good if they see what you must go through."

The pine leaves crumpled softly under Callista's moccasins. With Mystique by her side, she weaved her way through the trees then turned to face them when they were out of sight of the building. "Because you both fought so well yesterday, and losing you will be a great loss, I have brought these for you." She dipped her hand into a small bag she had slung over her shoulder resting just in front of her hip and pulled out four crystals, two red and two blue. "These should help you throughout your fight, to give you strength and let you be centered so that you will make the right decisions at the right time."

The cat yawned, showing off her pointed teeth, and stretched her long tongue.

"You could just not make us go." Kaine grabbed two of the crystals. "After all, you said you'll miss us so much, and we've proven ourselves to be strong." He gave her an endearing smile that would make most women swoon.

Callista's mouth twitched with amusement, and her eyes softened. She placed her hands on their shoulders. "I would love to keep you here. Unfortunately, to be strong as a community, we need everyone to have a familiar. Beating these opponents is the only thing that will allow you to stay. These will be like nothing else you have faced, and they are intimidating. It will be a tough feat to escape them." She handed the last two crystals to Samara. "I wish you both magical strength. If you are caught and eventually manage to escape, you will be welcomed back to this coterie, and you will have more time to find a familiar. If, on the other hand, you defeat the formidable opponents today, the same offer stands. Either way, you will need to bond with a familiar eventually to be of any use to us and these kingdoms."

The black jaguar moved to the bushes, her yellow eyes shining through them when she looked.

"Unfortunately, we must go, but don't forget to use the magic of the crystals. I hope they aid you." The head sorceress about-faced and led them farther through the trees.

Samara juggled the crystals in her left hand, twirling them one over the other, before putting them in her pocket. Her bow was strapped over her chest, her quiver on her back, and she had done everything she could to strengthen herself during the night, including charming a couple of arrows that she'd slotted against her thigh.

They fell silent as they passed through the pine forest and into the general forest. They weaved past the plain where Samara had planted her mulberry bush. Eliphas had been correct. The tree did lure animals, but none of them had wanted to bond with her. Only the previous night, she had spent more time next to the tree, trying to attract an animal, but none obliged.

Instead of a beacon of hope, the mulberry tree had become a reminder of her biggest failure.

Mystique circled them and went ahead. Her black tail was barely visible through the forest, sometimes disappearing behind low bushes.

The group was almost noiseless as they approached Samara and Kaine's impending doom. Samara brushed the thought aside and attempted to replace it with positive thoughts, filling her mind with ideas for them to work together to fight the enemy. Maybe because there were two of them, they would have a better chance—unless there were several contenders. Callista hadn't specified the details, which ate away at Samara's confidence.

She adjusted her quiver and bow on her shoulder, and the arrows rattled softly. The leather groaned when she tightened her belt, ensuring everything was secure. The fiddling probably also helped calm her nerves, making her think she was doing something constructive.

The toe of Kaine's boot got stuck in a root, and he stumbled, which was unusual for him. Samara glanced sideways at him, searching for any signs of fear, only to have him catch her eye and wink at her. Over the last few days, she'd started to think his charm was a way to cover his true feelings, which made her believe he was currently hiding his fear, especially since he stumbled again moments later.

After traveling for quite some time, Callista paused. Mystique had circled back and sat at the edge of a small clearing, her eyes eerily studying them.

Speaking softly, Callista asked her familiar, "Have you found something?"

The jaguar's body language was more rigid than usual. She flicked her tail from side to side with an air of annoyance. From the way the cat moved her head, it appeared as though she was talking to Callista.

Moments later, Callista nodded. "Hmm. Thank you, Mystique."

The familiar rose with her tail in the air and continued.

"Mystique has told me that the enemy is just ahead. If you don't want to announce you're coming, you'd better soften your footsteps. She says they're so noisy that a deaf mouse could hear you."

The jaguar often insulted the students, and Callista softened the blow in her translations, but the latest one still came across harshly. Samara had thought she was treading softly, and every new footstep she took made her stress more. At the same time, her worry seemed to make her steps louder, although she wasn't alone. Kaine was doing the same, his movement awkward, and more small branches cracked under his feet.

Pausing, Samara took a deep breath, trying to calm her nerves, then she fell in line behind Callista.

They passed another copse of trees. When they got to the other side, Callista stopped, and Samara nearly ran into her. Her jaw dropped as she looked up. Beside her, Kaine's reaction was the same. Before them were at least ten giant trolls. Samara had never seen them in person before, let alone fought them. She doubted Kaine had either. The trolls were at least twice their size and had bodies thicker than large tree trunks. Muscles bulged in their chests and arms. Samara swallowed, unsuccessfully trying to get rid of the lump in her throat. She didn't see how they could defeat so many trolls, even if there were two of them.

CHAPTER TWENTY-FIVE

Frozen in shock, Samara stared at the monstrous beings dressed in ragged loincloths. She couldn't believe they had to fight trolls. Callista had warned them that their opponent would be intimidating, but fighting creatures as large and numerous as those was ridiculous, even though there were two of them.

She gripped her bow, wondering if it was all a joke. When she looked at Kaine, his face was void of color, his charming demeanor utterly gone, and pure fear had kicked in.

When a hand landed on her shoulder, she jumped. She felt too nervous to laugh off her reaction when Callista stood between her and Kaine.

"I hate to do this," the sorceress said in a low

voice, "but it must be done. The great leader has requested the change."

Before Samara could process what she meant, Callista shoved her and Kaine into the clearing with the trolls. They flailed and struggled to remain upright.

Samara glanced over her shoulder to see Callista watching them, her face blank, as usual. With a wave of her hand, she put up a barrier, locking them in with the trolls.

When Samara faced her opponents, all ten trolls eyed them with amusement. Determination crossed the closest one's face, and he started toward them. Following his example, the others stepped forward. Anticipation and worry made Samara's nerves tingle and her arms numb as she called to her magic. She would need it.

But her magic didn't surface. Samara paused, twirling her fingers, as she called again to the magic, trying to place a barrier between the two of them and the trolls. One of the trolls passed right through the intended spot. She tried another time, but again, nothing happened, and all feeling left her face. Her magic was faulty.

She glanced at Kaine. "Help me construct a barrier. Mine didn't work."

His face still pale, he nodded. They worked

together, aiming for a place in the middle of the field. A moment later, their hopes were shattered when another troll passed through it, his giant footsteps quickly closing the gap between them.

"It didn't work." Kaine's face turned ghostly white. "What's going on? Even with us joined together, our magic doesn't work."

Samara shook her head. "I don't know. It's like we've been stripped of it."

"Surely not." Kaine peered over his shoulder, and Samara quickly followed suit. Callista had disappeared, and only the yellow eyes of Mystique stared between the branches.

Showing annoyance, Kaine waved his hand at the trolls. "Surely they wouldn't have stripped us of our magic to fight them. This is ridiculous. There're too many of them."

Samara's eyes widened. "How are we supposed to do that?"

"I don't know. It seems completely unfair." He scratched his temple, the worry lines growing deeper. "I thought we'd still have our magic when we came to this battle. Otherwise, why did we go to defense class for magic?"

Samara groaned. "Because it was our choice. We chose that lesson because we thought we would have magic to fight. We should have just spent our time in weapons training." Looking over her shoulder, she yelled back into the bushes, "Callista!" When she didn't see her, she called out again. "Callista! Have we seriously been stripped of our magic?" She waited, but nothing happened, though she could still see Mystique's eyes in the distance.

With no sign of their head sorceress, Samara pulled an arrow from her quiver and whispered an incantation over it. She nocked the arrow and said quietly to Kaine, "This is one way to test whether we've been stripped of all magic." She released the string, and the arrow flew straight toward the nearest troll and hit him in the thigh.

After a cry of pain, the troll yanked the arrow out of his thigh, broke it over his other leg, and tossed it aside.

Samara held her breath as she waited for the magic to take effect. But nothing changed. The troll kept up his pace, despite the blood trickling down his thigh.

"That isn't good. I put a stunning spell on that arrow. The troll should be immobile by now, no matter how big he is." Her cheeks lost all feeling as she watched the troll, and her lips barely moved as she said, "We've been stripped of all magic."

Without saying a word, Kaine pulled two of his knives from their sheaths on his back.

Samara grabbed another arrow, nocked it, and shot at the first troll's knees. Her aim was true but lacked the desired effect. Other than a little cry of discomfort, it didn't seem to bother the troll. He pulled the arrow out and broke it before throwing it aside.

Disbelief passed over Kaine's face as he looked at his knives, then at the trolls, who had almost reached them. "As if two little knives are going to do anything against these guys in hand-to-hand combat." He sounded disgusted by his choice of weapon.

"Just do the best you can. We'll work together. Let's aim for one at a time, unless all the trolls come at once."

Kaine flipped the blades in the air then caught them. His eyes were set on the trolls, as though he was weighing up something. He stilled the knives, and after a few moments of silence, he said, "I have an idea. I'll run and try to cut their ankles, and you aim for the eyes or the knees. Let's hope between the two of us, this will take them down."

Samara retrieved another arrow. "Since we have no magic, that sounds like the best plan." Panic rose in her. She hoped it had only been stripped away for the one battle, and if they managed to survive, they would get it back.

She pushed the thought aside. *One step at a time.*

Without hesitation, Kaine bolted toward the first troll, who was only a few feet away. He barely dodged the troll's swinging arm and slid on his backside, skimming across the wildland grass, leaving a trail through its beautiful flowers. Twisting to his side, he flicked his body around, aiming his knife at the back of the troll's ankle. Samara had to hand it to him. The move had taken some skill, proving how agile he was when he set his mind to it.

The troll roared, and his legs buckled, blood gushing out of his heel and over his bare feet.

Quickly, Samara nocked an arrow and aimed it at the heart of the troll closest to her. It shot straight in, the cry of pain ceased, and the troll fell lifeless to the ground. The next troll quickened his pace toward them, followed quickly by a third. Kaine jumped to his feet and sprang at the first one, zigzagging between the troll's swipes, dived between his legs, and sliced his blade across the back of one of his heels. Blood spurted everywhere, and the troll bellowed in pain. But Kaine didn't have a chance to relax after his victory. He jumped to his feet and headed for the next troll as Samara aimed for the crying troll's eyes.

She released the string, and the troll shifted at the last second. The arrow hit the troll in the bridge of his nose. She cursed and readied another arrow then let it fly straight for his heart. That time, the shot flew true. She pulled her eyes away from the troll just in time to see Kaine being battered by a troll as two others closed in on him.

Kaine flew a few feet, and a groan of pain escaped his lips when he landed with a thud. He dropped his knives, and it took him a moment to recover and unhook another knife from his back. He scrambled onto his hands and knees and attempted to get up. It took him longer than normal, his face distorted in pain.

Samara gritted her teeth, grabbed another arrow, and shot it at the troll stomping after Kaine. She didn't have a chance to aim for his heart, as the troll was facing the wrong way. Instead, the arrow landed in the lobe of his giant ear like an earring. She shot another arrow, and it hit the troll in the back of his neck, doing nothing to slow down the troll. He cried his annoyance, yanked the arrow out, and tossed it aside, as though it were only a little stick, and continued toward Kaine.

The troll's companion turned to pursue Samara, and she pulled the bow's string tight, trying not to let her tension affect her shot. The arrow would have to hit the troll's heart. She took a deep breath and released the string. The arrow hit the troll directly in the required place, piercing through his heart.

The giant slumped onto his knees. Samara inwardly cheered, glad all her practice had paid off. She pulled her eyes away from the deceased troll and snuck a glance at the one pursuing Kaine, only to find that he was towering over him. In her moment of panic, she remembered the arrows she had enchanted the previous night and pulled one from her thigh. She nocked it and shot it at the troll. It hit the troll's arm, causing him to roar with pain. He gazed at the impact point just in time to see the arrow before he fell onto his side, the arrow causing him to go limp.

Samara's spirits lifted. The arrows she had enchanted hadn't been stripped of their magic. It had done exactly as she had charmed it to do. As the troll fell, Kaine sat up and nodded his appreciation at her. He still seemed in pain from the latest troll's hit. Despite the small victory, they still had six trolls to go, and Kaine was injured. Their chances weren't looking great.

CHAPTER TWENTY-SIX

The six remaining trolls quickened their pace, all charging at once. Their footsteps thundered over the ground, and Kaine scrambled to his feet and bolted, his steps unsteady. After the blow he'd received, he must be in pain. He dived to the ground, aiming for the next troll's heel.

Samara shot at the troll, but because of the way it was facing, it was impossible to get him in the heart. The arrow hit the troll in the face, managing to annoy him further. He spun, swinging his fists low, and knocked Kaine straight into other trolls. Samara's brow furrowed with worry. She grabbed her last remaining arrow that she had prepared with magic and shot it at the troll who'd hit Kaine. It landed in the troll's backside, and his back straightened as he paused momentarily and yanked it out before he slumped immobile to the ground.

Another troll spotted Samara and charged toward her. She quickly nocked a regular arrow and shot it at the troll's eye. He swiped it before it hit him, knocking it off course. Whether it was by sheer luck or skill, she didn't know.

She nocked another arrow and found it challenging to decide whom to shoot next. One troll was nearly on Kaine and another almost upon her, with others behind them. Samara hit the one closest to her first and hoped Kaine could deal momentarily with the one pursuing him. She continued firing arrow after arrow, finding it hard to get a direct shot at their hearts.

Kaine was obviously doing his best to fight with his knives, but he was regularly hit because his weapon needed closer contact.

Samara reached for another arrow, only to find that she had shot her last one. Quickly, she scanned the ground and found one that had been pulled out of a troll. She picked it up, nocked it, aimed it at the next troll, and managed to hit it in its heart. He crumpled to his knees before falling face-first onto the ground, leaving four remaining.

Kaine struggled to move, his body badly bruised and his face swollen around his left eye and chin.

Each movement was slower and sloppier. A troll walloped Kaine in the side, and he landed on his stomach, groaning loudly enough to be heard from ten feet away.

A troll swiped at Samara, and she barely dodged it, feeling the brush of the wind against her face. Kaine struggled to get onto all fours. He grabbed a knife from his back sheath and threw it at the nearest troll, aiming for its heart. The troll dodged at the last second, anger plastered across his face, and he headed straight toward Kaine, ready to take revenge.

Samara tried her magic again. Even if she could only use it to call her whole arrows back, it would help. Her chances were slim, and her actions were fueled by desperation. Nothing happened.

In a moment of clarity, she remembered the small canteen of poison from a gympie-gympie plant she had collected. First, she needed to find another arrow. She scanned the ground and almost squealed with excitement when she spotted one a few feet away. Charging toward it, she somersaulted and picked it up, narrowly missing another strike. She fished for the small sack attached to her quiver and untied it. Dodging another blow from a troll, she quickly unlaced the bag and dipped the arrow tip into the moistened poison power, ensuring it was well coated. Quickly, she nocked the arrow and shot it into the next troll. Again, the troll roared and pulled out the arrow before he continued toward Samara.

As disappointment riddled Samara, she dodged a swipe. The poison should be working. Perhaps the size of the troll was making it either ineffective or slow to work. She chastised herself for her lack of foresight to make more spelled arrows. As if two spelled arrows would be enough. At the same time, she couldn't have known that they would be fighting more than one creature, let alone ten creatures at least twice their size, after being stripped of their magic. All the apprentices from the coterie working together would have trouble fighting ten trolls at once. She hoped the younger students would never have to face such a battle.

Exhausted, she dodged another swipe from a troll and allowed herself a glance around the plain then the surrounding forest. Her skin crawled when she spotted Mystique sitting in the shadows, her yellow eyes watching. Surely the cat could've gotten off her backside and come to help her and Kaine fight the trolls. Instead, she sat and observed them being wholly defeated.

If Mystique was still watching, maybe Callista was somewhere nearby. Or perhaps the jaguar wanted to entertain her perverted mind and watch them be destroyed and possibly slaughtered. The cat had never been friendly to her. She had only seen it be nice to Callista and no one else. It seemed the cat only put up with them because Callista told her to. Samara couldn't help wondering if the cat had a heart as black as her hide, the evil lurking underneath. Seeing the yellow eyes watching them only fueled her suspicion. She didn't know how the cat could be such a horrible creature and be connected with Callista, the savior of all the kingdoms, the one sorceress who wielded the magic to protect them. It just didn't seem to go together. She wondered if Mystique was just an evil unto herself or if, because she was like that, she was the perfect alter ego for Callista. Her sick nature would enlighten Callista as to the conniving thoughts of any plotter, putting the sorceress one step ahead of any evildoer in the lands.

Smashed from the side, Samara fell to the ground, pain radiating from her leg. Shoving her thoughts of Mystique aside, she focused on the battle just in time to avoid the swing of a fist. Something hard pressed into her leg, and she felt the spot, finding the two crystals Callista had given her earlier. She fished into her pocket and drew them out. The stones wouldn't do her any good without the use of magic. She could only think of one other use. She hurled a stone at one troll's eye then the second stone at another troll's eye. Both aimed true, and the trolls cried in anguish.

Suddenly, she was grabbed from behind and turned to look directly into a troll's face. It was massive. The troll gaped and let out a sour breath. She held back a gag and took in his sizable nose in the middle of his wrinkled face. Brown teeth showed under his parted lips. She wasn't sure if she had ever seen a creature so ugly.

Samara kicked and wriggled, trying to escape. The troll shook her. His tight grip made her think her ribs would crack. In her peripheral vision, Kaine was clobbered again by a troll. His body fell limp several feet away.

"No! Please leave him alone!" she screamed, knowing full well that she had no control over the trolls.

Her vision blurred as the troll shook her again, and the ones she had shot with arrows enchanted with stunning spells began to climb to their feet. Disappointment rocked through her. They were supposed to be stunned longer than that, but she had only enchanted them with a spell strong enough for a smaller being. Trolls were the last things she'd expected to fight.

The troll harassing Kaine whacked him again, and he fell to the ground, immobile.

"Please, leave him! Please! We're only fighting you because we were told we had to. We don't want to hurt you, but we had no choice. We were made to." The troll holding her dug his fingers into her ribcage. She felt like she could hardly breathe. "Please, let us live. We won't hurt you anymore."

The troll holding her looked confused. It seemed as though no one had talked to him before.

She begged again. "Please, let us live. Take us. We will work as your servants, if that's what you wish."

His large, bulging eyes scanned over her, and he snorted. "You are puny. What could you do for us?"

Samara gasped, trying to get some air into her lungs. "I'm sure we can work that out as soon as we heal." She cast another worried glance at Kaine's still form. She hoped he wasn't dead. "Please don't hurt him anymore. We promise not to hurt you."

"As the other troll said, you are puny. What can you do for us?" another troll asked.

A different troll picked up Kaine by his foot and dangled him. "Very puny."

Samara was grasping at straws, but she didn't know what else to do. "We have powerful magic. It was stripped from us before our battle. It should return as soon as we leave here, and we're not battling you anymore. We have also been trained in medicine. Maybe we can be of service to help heal you, or perhaps you want someone to wield magic for you for some other purpose. We could do these things for you when our magic returns, and we have healed."

The troll holding her rubbed an arm under his nose and sniffed. He eyed her, obviously thinking. He snorted loudly, hacking up something from his throat, and spat it to the side before looking at his companions behind him. One of them shrugged, spreading his arms wide, and grunted.

The troll holding Samara looked between her and the passed-out Kaine and grumbled.

He spun abruptly and headed in the opposite direction, back the way they'd come. The trolls still standing followed as they trekked through the bushes, away from the Sacred Flame coterie.

CHAPTER TWENTY-SEVEN

Birds scattered, and the forest fell silent as the giant trolls trampled the grass, carrying Samara and Kaine away from their home. It felt like they traveled half a day, knocking down bushes and small trees and sending animals scurrying. Hooked under a troll's arm, pressed against his smelly body, Samara longed for the trip to be over. Even with the troll's extended stride, it took them quite some time to get to where they were going. She wondered if the trolls lived in Wraeyanor, ruled by witches, or in another realm. Perhaps they lived on the outskirts. Samara had never been out of Wraeyanor. She had never even left her little village before being accepted into the Sacred Flame coterie. Her nerves were getting the better of her. If she managed to escape, she would need to know how to find her way back to the coterie building.

"Where are you taking us?" Samara asked.

The troll squeezed her tighter around the chest, causing her ribs to ache. Breathing hurt, and it was even worse when she accidentally caught a whiff of the troll's rancid underarm.

After several more steps, the troll's bicep grew slack, giving her more breathing space.

"You could at least tell me where we're going. Don't you think? I've never been anywhere like this before."

"We are going to our homeland," the troll grumbled, and his chest rumbled behind Samara's back as he squeezed tighter, causing her ribs to ache again. His answer was the most intelligent one she'd been given so far, and she was probably not going to get much more.

Still, she persisted. "Is that within Wraeyanor, or is that another realm?"

"Wraeyanor," the troll said, his voice deep and rough. "Stop talking!"

Each stomp forward vibrated through every single bone of Samara's body. She glanced at Kaine and felt a little better that he had remained passed out for the trip. It would probably block out most of the pain from the bumpy ride. Selfishly, she was glad he was with her through the ordeal. She hoped his injuries were mainly superficial, and she would be able to heal him when they arrived and their magic returned. His head slumped forward, and his brilliant blue hair seemed to bob with each movement the troll carrying him made.

Samara tried to focus on the landscape, attempting to memorize all the hillsides and valleys they passed through. Although the more she saw, the more she knew it would be impossible to remember them all. They had traveled so far. Concentrating on more memorable points, she committed them to memory and hoped it would be enough to guide her way home.

The journey was slow and tedious, but at least they were still alive, for the moment. Perhaps if she played her cards right, things would go well for her and Kaine. She cast him a worried glance. He was still unconscious.

They entered a small village with scattered huts big enough to house a couple of trolls each before being carried to a large stone building. The structure was rough, bulky, and unattractive, with stories held up by thick stone pillars. Inside, they passed sparse, bulky furniture as they were carried directly to the stairs and descended many levels. The lower they got, the mustier and thicker the air.

Samara could only imagine that they were taking them to the dungeons. She had heard of dungeons but had never seen any. The only building she had seen that was similar in size was the building that housed the Sacred Flame apprentices, although it was far more aesthetic and had much more furniture. Underneath, the building was dark and dreary. The farther down they went, the fewer sconces on the wall, and the walls grew damp, some places with trails of water.

Eventually, they stopped descending and entered a room on the right filled with cells fronted with steel bars. Some were empty, and others had beings curled up in the corners, looking very dejected and almost starved. Samara struggled to see through the dimness. She wondered if any were from the Sacred Flame coterie from past years' tournaments, ones who couldn't find familiars and had lost their battles.

Chains rattled against the metal bars, and hinges squealed as they drew back the door. They tossed Samara into the cell and slammed the door behind her with a clack. A click sounded as the lock fell into place. The troll who'd carried Kaine walked several more steps to the cell two doors down. A loud thump followed as he threw Kaine onto a hard makeshift bed. Samara couldn't see him, as there were rock walls between each cell. The gate squealed its protest as the troll slammed the gate shut. As an added security measure, they chained the doors to the barred walls and sealed them with more locks.

Then without a word, the trolls left, ascending the stairs and leaving them in semidarkness. The flame of a lone sconce flickered against the wall, highlighting the shadows and making the whole area seem eerie and unwelcoming. Samara sat on a stone bench that had a few handfuls of straw thrown on top in what was supposed to be her makeshift bed. It was not much softer than just stone alone. Fatigue took over her every limb, and there was nothing she could do for Kaine at that moment. She curled up on the bench to try to catch some much-needed rest.

Even though she was exhausted, her mind wouldn't stop spinning. She hoped she could deliver her promise to the trolls, and they would keep them alive for longer. If only Kaine would get better to help her. She didn't know what condition he was in, how many bones were broken, and how bad his injuries were. The trolls wouldn't let her go anywhere near him.

A moan sounded not far away. It didn't sound like Kaine. She supposed it was probably the long-term occupants moaning over their uncomfortableness or their aching bodies.

Samara lay still. She didn't want to speak to any of the occupants as her mind processed the day's events. One particular thought kept churning through her mind. She didn't understand why Callista had stripped them of their magic. She wondered if every apprentice had faced the same situation before they went against their formidable opponents. It didn't seem fair. She understood they didn't have a familiar, so they couldn't accentuate their magic, but they still had magic, which would have been strong even without a familiar.

It felt unnerving to remember Mystique sitting in the forest, her yellow eyes watching their performance as they got slaughtered. That alone was sadistic, and the jaguar seemed to enjoy it. She hoped it was just the cat and that Callista had been long gone because she couldn't bear to watch what would happen to the students.

A groan sounded from a couple of cells down. It was different from the cries from before, and she wondered if it was Kaine finally coming to. He would be in enormous amounts of pain, and she could only imagine his shock when he realized he wasn't dead. She wasn't sure exactly how good his healing skills were or if their magic worked in the cells. Her cheeks turned numb as panic set in. Maybe their magic still didn't work. Or perhaps their magic had been permanently inhibited. If it hadn't, they would be able to open the cells and escape.

She sat upright and brushed some of the straw from her leather clothes. Her quiver and bow had been taken from her. She was weaponless and possibly magicless. Focusing on the cell door, she concentrated on the lock securing the chains. If she still had magic, she would be able to open that lock. After peering through the bars to look for guards, she clasped the lock and whispered, "*Aperti.*" She waited, only to be disappointed. She was about to trudge back to her uncomfortable bed when a glimmer of hope made her return to the lock. Maybe it had opened without a sound. She pulled on the clasp, willing it to open, but it didn't budge.

The only sound was the chains rattling against the bars as she took her frustration out on the lock. As an added measure, she tried the lock on the door. If it had unlocked instead, there was a minor chance she might be able to squeeze out of the thin gap. "*Aperti,*" she whispered. Nothing happened. She was stuck in the cell.

Panic started to rise. She didn't know how they would escape if their magic wasn't working. Nor did she know how Kaine would survive without magical healing. It wasn't as though the trolls would send down a doctor. She hoped Kaine's injuries weren't as bad as she feared.

She remembered the promise she'd made to the trolls to save their lives. Samara had said she would do magic for them if they kept them alive. She hoped the loss of magic was only temporary. If her magic didn't return soon, she couldn't fulfill her promise.

CHAPTER TWENTY-EIGHT

A strange noise sounded in the darkness. Samara bolted upright, on high alert. Her sides ached, and her body was cold and rigid from lying on a mostly stone bed. The wall sconce had burned itself out. She missed being able to ignite a flame using magic.

Something scraped outside her cell, and her eyes widened. She struggled to see, but her eyes hadn't adjusted yet. She gripped the stones on her bed until her joints ached.

The consistent noise of dribbling water remained.

More scraping reverberated through her cell, and she squinted, wishing she had night vision. The sound seemed to originate right outside her cell. Not being able to see anything was setting her nerves on edge. After a while, her eyes adjusted slightly to the darkness, aided by a dull light in a room up the stairs. She still couldn't see anything unusual. The extra light slightly eased her fears, and she stretched out on the rough bed, trying to rid herself of some of the aches and pains. Working the stiffness out of the muscles made her feel slightly better and more relaxed until another strange sound echoed in the darkness. That time, it seemed to be clinking against the metal bars.

Holding her arms in front of her chest, she readied to defend herself. It sounded as though something was coming into her cell, except the cell door remained closed with the chains across it. She listened to the other beings in the cells. None of them were stirring. A snore came from the cell next door, and a moan sounded from another one, interrupted by the jerky yells of a nightmare. They were not the sounds that had disturbed Samara from her sleep.

It happened again. Sharp clacking sounded from the bars of her cell. Although as much as Samara looked, she couldn't see anything.

Waiting on her uncomfortable bed, she shifted her legs over the side, keeping her arms raised in defense. It irked her that she couldn't find the origin of the noise. Determined to get to the bottom of it, she stared at her cell bars and thought she saw a glimpse of red. They were like two small dots that seemed to glow. She narrowed her eyes on that area, waiting to see if she could glimpse the red again.

She didn't know whether it was night or day. The cells had no windows. It felt like night, but it was hard to know in a dungeon.

Voices echoed upstairs, and light flickered within the stairway gap, enough to catch a glimpse of something black pasted against the cell bars. In the middle were those two red dots. They looked like eyes.

Samara gasped and recoiled before she steeled her nerves and prepared to fight. The red eyes disappeared then reappeared again, focusing on her. She bit her tongue, trying to swallow her fear. She'd never seen anything like it. The thing was some kind of animal, and rising from its black flesh were too many horns to count. It had a long snout like a hound, no ears, and membranous black wings. The creature was about half Samara's size and had an extensive array of sharp, pointed teeth and long claws. Everything about the creature screamed danger, and its red eyes were fixed on her.

Suddenly, the dungeon seemed empty, and all the other noises were blocked out, as though it was just Samara and the creature. Samara backed into a corner, taking comfort from the cold stone walls defending her back and sides. When the red eyes didn't move, she sat and pulled her knees up to her chest, hugging them tightly, as if that would give her comfort. She didn't know what else to do. She had no weapons or magic, just two hands and two feet to fight with. Not even anything in her room could be used as a weapon. Whatever the creature was, surely the red eyes and horns indicated it was dangerous.

The dungeon fell into darkness after the torchlight passed, and the red eyes remained fixed on her, sending a tremor of fear running through her body. It seemed as though half the night had gone by with her trapped under its gaze. The eyes thinned to a squint before opening wide again. Concerned, she imagined the red-eyed evil creature had come to take her soul. Eventually, the eyes shifted and moved closer. Samara shrank back a little more and pressed harder against the stone. She wished whatever it was would go away. It must be some strange creature that the trolls kept to watch over their captives and keep them in line. Whatever it was, it was working. She was scared out of her mind.

The eyes shifted for a moment, as though the creature was assessing the others in the dungeon, then returned to her. She wondered if it was checking that it wouldn't be disturbed as it took her life. Digging her heels into the hard floor, she pressed herself back and wished the wall would devour her.

The creature huffed, throwing Samara off guard.

Why are you cowering, child? the creature grumbled in a harsh male voice, sounding closer than the doorway.

Samara jumped at the sound. The voice was quite loud, and she was sure it would wake the others in the dungeon. But when she looked into the other cells, no one had stirred. Everyone was still sound asleep.

When she didn't answer, impatience laced the grumpy voice. *I asked you why you are cowering.* The creature shifted closer. *You act as though I'm aggressive or something.*

She didn't answer. He certainly sounded aggressive.

The creature shifted on the bars. *That's stupid! I'm only aggressive if you attack me.*

Tension rocketed through Samara's body, and she remained where she was, unsure how to react. She couldn't see what the creature was, let alone trust it. But that it was talking to her was strange. She didn't think animals could speak—if he *was* an animal. Perhaps it was some other evil being in that realm.

Shifting his claws around the bars, the creature

rolled his eyes. *Stupid rise of the full moon. What have you gotten me into this time?* he mumbled. Narrowing his red eyes on Samara again, he asked, *Are you stupid? I told you I'm not aggressive, yet you still cower in the corner. What are you afraid of?*

Her cheeks numb and her lips barely able to move, Samara stared at the red eyes. Eventually, her mouth relaxed enough to talk. "I can't see you properly, and I don't know what you are. All that I can see are your red eyes."

Grumbling, the animal let out a huff. Then came scratching and clamoring sounds, and suddenly, a burst of fire shot through the air and ignited the sconce in the wall, illuminating her visitor. As he clung to the wall's stones, the red-eyed creature turned to her, allowing her to see him more clearly. He looked like an oddly shaped bird that had lost its feathers, except he was far from a bird. For one, birds didn't have teeth or horns. Perhaps he was an enormous bat, except he wasn't covered in fur, and the fiery red eyes sent chills up her spine.

Her visitor's eyes glowed a deeper red as he caught her reaction, and he scrambled down the wall then climbed the bars of her cell to the horizontal one that secured them together. The claws clinking on the bars confirmed what Samara had heard earlier.

"What are you?" she asked when the animal only sat and stared at her.

You're kidding me. Right?

Slowly, Samara shook her head. "No!"

More grumbles reached Samara's ears. *Come here, and let me have a good look at you.*

When Samara hesitated, a small fire passed through his lips, and his eyes narrowed. *I said I wouldn't harm you. So come.*

Slowly and hesitantly, Samara unfolded her legs over the side of the stone bed, accidentally pushing bits of straw to the floor. She would need to collect them later. Her bed was already too hard with them. Her boots hit the ground, and she ambled toward the creature, hesitation in every step. She had no way of knowing what the creature might do. She shouldn't just trust a strange creature, but deep down, something told her that despite his fierce appearance and spooky red eyes, the creature wouldn't hurt her. She followed her gut instinct. Even so, when she reached the edge of her cell, she stood just out of reach of her visitor.

His pointy little head moved in all directions while he studied her before sliding through the bars and getting a closer look. She flinched back, but he didn't lunge at her. He clicked his tongue, giving Samara a closer look at the array of sharp, pointy teeth. She had no doubt that one bite would inflict a lot of pain.

After he had studied her further, the horns on his forehead bunched into a frown, and a deep rumble reverberated up his neck. *Pink hair and a trace of pink around your irises. From this, I assume you're a witch of some sort, probably one of the ones from the Sacred Flame coterie.* All pleasantries left the animal's voice when he mentioned her home. Instead, it was full of disapproval.

Samara didn't understand the creature's distaste for where she had come from, yet she didn't let that disturb her. She studied the animal as much as he was studying her. Long talons wrapped around the bars of the cell, and every wing rib had spikes on the end that looked dangerous and painful. Not to mention the hideous amounts of horns on his body and head, like he had a short, spiky haircut.

Samara nodded. "Yes, I am an apprentice witch." She took a deep breath and corrected herself. "I *was* an apprentice witch from the Sacred Flame coterie. But now I'm a prisoner of the trolls because I failed to get a familiar. What are you? I've never seen anything like you."

The creature huffed, and his face distorted with disappointment and disbelief. *Then they really do breed you dumb there, don't they? Either that, or they keep the truth from you, and you're incredibly naive.*

Samara didn't like the insinuation that she was stupid, but she pushed it aside, determined to learn more about the creature. "Is the Sacred Flame coterie acquainted with creatures of your type?"

Oh yes. They are exceptionally knowledgeable about my type.

Samara found the creature's grumpy attitude to her just as baffling as her coterie knowing about his type and not educating them about them. "I'm sorry. They haven't taught us about you."

That is surprising, considering we're classed as your enemy. What's even more surprising is that I was drawn down here. The creature's tail flicked sharply. *The rising full moon is messing with my senses and has me doing things I wouldn't usually do. I've been watching you all day and all night, and I cannot understand why I was drawn here.*

"Sorry, I can't help you with that. It certainly wasn't me, as I was stripped of all my magic before being ordered to fight the trolls." Despite his rough exterior and belittling nature, the creature was growing on Samara. "But you still haven't answered me. What are you?"

The creature chuckled sardonically. *I'm a dragon, of course.*

"You're a dragon?" Samara said the word like it was foreign to her tongue.

Wow! That's ironic! The dragon shook his head. *They must be trying to keep you in the dark until it's too late.*

Samara frowned. "What do you mean?"

Haven't you heard? We're the evil of all the realms, the dragon said dramatically, spreading his wings wide. *That is why we are exiled and must live in hiding, especially in this realm. According to your coterie and the leading sorcerers and sorceresses, we are the greatest evil.*

The dragon's sarcasm didn't escape Samara. She shrugged. "That's not what we've been taught. They said that elf shifters were our enemies because they caused trouble throughout the lands. As for you, you look ferocious and all, but you're only little."

The dragon chuckled in an unpleasant way again. *Dragon moon! You really don't know, do you? We come in all shapes and sizes, from tiny ones to enormous breeds that can destroy whole villages.*

Tilting her head to one side, Samara said, "That may be so, but I think you might find you're wrong about your kind being our greatest enemy. Callista is training us to fight elf shifters who change into dangerous nameless creatures and hold strong magic. She can't be leading us against animals."

The dragon hooked his tail around one of the

bars. *Then she is hiding from you what she truly believes and only telling you part of the story. Either that, or you're particularly dumb.* With squinted eyes, he stared at her. *But there's something about you I like. So despite your idiocy, I'll be back.* He climbed down the cell and headed for the stairs.

Samara called, "Wait! You haven't told me your name."

Bearing a disgruntled expression that Samara was starting to think was put on, he grumbled, *My name is Ulrieg. What is your name?*

"Samara."

The dragon inclined his head, spun around, and vanished before her eyes. His talons scraped up the stones in the opposite direction as he left the dungeon.

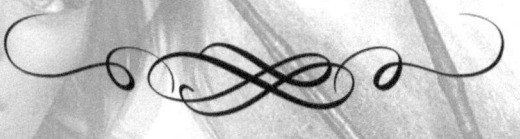

CHAPTER TWENTY-NINE

Attempting to get comfortable, Samara wriggled on the thin straw covering her stone mattress. A single sconce shone dully in the dank dungeon, and Samara silently thanked her strange dragon friend. At least, she assumed he was a friend. Despite his rough and sometimes-demeaning personality, something about him struck her as sincere. She had a sneaking suspicion that his coarseness was mainly just a show. Only time would tell.

Strangely, she missed his company. It could be because, with Kaine unconscious, she felt alone. One thing was for sure—not only was he a strange creature, but a dungeon was a strange place to meet one. She wondered if he was a hallucination. Nobody else in the dungeon had seen him or stirred when the creature was there.

Thunderous footsteps echoed down the staircase as a thick-set troll descended into the main area, carrying a large tray and three bowls. He shoved one through the food slot at the base of each cell door, making the soup spill over the side in the process, before stomping back up the steps without a word. The thought of food made Samara's stomach grumble, and she scrambled to her feet to grab the bowl then spooned the food into her mouth. To call it soup would be an overstatement. Highly watered down, it tasted disgusting, making her want to regurgitate the contents. But Samara hadn't eaten since before the big battle and was so hungry that she ate it anyway. She'd thought the battle was the previous day, but perhaps it was longer.

The occupant in the cell next to hers grabbed their bowl. She still couldn't see or hear any movement from Kaine's cell, and worry ate at her. She called, "Kaine, are you awake?" As she waited for an answer, she scooped more spoonfuls of the runny meal before abandoning the spoon and drinking straight from the bowl. The lukewarm liquid slightly abated her hunger.

A groan reached her, and she took that as Kaine's delayed response. "Make sure you get up and get some food. You need to get your strength up so that you can heal."

A moan filled with anguish was her only answer.

"Kaine. Can you hear me?" Trying to see his cell, she squinted. The light from the sconce wasn't strong enough to shine into all the cells.

"If you're talking about the blue-haired guy over there, he ain't moving" came a male's coarse voice from the cell next to her.

Samara pressed her cheek against the bars of her cell but couldn't see anything.

"Ya won't be able to see me from there. If ya go to the middle of the wall, there's a small stone that's come loose. You can see me from there."

Samara scanned the wall, running her hand over the surface until she felt the loose stone. She could see a peephole already there, and the person on the other side shifted back and stood in the middle of the room. He was a short, stocky dwarf with legs too short for his torso. His dark hair stopped below his shoulders, and his beard was unkempt. His thick bones were visible through his thin skin, making him look malnourished.

He spread his arms wide. "Well, can you see me? If you can't, ya probably looking too high." He grinned, showing off his half-rotten teeth.

"I can see you," Samara said. "How long have you been looking into my cell?"

"Only a couple of minutes since y' were hollerin'."

"Hi," she said tentatively. It made her uneasy to think someone could be watching her without her knowing. At least the man had told her. "Has the guy next to you woken up yet?"

He shook his head. "I haven't heard him move at all. He just lies there and moans. Although I'd happily eat his food if I could reach it."

Samara cursed under her breath. "How's he supposed to heal if he's not moving or eating?"

"If ya ask me, he's already on his deathbed. He ain't got long."

Samara's stomach whirled with worry. Kaine needed healing, and she didn't know how to get it to him, nor did she have her magic. "Do the trolls ever send a healer down here?"

The dwarf scoffed. "As if! If we survive, we get to survive. If we don't, we don't. Often, it's like they bring us down here for a slow death instead of just killing us."

Worried, Samara played with her spoon, wishing she had more food. She would have to pay close attention to her health so that she could escape. "How do the trolls expect us to perform magic for them if they leave us down here to rot without any care or proper food?" Using her spoon, she worked away some of the mortar around the stones to widen the hole between the cells.

The dwarf shrugged. "Like I said. If you live, you live. If you don't, you don't. That's the way it is around here."

Samara threw her spoon into her pewter bowl, making it clang. Her mind spun as she tried to devise a plan of action. She had no magic to unlock the locks. But she would have to get out somehow. And she had to help Kaine. She peeked at the dwarf through the gap again to find him sitting on his bed, his face sad. "How long have you been here?"

The dwarf shrugged. "Hard to say. I can't see anything to tell if it's night or day. I don't know what cycle the moon is on or if it's a different season. By guessing, I would say I've been here 'bout a month. The only way I figured that is by the meals that I've had."

"Do they bring us three meals?"

The dwarf scoffed. "No! We're lucky to get one a day. Why do you think I look so skinny? I used to have a nice big belly." He rubbed his flat stomach in a circular motion.

Her heart sank. That wasn't going to help her stay healthy. "What are you in here for?"

"I wandered into the wrong area, didn't I. Me name's Thongret."

"Samara. And that's Kaine on the other side of you."

"How'd you get here?"

"We had to fight the trolls."

He gazed toward the hole in disbelief. "Now, why would you have to do that?"

She scratched at the stone on the wall. "We're from the Sacred Flame coterie, studying under the head sorceress. We're required to get a familiar, but we weren't able to. Because of our age, our time was up. Fighting the trolls was our final chance to prove our worth. Except right before the battle, we were stripped of our magic and had to fight the trolls without it." Saying the words out loud filled Samara with depression.

Thongret whistled. "Sounds like ya weren't very appreciated."

Irritated, she replied, "No! We were very appreciated. It's just that we had to prove ourselves because we didn't have familiars. We must prove we're strong enough to serve under the head sorceress to protect the realms."

He shrugged. "Don't take offense. I'm jus' sayin' it like I hear it. It sounds to me as though you're not appreciated. And you were backstabbed when they took ya magic away. The trolls can't take away your magic. It had to be a sorceress."

Crossing her arms over her chest, Samara shook her head.

A clicking sound on the bars, like before, grabbed her attention, but she couldn't see anything in the dim light on the other side of the cell.

I tried to tell you. I'd have to agree with him.

Samara blinked, and the glowing red eyes cut across the room from where Ulrieg clung to the bars.

"How do you know so much about our coterie when we've heard nothing about you?" she asked the dragon.

"I dunno what you're talking 'bout," Thongret said. "I don't know nothin' 'bout ya coterie." Frowning, Samara spun around to peek through the hole and pointed at the dragon. "I was talking to him."

Thongret jumped off his bed, walked to the edge of his cell, and peered into the main room. "Hate to tell ya this, love, but there's nobody there." He looked back at the gap in the wall with sorrow and suspicion. "Maybe you're startin' to lose it. Maybe they hit you over the head in ya fight."

She turned back to the front and saw the dragon hanging from the bars. There was no mistaking those red glowing eyes. "No, there's a dragon over there."

The dwarf gazed to the left then to the right. "There ain't any dragon over there, love. Sadly, ain't no dragons in this realm. They've been forbidden."

Her jaw dropped. She found it hard to believe that the dwarf knew about dragons when she didn't. She wondered if the others in the coterie also knew about them.

Wow! Ulrieg said from the edge of the cell. *You really are slow in learning, aren't you?* He adjusted his grip on the bars. *The dwarf can't see me. I'm invisible to everyone unless I want them to see me.*

"Is that how you said you watched me all day? Because I haven't seen you in here." The notion was hard for Samara to understand, although she knew the way he had disappeared the previous night wasn't normal. "So you're telling me you've been invisible until you decided to expose yourself?"

He spread his wings as though throwing his hands up in the air. *Oh, now she's started to cotton on. Yep. They really do breed them bright these days.* Sarcasm oozed through his voice.

Thongret cleared his throat. "Love, I think ya really startin' to lose it. Now ya talkin' to yourself."

Samara eyed the dragon then the wall the dwarf

sat behind, considering his words, before turning her attention back to Ulrieg.

He's right, you know. You do appear as though you're losing it. You must learn to speak to me without everyone else knowing what you're doing. His talons clicked on the bars as he adjusted his position.

Samara wondered if the dwarf could hear him. Surely he must hear the talons. She peeked through the hole and saw that Thongret wasn't reacting to the dragon's words. As for the talons, she gave him the benefit of the doubt. Since he was in the next room along, they might be muffled by other noises. It seemed strange that she could hear Ulrieg, and the others couldn't. Her brain ached with confusion. She shouldn't be surprised, considering she could perform magic.

The dragon's glowing red eyes remained fixed on her. *Well?* He lowered himself to rest on the horizontal bar. When she didn't answer, he huffed out steam.

He held something out in his talons. *I brought this for you.* Ulrieg waved his leg up and down as though to grab her attention. *I figured you'd be starving. I've seen what these trolls bring their prisoners.*

Curious about the nice gesture, Samara moved toward the bars. In a claw slightly smaller than Samara's hand was a large hunk of bread.

Not wasting a second, she snatched it up and took a bite. It tasted so good after the disgusting soup. She almost moaned when she said, "Thank you!" She surveyed the dragon with amusement and gratitude. It was starting to look like her gut instinct about him had been right, and his gruffness was mostly for show.

"What have you got?" It seemed strange that Thongret didn't miss the sound of someone eating.

"Just a piece of bread I found." She devoured mouthful after mouthful until she was full, then she broke some off for Thongret.

"Here! I saved you some."

The piece was whipped out of her hand in seconds.

"But please help me look after my friend on your other side if you can."

His chewing was broken up with muffled words. "I'll do my best, but I can't do nothin' if he don't regain consciousness. I can't reach him and force him to eat." He waved the bread outside his cell so that it was visible to Samara from her bars. "But thanks for the bread."

CHAPTER THIRTY

The sound of trickling water constantly filled Samara's ears, and dampness permeated the air as well as the stone floor. It smelled as though some of the pipes had cracked a while ago, and no one had fixed them. The scent began to seem less invasive, although it was probably just that her nose was getting used to the smell.

A groan sounded again a couple of cells away. Holding on to hope, Samara called out again. "Kaine, are you awake?"

No response other than another pain-filled groan came.

Samara gnawed her bottom lip. Kaine's lack of response was bothering her.

"He hasn't moved since you got here." Thongret tapped his foot impatiently. "I don't think there's hope for ya friend."

Struggling to swallow the lump in her throat, Samara didn't say anything. She had tried to save Kaine during the fight and didn't want him to die from his injuries days later. She wished she could be closer to him and had her magic and potions to help him. "Can you not reach him at all?"

"No! His bed's right across the other side of the cell. There's no chance for me to get to him." Thongret lightly hit his head against the bars. "If only me head would fit through these bars. With the amount of weight I've lost, me body probably would."

Samara's shoulders slumped. She felt so lost without her magic. So many limitations had been placed on her and her plan to escape and return to the coterie.

She inspected the chains and the two locks. Though she didn't know how to undo them without magic or a key, she was determined enough to give anything a try. Feeling around the floor, she searched for sticks or small pieces of metal that she might be able to jiggle in the locks. If she was lucky, it might shift something within.

But luck wasn't on her side. The only thing she found was straw, which was too thin and weak to do anything.

Heavy footsteps thumped down the stairs, and

she lowered the chain, making sure it didn't rattle against the bars, and backed away.

Darkness blanketed her as she sat on her hard bed. She hoped they were bringing food. Instead, the troll stomped to the cell next door and unlocked the gate. Something was off, and the hinge squeal sent terror through her body.

"Hey, me ol' friend." Thongret sounded cheerful, and she was sure it was an act. "What can I do for ya?"

The troll didn't answer. Samara peeked through the small hole in time to see the troll grab Thongret by the elbow and pull him toward the door.

"Come. Your time is up. You've eaten way too much of our food already." The troll's voice was deep and gravelly.

Quickly, Samara backed away from the hole distraught that she couldn't help him.

The troll dragged the dwarf into the main area, and Samara could've sworn that his face had turned white under the sconce's light as he was dragged up the stairs. She didn't know what to do and felt so helpless. He was the closest thing she had to an ally, even though she knew nothing about him.

"Where are you taking him?" Samara yelled. It was a feeble effort, but she had to try something.

Unsurprisingly, the troll ignored her question and dragged Thongret up the stairs.

The last thing she saw of the dwarf was his pale face as he called over his shoulder, "Good luck to ya, love. I hope you find what ya after."

She didn't know what to make of the situation. It crossed her mind that the trolls were holding them in the cells until they decided to slaughter them. Clasping the cell's bars, she watched until she couldn't hear his progression. Her knuckles were white, and shock had stripped her face of all feeling. Perhaps she or Kaine would be next, especially if they didn't recover their magic or get ahold of any weapons. A hot tear trickled down her face. They had to get out of there, yet she didn't know how to help Kaine recover.

A gruff voice cut through the darkness. *I still don't know what it is. But despite your being so naive and stupid, there's something about you that keeps drawing me. Perhaps it's the effect the full moon has on me. Sometimes I despise how it messes with my senses.*

Samara's heart warmed when she heard the dragon. "Is that so? And when is the full moon?" She gazed along the bars of her cell to see the bright-red eyes come into focus less than a foot away. She startled and pulled her hands away from the bars. "Where did you come from?"

Ulrieg rolled his red eyes and sighed. *I thought we covered this. I can turn invisible.* He faced the other direction and muttered, *I don't know why I'm so keen on her. She's short a few brain cells.* He turned back around.

She smiled and moved closer. "You're a little bit grumpy, aren't you? Is that your normal state of mind?" She placed her hand on the bars again, daring herself to get closer to him.

Wingless flight! he cursed. *Again! The answer is right in front of your nose.* He shook his head and whacked his forehead with his open paw. *Dragon Moon! What are you getting me into?* He gazed up as though looking at the moon. It looked as though he was asking the universe a question.

Undeterred, Samara smiled and nodded. "Yep, you're a grumpy one." Moving closer to his ear, she whispered, "It's all right. You don't have to say it. I like you too. Despite your rough exterior, you're growing on me."

Ulrieg's jaw dropped. *I'm growing on you?* He shook his head.

"Exactly. Despite that you're always grumpy and rude, it's nice to have your company down here." She stood so close to him that only the thin line of bars separated them. She didn't want to be presumptuous and touch him. It felt right to allow him to do that first if he wished. "Although can you do me one favor, please?"

With wide eyes, Ulrieg tilted his head to one side as though weighing her up. After a pause, the surprise vanished, and he asked, *What is it?*

"I need to help my friend over there in the other cell. He hasn't moved since we got here, and I'm worried for his health."

And what do you expect me to do? Ulrieg hissed.

"I need you to go over and see if he has any open wounds. If he does, I'll need to ask you to find some herbs and stuff for him."

What am I? A nursemaid? Ulrieg shook his head. *I've come here for you, not him.*

Grabbing the bars, Samara leaned back and said coyly, "Well, if you want to be my friend, I need you to help me look after him. He's also my friend, and like me, he's from the coterie."

All the more reason to leave him here and let him rot.

Samara frowned. "That's not very nice!"

I shouldn't even be near you, Ulrieg grumbled. *You're from the coterie. I trust nobody from the coterie, but something keeps bringing me back to you.*

"Why don't you trust anyone from the coterie? Have you met anyone from there besides me?"

The dragon shook his head.

"Exactly! They have been very good to my family

and me. I need to get back there so that my family will still be looked after. The longer I'm here, and the longer Kaine's here, the higher the possibility that our families won't survive. The coterie will no longer look after them if we're not active members."

Yup! That sounds like loyalty. I see that I'm going to have to sit down and give you a one-on-one about why I don't trust them. But right now, you need to get out of here.

"What?" Samara asked.

As I said, something keeps pulling me to you, and I couldn't live with myself if I left you here to die. So. He took a deep breath. *I'm going to break you out.*

"How?"

The dragon held up a key and dangled it in front of her. *With this, of course. I flogged it off the guard when he was distracted with dragging the dwarf away.*

Ulrieg first unlocked the chain, which Samara helped him unwind, then worked on the lock for the gate with another key. Their skin touched, and a spark shot into Samara's skin on top of her hand between her thumb and forefinger.

"Ow!" Samara pulled her hand back. "Did you scratch me?" She grabbed the spot, confused about the pain.

If I scratched you, you'd know it. Ulrieg had also

pulled back. *I thought you sparked me with your magic. I got hit too.*

"That can't be right. My magic doesn't work."

They brushed it aside and got back to work on the lock. After another turn of the key, they were rewarded with a click, and they swung the gate open slowly, trying desperately to dampen the squeak of the hinges. Samara stepped through the passage.

Come on! Let's go! Ulrieg called as he started to climb the stairs. *I'll keep watch and help you make your way through the building.*

Samara froze. "I'm not going anywhere without Kaine."

What? Ulrieg hissed.

"I told you I'm not going anywhere without Kaine. I couldn't live with myself if I left him here, and I escaped."

You have to live with yourself. Ulrieg scurried down the stairs and grabbed her ankle, and when she didn't move, he pulled on her hand in an attempt to draw her forward. *Come on!*

Samara shook her head. "No!"

Ulrieg grunted, his many horns standing on end. *I told you I'm not helping anybody else from the coterie.*

Although Samara had to admit the dragon did look intimidating at that moment, she wouldn't give up. She yanked her hand out of his grasp. "Then I'll get him myself. You run along, and I'll take my chances. Thanks for helping me escape."

Fine! He gritted his pointy teeth, making him seem more vicious. *You really are a dumb one, aren't you?* He waved his wings toward Kaine. *He's half-dead anyway.*

Samara balled her fists on her hips. "As soon as I get him out of here and back to the coterie, he has an exceptional chance to survive. Somebody could heal him." She took the key from the dragon and headed toward Kaine's cell. "I'm going to grab him whether you like it or not. Run along, and keep yourself safe." She waved a dismissive hand at Ulrieg. "I like you and don't want any harm to come to you, but I cannot leave my friend here."

The dragon's shoulders slumped, and his fiery-red eyes glowed brighter. *Dragon Moon! What have you gotten me into? Stupid heightened emotions,* the dragon hissed before turning around, snatching the key from Samara, and heading toward Kaine's cell.

As he worked on the lock with Samara's help, he said, *I hope you can carry him if he can't walk. 'Coz I'm not that kind of dragon. I'm only about half the size of you, and there's no way I could lift him.*

The lock clicked, and Samara charged into the cell to Kaine's side. Pressing the back of her hand against his forehead, she could feel the heat of a fever. She gasped. "We have to get you back to the coterie. I wish I had my magic to do something to help."

She grabbed his arm and yanked him into a sitting position, and he moaned, his eyes opening the slightest bit. "Can you walk at all?"

Her only answer was a moan, and his body fell limp. Though she was strong for her size, Kaine was much taller and heavier. Worried, she didn't know how she would get him up the stairs and out of the building.

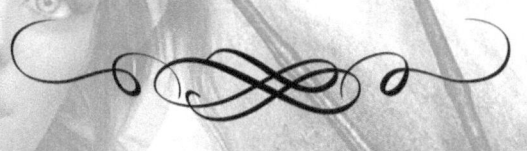

CHAPTER THIRTY-ONE

Struggling to hold Kaine upright, Samara assessed him as well as the spot where the dragon had touched her. The warming sensation grew and traveled up her arm to her shoulder and to her brain. It felt euphoric and strange, similar to how her magic used to feel. After passing through her brain, it weaved down her spine, immediately giving it more strength.

She squinted at Ulrieg. "Are you sure you didn't do anything to me? I feel different, and it's starting right at the spot we touched."

Ulrieg clasped his front talons. *I was thinking the same thing about you.*

"I could've sworn you pricked me or something. But now it's a different feeling. It's warm." Samara looked at her hand and spotted a mark on the spot where they'd touched. In the dim light, she couldn't make out what it was. Although there was no mistaking that she felt stronger, and it was also like she could feel the magic flowing through her veins again.

She decided to give it a try. Placing her hand on Kaine's head, she whispered an incantation, willing him to wake up. Warmth shot out of her hand and into Kaine's forehead. She continued her incantations, and eventually, Kaine's eyes opened.

"S-Samara," he slurred. "What's going on?" He took in the dark and dreary cell. "Am I dead?"

Tears of joy welling in her eyes, Samara shook her head. "No, but we're in a dungeon, and I'm trying to wake you up so we can escape. Do you think you can walk?"

He groaned as he tried to process everything then shifted. With a lot of moaning, he attempted to rise to his feet, and as soon as he was high enough, Samara hooked her shoulder under his arm to give him some support, and she wrapped his arm around her shoulders. She helped him out of his bed then out of his cell. They stumbled slightly, and Samara tightened her grip, bearing more of Kaine's weight so that he could walk. With Samara's nerves on edge, they slowly made their way up the stairs. Ulrieg scrambled up first to keep watch. He disappeared, and she hoped he had only turned invisible to help guide their way. She needed his help, even though earlier, she'd acted like she didn't.

Several minutes later, Ulrieg appeared out of nowhere, holding her bow and quiver. Grateful, she took them from him. "Thank you. I needed these to help us get back to the coterie." She cast him a sly look. "You *have* been watching me the whole time I've been here."

Ulrieg grumbled at the mention of the coterie. Samara ignored his protests. The quiver didn't have any arrows, as she had used them all in their battle against the trolls. She would have to make some more. "Did you see Kaine's knives as well? There should be several knives in a sheath that would be carried on his lower back."

What? You expect me to get his weapons also? He's the enemy.

She pushed her mouth into a thin line. "He's not our enemy. He's my friend, and I need his knives to help protect us and also to make more arrows for our trip home."

As Kaine groaned and opened his eyes, Ulrieg suddenly disappeared.

"Ulrieg!" Samara called in a whisper.

Looking confused, Kaine asked, "Who's Ulrieg?"

"He's a dra—"

Something blocked Samara's mouth, and her eyes widened. Her lips had been forcefully sealed. She attempted to shake herself free.

"Are you all right, Samara?" Kaine asked.

You and I need to have a talk.

Her eyes wide, she searched the area for the dragon, but her lips remained sealed shut. She nodded.

He can't hear me. I've made sure of that, but you need to act as though I'm not here in front of him. I will get his knives, but you're not to tell him where you got them.

Samara nodded again, trying to ignore Kaine's curious stares.

Now, remember. Act as though I'm not here. If you talk to me, you do it discreetly, away from him. He's not to know I'm here.

Since she didn't have a choice, Samara sighed and nodded. She didn't understand, but she hoped that the dragon would explain it to her later. He was an odd creature, but he had helped her, and there was something warm about him despite his gruffness. She had learned over the years to take the bad with the good when it came to being with other beings.

When Ulrieg released her lips, she kept her promise and asked quietly, "How are you coping, Kaine? Can you make it up the stairs all right?"

He groaned softly, and she shushed him. "We

don't know where they are exactly. We just need to be quiet and get out of here. We've been held captive for the last few days."

"Really?" Kaine's eyes were glazed, and it worried her. She had to keep his mind busy and get them out of there so that she could work on his injuries properly.

Samara nodded. "We lost the challenge."

Kaine attempted a charming smile that fell flat. He looked more like death warmed up. "I figured that."

The light from the sconces increased as they conquered the top of the stairs, but the higher floor was still quite dark, with no windows or external doors. Many passageways branched off, and she didn't know which way to turn. She took a risk and went right.

Kaine's attention was directed momentarily to the left, and a sheath and knives were shoved into her hands.

Quickly, she bent over, lowering Kaine slightly with her, and pretended to pick up the weapons from the floor. "Ha. Look what I found."

Kaine's face lit up, almost bringing back some of its color. "My knives! What a strange place to leave them." He glanced around as though he could piece together why they were there then shrugged. "I knew you were my lucky token."

The compliment warmed her, but she scoffed. "Perhaps it's because these guys are short of a few brain cells and leave weapons in any old place."

With Samara's help, Kaine strapped on his knives' holder.

They walked farther and found another passage that looked like it could be the main one and went through it, making sure they kept to the walls and listened for heavy footsteps.

"What would I do without you, Samara? You're my knight in shining armor." He gave her a half-lidded smile but still managed to weave in some of his charm.

She chuckled and shook her head. "Save your energy. I may need your help later."

"All right. But I will make it up to you when we get out of here."

"There's no way I could leave you behind."

Wingless flight! Give me a break!

Samara looked for the dragon but kept her promise not to respond in front of Kaine.

The dragon called, *This way.* Even though his voice was projected inside her head, it sounded as though it had come from down the hall. She followed it down another corridor. Each time they heard a faint sound, they found a crevice or spare room, pressed into it, and held their breath as they waited for the trolls to pass. When they reached a room with outside doors, she breathed a sigh of relief but didn't let her guard down. She could relax more when they were out of the building and not at risk of being recaptured.

CHAPTER THIRTY-TWO

Kaine and Samara staggered out of the building and into the open. The full moon lit the sky, casting eerie shadows over every building and tree. Samara couldn't see the dragon, but she was confident he was still around. A commotion rose behind them, and she peered over her shoulder to see a flurry of activity. Cries of alarm had everyone running inside. Their escape must have been noticed, despite hardly anyone coming to visit them.

The warmth traveling through her body had grown. Her magic was returning, and after the break, it felt stronger. She cast a spell that shielded them and made them blend into their environment right as several trolls charged outside. Not being

KATRINA COPE

able to find them inside, they'd vacated the building and stomped over the grounds.

This way, Ulrieg called from the right. She swayed under Kaine's weight and led him in the direction of the dragon's call. He moaned, and Samara continued injecting him with light healing power, hoping to heal some superficial wounds and keep him going until they returned to the coterie. Their healing would be much better than her novice experience. Still, she tried to heal the more severe wounds, at least enough that they were no longer critical. She couldn't remember feeling so strong before.

"Do you know where you're going?" Kaine asked.

Samara had to tell him the truth. "No. What makes you think I would?"

He held out his palm face up. "You seem to be following something."

Samara let the silence fall for a minute as she thought of an answer. "Just following my gut. I have this feeling we're supposed to go this way. I was awake when they brought us here, although it wasn't easy to see."

Kaine seemed to believe her. A gruff voice sounded in her head. *I can't believe he fell for that. You must all be as naive and stupid as one another. Hard to believe, since the coterie was supposed to be a place for intelligent witches and sorcerers.*

Samara glared at the spot where she thought Ulrieg was. She longed to answer, but she had promised not to give him away.

Light cut through the sky as the sun rose. The new light blinded them after they'd spent an extended time in the dark. Shielding her eyes with her spare arm, she weaved through several bushes. Because of Samara's disguise, the trolls had followed a different direction, allowing them to escape. Kaine slipped slightly, and Samara moved him to her other arm to give him extra support.

"What's that?" Kaine ran his finger over Samara's skin between her forefinger and thumb, where she had felt the spark when she and the dragon touched.

She gazed down at her pale skin and saw something similar to a bird's claw. After an inspection, she blanched. It looked like a dragon's talon. Thoughts scrambled in her head. It looked like Ulrieg had marked her. He had been blaming her for the shock, yet he was the one who'd marked her. She stroked it with her thumb.

"Do you know where it came from?" Kaine's voice cut through her whirlwind of thoughts.

Shaking her head, she brushed it again. It didn't smudge at all and was like a faint tattoo. "I have no idea."

Guilt wracked her. She hated to lie to Kaine and didn't know why she trusted Ulrieg more than Kaine when she had just met the dragon.

Kaine shrugged. "I like it." His eyes met with hers, and he smiled.

Her heart skipped a beat. Some color had returned to his face, though he still looked worn out. She didn't know how to maintain their friendship while acting like a dragon wasn't nearby. She rubbed the mark again. As soon as she could talk to Ulrieg properly, she would ask him about it.

Ulrieg's voice cut through her thoughts. *All right. It should be safe to put him down.* She wanted to glare at the dragon for thinking he could boss her around, especially since he hadn't told her the truth. But again, she held her tongue. He had saved them, and she was grateful for that.

After putting Kaine on the ground with his back pressed against a large tree, she studied their surroundings. They were deep in the bushes, making it more difficult for the trolls to find them. Kaine's face remained pale, and he had dark circles under his eyes, despite some color returning after being injected with healing magic. Although his injuries and lack of food over the last few days didn't help his healing pace. She pressed the back of her hand to his forehead. He was still burning up.

"I'm going to search for food and healing herbs. Stay here and rest. You should be safe. I'll establish a cloaking spell around you to make it seem like you're part of nature."

He nodded, looking exhausted. She pulled her eyes away and stood. His weakness tore at her. Usually, he was strong. Before she left the area, his eyes drooped with sleep and fatigue. He needed help as quickly as she could find it.

Come this way, the dragon demanded.

Determined to get answers, she followed the sound of his voice. She was certain that, because of his lack of social skills, he would be leaving soon. He clearly didn't like people.

She cast one last look back at Kaine. His head lolled to the side, and his eyes were closed. If he weren't already asleep, it wouldn't be too long.

Samara searched for medicinal plants for Kaine's wounds, berries, and anything that could be eaten without cooking. The more time she was alone, the more she thought about her encounter with the dragon. She couldn't explain why she trusted the strange creature, although it felt right and more substantial than the trust she had felt for any other being. It had grown since their touch, and she felt different somehow. She didn't understand why her magic had returned after their contact. Kaine's magic hadn't suddenly returned at the same time. It sent her into a world of confusion.

Absentmindedly, she ran her thumb over the dragon's point of contact with her skin. Ulrieg turned visible, sitting on a branch at her head height. The multihorned black dragon and his fiery-red eyes appeared like something out of a nightmare, especially when his lips pulled back, exposing his vast array of sharp teeth. His eyes held a meanness she hadn't seen in a creature before. They reflected his abruptness and sarcasm, counteracting the kindness he had shown her.

Samara gazed at the mark and wiped it again with her thumb, almost like a nervous habit, before staring back into his eyes.

Confident they were out of earshot, she said, "You left a mark on me. What does it mean?"

Ulrieg frowned, and his horns bunched, making him seem angry. *What do you mean?*

She thrust out her hand with the mark facing up. "I got this right on the spot where we first touched. Did you get anything?"

Ulrieg violently shook his head, and she backed away, determined not to get hit by his multiple horns.

She stroked the mark again, wistful. "I feel different after we touched too. How about you?"

The red eyes turned cautious. After a long pause, he said, *I guess I do feel stronger.* As if to prove a point, he jumped from tree to tree, occasionally gliding between branches, before he flipped and landed on the ground and returned to a tree branch. *Are you sure we can't just leave him there, and you and I live our own peaceful lives?*

Samara stopped in her tracks. "What do you mean by you and I? I thought you would want to go off by yourself."

Wow! Keen to get rid of me already? Ulrieg wrapped his wings around himself like a cocoon. *That's nice! Nothing like a grateful thank you. I guess I only saved your life. Nothing too extravagant.*

"No. That's not what I meant. I quite like your grumpy company... somehow." She spread her arms wide. "I just thought you would be on your way. You don't seem like you enjoy others' company."

As I said already, something about you is drawing me to you. To be honest, it's rather frustrating. But I'll be with you for a bit longer.

"Is that why you marked me?" She held her hand

out to him again. The mark looked precisely like his front claws.

After descending the trunk to Samara's height, Ulrieg studied the marking. *It does look like a dragon's talon. You can't take that back to the coterie.*

"Why not?"

Do you honestly not know anything about the dragons?

Samara shook her head.

He whistled and jumped to the next branch over in line with Samara's head height. *I can't believe you don't know anything about dragons or Dragoria.*

"Drag what?" She squeezed her wrist as uncertainty flooded through her.

Dragoria. Disbelief flashed in the dragon's red eyes. When her face remained blank, he gasped. *Dragon Moon! You seriously don't know anything about Dragoria, the lost dragon realm?*

Speechless, Samara shook her head.

Honestly! How can you be so naive? Ulrieg's demeaning tone had returned, and it ate at Samara's patience.

Crossing her arms, she cocked a hip. "I don't understand why you're getting so snarky with me and making me out to be stupid. Why am I supposed to have heard of this realm?"

Mouth agape, the dragon stared at her, his red eyes blazing. After a while, he said, *You're led by Callista, the great sorceress. Yes?*

Samara nodded. "Yes. She's nice to us and looks after our families when we're training to serve in the coterie."

Ulrieg balked. Many emotions flashed over his face. *And has that sorceress told you about some great evil among the lands?*

Frowning, Samara nodded.

And how this evil was conquered by a member of the Sacred Flame coterie. And how they defeated that great evil and banished it for good, but it is her responsibility to continue monitoring it and working on keeping it secure?

"Well, yes. Of course. Except it was Callista who defeated it with the help of her understudies. What are you getting at?"

Hmm. My mind boggles. When Samara gazed at him in confusion, he quickly went on, *Someone with powerful magic cloaked Dragoria, banishing it from all the other kingdoms. It is the land of the dragons, and it has been hidden from all realms by a great magician claiming Dragoria is a source of great evil.*

"Are you trying to tell me you're evil?" Samara asked. "It would explain why your eyes are rather malicious looking."

The dragon leaned back and whacked his forehead with his front claw. *No. That's not what I'm saying.* His talons squeezed the branch tighter, making marks in the bark. *I'm saying the strongest magicians are from the Sacred Flame coterie, are they not?*

"As far as I know."

So doesn't that make you wary of their loyalties?

"No. Because they have never mentioned Dragoria specifically, only a great source of evil, nor have they told us they sealed off some realm. Are you sure this realm exists?"

Dragon Moon! They have really pulled one over on you. I cannot believe the coterie convinced you to be this stupid.

Hooking a pink strand of hair behind her ear, she sighed. "I still don't understand."

Ulrieg took a deep breath and leaned closer, leveling his fiery eyes with hers. *Do I look evil to you?*

She tilted her head to one side. "To be honest, right now, you kind of do."

He snorted, and steam coated Samara with perspiration. *I mean, do I look like I could be something evil enough to destroy kingdoms?*

Samara looked at him long and hard. Despite all the roughness of the dragon, her heart was still telling her that deep down, he had a soft soul. "I haven't seen anything from you that says you're evil. You look rather rough and scary, and you're often rude and insulting. I'm starting to write that off as your mannerisms. Other than that, you've helped me."

Clearly, we need to talk. It will take a while, and you need to get back to Kaine, if you're so intent on looking after him. Do you mind if I hop onto your arm?

Instantly her gaze dropped to his sharp talons, then she eyed the soft skin of her arm and felt the exposed area along her shoulders.

I promise I'll be gentle.

She lifted her arm as an invitation, and he gently climbed on hooking one claw on the leather at her shoulder. That way, she could continue her search for food, medicinal plants, and branches to craft into arrows.

As she suspected, he was heavy. His talons scraped her skin. Still, he labored not to hurt her. Her arm burned with exhaustion, and when she lowered it to cope with his weight, his talon lightly sliced her skin. Blood trickled down.

Sorry. He wrapped his wings around her, digging the wing rib spikes into her tunic, and took a big step, putting his weight on her leather-covered shoulder with one talon, then placed the other on her quiver. His back feet dug into the bottom of the quiver. Once he'd established his position, he folded his wings, radiating warmth from his body.

Now. Let me tell you the dragon side of the story and what your coterie hasn't been telling you.

CHAPTER THIRTY-THREE

The dragon clung to Samara's shoulders, resting heavily on her back, his head near her ear. *Many years ago, there were four kingdoms—Wraeyanor, Slosiaran, Clialarion, and Dragoria.*

A branch snapped under Samara's feet. "I know of the first three. They're the kingdoms that the Sacred Flame coterie and Callista protect. Yet never have I heard about Dragoria."

It's a magical place, he said wistfully.

"Have you been there?" Samara turned to look at him, and her cheek brushed against him, making warmth shoot to her stomach.

Unfortunately, no. All of what I'm about to tell you happened before my time. I'm just passing on the story that has been passed to me by other dragons.

"You speak as if there are many dragons." Samara stopped to pick some berries.

There are but not many in the realms that aren't Dragoria.

She placed the handful of berries in a pouch. "Then tell me more."

Dragoria is filled with dragons of varying breeds and sizes. Some are very small, some are extremely large, and some are my size. But don't let the size of the small dragons deceive you. They have a unique kind of magic that was ignited when they were in the company of the dragon elf. Together, they were the guardians of the realms. Their union created extraordinary magic and made them a force to be reckoned with.

Samara broke off a branch with the perfect thickness and length for an arrow. "A dragon elf?"

Yes. They are elves of a peculiar breed. When the dragon elf and the small guardian dragons are united, the dragon elf can shift into a full-sized dragon, and the little dragons can turn into giant dragons. It's part of the magic manifestation of their bond.

A rabbit darted in front of them, and even though she had crafted a couple of arrows already, Samara couldn't bring herself to kill an animal, especially after spending a significant amount of time with them while trying to find a familiar. If she did hunt an animal, she would be afraid that she had killed her or Kaine's familiar. With that in mind, she decided to stick to food from the plants. The other advantage was that they wouldn't need a fire to cook them. "Okay. But wouldn't a permanently large dragon be just as much of a threat, if not more, as a tiny dragon that can turn into a large dragon?"

The large dragons are formidable enemies. That is no doubt, except they are more about brute strength. The smaller dragons, on the other hand, are clever and craftier, and combined with the magic held by their dragon elf, they are almost unstoppable.

Samara stumbled across a large walnut tree laden with nuts.

Ulrieg jumped off her back, helped her gather the nuts, and put them in her quiver. *Overall, the dragons of Dragoria and the dragon elves ruled over the realms. Their role was what Callista claims she and her understudies of the Sacred Flame coterie do today—as guardians of all the realms, they kept the peace. But the great magician I mentioned earlier didn't like this. They wanted the power to rule the lands. Working with a greater evil they found hidden in a chasm, the magician plotted against Dragoria and gathered powerful magic from throughout the kingdoms in the form of artifacts and crystals. They banished Dragoria from the other realms, creating a barrier that could not be passed or seen, leaving* the realm of the dragons cut off from all the other king-doms and halting their protection.

"That doesn't make sense. Why would a greater evil want to help this magician?" Samara threw a few more nuts into her quiver.

Ulrieg flew to the top of the tree and knocked many of the nuts to the ground, making it easier for Samara to gather them. *The evil sought to destroy the kingdoms many years before this magician was born. The Dragorians and the dragon elves fought this evil, trapped it in this chasm, and brought peace to the lands. Laden with envy and greed, the magician sought out this evil and promised to free it to do as it wanted, as long as they could rule the realms. They plotted, labored, and fought the dragons. Eventually, they realized they could banish Dragoria forever, if they got certain elements from the different kingdoms.*

"Was the magician male or female?"

We don't know. Their face was always covered, and they wore a large cloak, concealing their identity.

They finished collecting the nuts, and after Samara returned the quiver to her back, Ulrieg climbed on top.

After careful planning, the magician gathered these elements, using their strength and the force of the evil, and sealed off the land of Dragoria so that it could never be seen again. They also concocted a plan to extradite all the dragon elves back to the kingdom of Clialarion, stripping the dragon elves and guardian dragons of their magic, inhibiting the dragons and Dragoria from rising again.

"And you're claiming that the head magician of the Sacred Flame coterie was responsible for this?" Samara asked.

Yes. Sadness was etched in his voice.

Samara stooped to pick some herbs for healing. "That's a sad story. But it's completely different from what I've been told."

Clearly, the story has been twisted for you. He huffed. *You didn't even know what a dragon was. Either you're incredibly naive, or your position is so low in the coterie that they haven't told you the truth. Dragon forbid they tell you about the missing magnificent dragons.*

Though Samara was annoyed, she found it hard to be mad at him. She pursed her lips. "Hmm. Did I mention I'm only an apprentice and in training? So I don't know everything there is to know. Besides, everyone at the coterie is working toward making the kingdoms safer. They use their training and strong magic to do good, not evil. Our head sorceress, Callista, goes out of her way to ensure the peace is kept. She often travels to the borders to check on her commanders. If you ever meet her, you'll see what I mean."

Uh-huh. I'm certain you're wrong.

"How are you so certain that the stories you've been told are correct? When did you say this happened?"

About four hundred years ago.

"Are you telling me you're four hundred years old?" She raised an eyebrow at him.

He pulled his head back. *Excuse me? I'm only thirty summers old. Wingless flight! Way to make someone feel old.*

She smirked. "My point is that you weren't there. The only way you would know for sure is if you were. There are sorceresses and sorcerers in the coterie that were alive at the time. They should know the truth."

Humph. He rested his head back on her shoulder. *There's a large berry bush several trees to the right.*

"Thank you." She went in search of the bush. "How do you know this story anyway? If, as you say, all the dragons were trapped in Dragoria, then how are you here, especially since you're so young?"

Not all dragons were in Dragoria when it was cut off from the other lands. They were in all the kingdoms. I'm one of their offspring, but my heart yearns to visit my motherland.

"Is that why you're so grumpy and sarcastic most of the time?"

No. That's just my natural charm. And that charisma goes right to my core.

He exposed his vast array of sharp teeth, and Samara pulled back, her heart racing at the daunting display. His mouth was very close to her face.

Geez! Relax. That was me smiling.

Her heart slowed. "Oh. I didn't know that was your thing." She found the berry bush and started filling another small sack and Ulrieg climbed off her back to help her. They would need as much food as possible to get back to the coterie. "I think you'll find that our side of the story is correct. But I'm happy to wait and let you find out over time. You don't have to take my word for it. I understand we have just met and that it's wise not to believe a stranger."

The dragon tilted his head to one side. *That's the smartest thing you have said since I met you.* He waved the tip of his wing. *The last part about trusting a stranger, not the part about you being right.*

"Gee, thanks. So full of compliments."

You're welcome.

"Besides being a dragon, how do you think you know so much about this anyway?" She dropped another handful of blackberries into the sack, the dark juices staining her skin.

Some of my parents' great ancestors were trapped in Dragoria. My grandparents were locked out of our natural realm. *It all happened so fast when they were cut off. Some of my family is still there, and we cannot get to them.* Now that he was off her shoulder and over the other side of the bush, the real pain was evident in his red eyes.

"If there are so many dragons in the realms, where are they?"

I know for sure that my immediate family members aren't the only dragons. There are many. Before Dragoria's segregation, it was normal for dragons to be everywhere. They often acted like guardians, watching for any trouble in the kingdoms. Now, the descendants of those dragons are in hiding. Unlike me, they cannot turn invisible. I've been told they're hunted by the Sacred Flame coterie and its leaders. Dragons go missing regularly, never to be seen again. Our kind fear your coterie's leader and their followers. That is why it's puzzling that the moon guided me to help you. He picked up a couple of straight sticks and handed them to Samara.

We know our realm is somewhere, and sometimes we can sense it. But we cannot seem to find it, nor can we break through the illusion when we visit the place rumored to be the border of Dragoria. It's completely hidden from us.

Samara placed the sticks in her quiver, and Ulrieg climbed onto her back and hung from her shoulders. "I can see you honestly believe what you're telling me." She frowned. "Actually, I think I can sense it. That's weird." She progressed a few more steps before she spoke again. "And I know it brings you pain. If what you say is true, perhaps there was someone else who did all this evil to your kind. I find it hard to think Callista did this. Maybe there was another sorcerer in charge of the coterie back then. I don't know. I'm only eighteen summers, and I grew up in a small village and spent the last year at the coterie, training under Callista. Perhaps the great evil that Callista is working so hard to get rid of did this to your kind, and the dragons and the Sacred Flame coterie are working together and don't know it. Perhaps the evil behind all of this is trying to set us against the Sacred Flame coterie."

Pfft! I doubt it!

"I think you'll be surprised," she said in a singsong voice. "Why don't you come back to the coterie with me and see for yourself? I'll prove that Callista is pure and has the best intentions for all beings. She's not there to hurt people. She protects the realms and the kingdoms. What do you say? You're grumpy and often rude, but I kind of like you. Besides, you saved me. Maybe together, we can get to the bottom of this, and I can prove to you that Callista is good."

Ulrieg leaped off her shoulders then jumped

from branch to branch before stopping on one at Samara's head height, and his talons dug into the bark.

I accept your challenge. Although I still think you're incredibly naive.

"Fantastic!" Samara was surprised by how happy she was to hear him say he would come. She looked down at the mark on her hand. "Perhaps together, we can work out what this is."

Ulrieg returned to Samara's back, and they trekked farther through the forest. The horns on his forehead bunched together. *There's something I don't understand.*

"Oh? What's that?"

Why were you and Kaine put at risk and made to fight those trolls?

Saddened, Samara replied, "We don't have familiars. Because of that, our magic is weaker than others', and we're considered feebler and a risk. We had to prove ourselves against these enemies. That's the rule of the coterie. If we don't have familiars, we're tested against a formidable opponent." She rolled her neck. "Would you mind flying for a bit? You're heavy, and my back could use a rest."

The dragon pushed off her shoulder and circled above her between the trees, often stopping on low branches to stay close.

Samara continued, "We failed. Clearly. But Callista said we could return for a second chance if we escaped, as that is also proof that we have strength. Although we each still need to bond with a familiar to be able to stay permanently."

If that's supposed to support loyalty, then that's absurd. Why would you even go back? He landed on a low branch to let her catch up.

"I'm concerned for my family. Without the coterie, they won't have enough food to survive. I need to return before Callista denies the funding or access to the farm they're managing."

Sounds ludicrous to me. I'd be running and finding another way to help your family. Ulrieg found another straight stick and hovered in front of her, holding it out.

"Thank you." She took it from him and placed it with the other sticks and walnuts in her quiver. After collecting more nuts, Samara put them in her quiver as well. "I think this will do for a while. We should get back to Kaine and check on him. I also want to craft these arrows before I need them."

When they neared Kaine, Ulrieg turned invisible. Samara could hear him rustling in the trees, and she found it comforting to know he was close by, flying high to watch out for trolls. Kaine was awake, although he still looked groggy, and his handsome face was distorted by the many bruises. Samara checked on his wounds. Some had started to heal, while others looked infected. Using a stone, she cracked open several walnuts and gave them and a large leafful of berries to Kaine to eat then set to work on his wounds. Using the same stone, she crushed some bay leaves on a larger rock and placed a poultice on the infected wounds. She could heal minor wounds but not once they had become infected.

Kaine eyed her quiver, which rested against a large rock, exposing its contents and the sacks of berries attached. "I can't believe you found this much food in such a short time." He tossed another nut into his mouth and chewed. "How did you know what to collect and where to find them?"

"Seriously? You know we've been doing a class called Herbology, right?"

The shock in his eyes made her think about what she had said. She sucked in a breath. She almost sounded like Ulrieg and very unlike how she had ever talked to Kaine before. He must be rubbing off on her. Giving Kaine an apologetic smile, she said, "Sorry. I guess I'm tired after everything we've been through. You're probably not thinking straight because of your head injuries."

I thought you were being too nice. You could've been harsher. Clearly, he's an imbecile.

Samara scowled over her shoulder, trying to hide it from Kaine.

His eyes fixed on her as he swallowed his mouthful, and her heart skipped a beat. "I understand, honestly. I was in the same classes as you. In fact, I've been at the coterie longer than you, so I should know better."

Peeling back the split in his brown leather pants, she winced. Red lines circled the long gash on his leg. "We really have to get you back to the coterie as soon as possible. You need to be healed by a powerful healer." She covered the cut with the bay leaves and held her hands over the wound. "*Mendamora,*" she whispered.

The ends of the wound sealed slightly, but the infected parts remained the same.

The whole time she worked, Kaine watched her, his eyes falling to the mark on her hand. "Are you sure you didn't bond with a familiar?"

Pausing, Samara frowned. "What?"

He nodded at her hand. "That new mark. When Paxton got his familiar, he got a little mark. Not long after he bonded, he showed it to me. It looked like a faint tattoo. His is on his torso. It looks similar to the one on your hand, except his is a frog's foot."

Samara's mind spun, and she didn't know what to say. The only animal she had come close to was the dragon.

"Another reason I think that is because you've retrieved your magic when I haven't."

Her brow furrowed. She'd gotten her magic back when she was in the dungeon, and it was different somehow. But if the dragon was bonded with her, surely he must know or feel it too. Annoyed that Ulrieg might have known and didn't tell her, she turned to face the treetops. He would be there somewhere, invisible among the branches.

I know! I was appalled to be bonded with you too!

Her scowl deepened. After all the time she'd spent searching for a familiar, her initial joy had been robbed from her, thanks to a belittling dragon.

All right! Don't get your tail twisted. I'm pretty sure we're bonded. I didn't know at the time, but the more I think about it, the more I think he's right.

Samara's eyes narrowed.

I didn't say anything to you yet because I wasn't sure, and I'm only just working it out. I'd never heard of bonding with a being before. His tone had softened.

Removing her scowl, she returned to tending Kaine's wounds, unsure what to say.

But don't tell him it's a dragon. It's the last thing you need before returning to the coterie. I know you don't believe me about this yet, but play along for now. Tell him your familiar is only an owl, and you didn't think much of it because you had already been through your battle of proving yourself.

Samara turned her head away from Kaine and muttered, "And where am I supposed to get an owl from?"

I'll sort that out. Tell him it's in the trees somewhere, and it'll come down later.

Samara cleared her throat and passed Kaine some more fruit, noticing his eyes keenly followed her marked hand. "I bonded with an owl. I didn't tell you straightaway because you were so sick, and I didn't want you to feel like I was rubbing it in."

He placed a hand on her arm, which warmed from his touch. "Don't be ridiculous. I'm so happy for you. How did it happen?"

She shrugged. "He just came into the dungeon. It happened so easily that I think we've been trying too hard to find our familiars, and they've probably been running away because of our desperation."

When he smiled, even with a bruised and swollen face, it still made her heart skip a beat. "Where is he now?"

Gazing up at the treetops, she said, "He's up there somewhere. You know what they're like. They like to hide during the day and only come out at night."

She sighed deeply to release some pent-up stress. "I think that's how I managed to break us out of the cells and start using magic again. My magic does feel slightly different, stronger after the bond. It hasn't all returned. But I can feel it coming back."

A strange call sounded above, which Samara guessed was supposed to sound like an owl. She hid her expression behind her hand. It had to be Ulrieg trying to reinforce her story.

"That's wonderful!" Sadness spread across Kaine's face, making Samara think that it upset him a little. "You'll be able to return to the coterie. I just need to find mine."

Samara nodded. Not that long ago, she'd felt the same way. "We'll keep an eye out. But if you don't, I'll insist that Callista take you back anyway. We've proven how strong we are. We deserve to stay there and live to serve under her to protect the kingdoms."

CHAPTER THIRTY-FOUR

Where is your coterie building?

Samara sat a good distance from Kaine, using one of his knives to fashion her arrows. Pausing, she gazed at Ulrieg, who was behind a bush, out of Kaine's sight if he happened to wake. The shadows hid his black body well. His wings were furled by his sides, and his pointed tail was wrapped around his body as he watched Samara with curiosity and skepticism. She didn't blame him. They were both in shock over their pairing. She had never heard of dragons, and he hated everything to do with the coterie.

"You'll find out soon, I hope." She sliced more wood off her arrow tip.

Really? And I thought we were heading to Dragoria. He huffed.

She raised an eyebrow at him. "Why do you ask?"

Because I'm a curious dragon. When her eyebrow rose, he said, *If I can scout ahead and find it, I'll be able to direct you from the sky.*

"Now, was that so hard?" She smirked. "It's an excellent idea, but I don't know if you'll be able to see it. It's hidden by magic."

That would explain a lot. I've heard of it but can never find it. He scratched behind one of the horns on his head with his back foot.

It felt traitorous to tell an outsider the location of the coterie. She pursed her lips in thought. He was her familiar, and others told their familiars where to find the coterie. Besides, something about him, probably the bond, made her completely trust him.

"It's surrounded by a small forest of pine trees that's different from a normal forest like we're in now. As you probably won't see the building, there will be a plain in the middle of the forest with a few straggly trees."

I guess that kind of makes it easier. What direction is it in?

"Judging from the moss growing on the trees on our way here, I think it's south." She finished the arrow she was making and put it in her quiver.

All right. That should be enough for me to find it. I'll

be back as soon as I can. He launched into the air and turned invisible.

Samara continued crafting her arrows until she heard Kaine stirring. After packing up her remaining sticks, she headed back to find him awake, his eyes wide as he searched the area for danger.

"You're awake!" She laid her quiver against a rock not far from him and felt his forehead. It was still hot.

"Since my lovely rescuer has left me to fend for myself, I thought it was best to stay awake and observant. You never know if they'll come looking for us."

Bewildered, she said, "I was only a few feet away."

"I know." He grinned and waved his hand. A slight spark ignited. "I'm slowly regaining my magic, but I can't say it'll help me defend myself against them if they do come. At least I could hide."

Samara smiled at his attempt then fished for her pouches. "At least that's a positive sign." She handed him some more food. "Eat some more before we go. It should help build your strength. We'll wait until it gets a little darker and try to travel under the night's cover and remain in the shadows."

She injected some healing light into his forehead

KATRINA COPE

in an attempt to reduce some of the fever. The heat of the magic traveled down her arm and through her hands as it passed into him. His blue eyes never left her face, making her feel self-conscious, even though he wasn't scrutinizing her. Controlling her emotions, she finally gazed back.

Instantly, he plastered on his customary charming grin. "So, did I impress you with my heroism and fighting skills against the trolls?"

Samara finished injecting the healing power into him and pulled away but remained squatted next to him. She tilted her head to one side. "You know that one time you lay passed out?"

He blanched.

"Yeah, that was very heroic," she teased.

Kaine groaned and looked at the ground, embarrassed.

She touched his arm. "I was joking. You fought brilliantly, especially since you only had your knives. The way you dived down and cut their heels was rather impressive. It's just that they got to you. And after that, you didn't stand a chance." She said more seriously, "We both didn't stand a chance without magic. Though at least I had two arrows that were already spelled. That helped to delay the inevitable for a little bit. But unfortunately, we were still captured. There were way too many of them. And we weren't prepared for not having any magic."

He ran his fingers through some side strands of her pink hair. "My beautiful companion saved the day."

Samara's cheeks warmed, and she stood. To change the subject, she handed him some more berries. "I couldn't find a river, so I don't have any water to give you. I suggest you eat some more of these to keep your hydration up."

She was forced to look at him when he didn't take them straightaway.

Amusement shone in his eyes. As soon as he grabbed the berries, Samara turned away to hide her embarrassment.

"You're not very good at accepting compliments, are you?"

Samara wrung her hands then sat opposite Kaine with her back against the tree and rested her arms on her knees. "I like compliments. I just know that you hand them out quite readily to all the female apprentices. So pretty much anything you say to me, I take with a grain of salt because I've heard you say it to lots of young women. We'll be back at the coterie soon, and you'll be doing it again, as though talking to every female is a game to you."

His jaw dropped, and he seemed as though he was going to say something, but she cut him off.

"It's okay. I know that's who you are. And you mean well, but you play with people's hearts." She raised her chin slightly.

"That's a bit harsh, isn't it?"

She shrugged. "I'm just telling the truth. We're friends, and I like that. I don't want to change it. But to protect my heart, I'm reluctant to believe what you say."

The dark circles underneath Kaine's eyes looked darker, and she felt guilty. Perhaps Ulrieg was rubbing off on her too quickly.

Softening her tone, she said, "Why don't you sleep, and I'll stand guard. You need to rest and get your strength back."

Relief washed over his face. "See? You do care."

Samara's eyebrows rose. "Because I can't carry you back to the coterie. You're way too heavy."

"Nice!" Kaine retorted, but he didn't look at all upset.

Samara chuckled. "You know I care."

Kaine nodded. "I will take your advice, though. I'm feeling quite tired. But don't tell the ladies back at the coterie. Instead, tell them how valiant, strong, and handsome I was."

She smiled. "I'm sure you'll have fun telling them

yourself. You've never held back from showering yourself in praise."

His eyes drooped, and Samara stood watch, listening for unusual noises, and worked on finishing converting her last few sticks into arrows. Birds chirped joyously, lulling her into a sense of security. If the trolls were coming, the noise in the trees and thumping footsteps would scare the wildlife away.

Brilliant orange, red, and blue hues spread across the sky as the sun descended, and she wondered where Ulrieg was. Surely a dragon's flight would be as quick as a bird's flight, if not faster. She hoped he would find the position of the coterie from her description. It would be hard to find something invisible, just like him. She pondered how the dragon thought he was going to be able to find an owl to act as her familiar. The bird would be wild and undoubtedly independent. It seemed like an impossible task. She wished she could tell everyone the truth. Having to tell everyone a lie was robbing her of enjoying the bond. Except deep down, she was excited to have a dragon as a familiar. She would respect his wishes until who'd told the correct story came to light.

Purple edged its way into the colors of the sky. Listening to Kaine's even breathing and the pleasant sounds of the forest lulled her into relaxation. Exhaustion took over her body, and her eyes drooped. Her head jerked to the side, waking her for a moment, and she fought to remain on guard, but the exhaustion won the fight again. It had been a long day, and they had a long trip ahead of them.

A large crack sounded behind her, and she snapped awake. The setting sun blinded her momentarily, and her heartbeat quickened when she realized the birds were quiet.

CHAPTER THIRTY-FIVE

Samara sprang to her feet while retrieving an arrow and nocked it. She spun, alert but her eyes still crusted with sleep. Kaine hadn't moved. He was opposite her, still fast asleep, as he should be. She chastised herself for falling asleep on duty, even if it had only been for a moment. Because she was napping when the crack sounded, she wasn't sure where it had come from. She circled, searching for any sign.

A movement came from above, and Samara pointed her arrow up.

Dragon Moon! Jumpy much? Relax. It's just me.

The sarcastic voice of Ulrieg was a welcome sound.

Don't get your tail all twisted. You needed your beauty sleep, so I left you alone. All the kerfuffle you just heard was my catching your owl. You know, your pretend familiar.

His black form appeared above her. He looked frustrated and something was wrapped in his wings. *I'm trying to work out how to make him stay.* He feathered out the top of his wings, and from within the black membranes and rib hooks, an owl peered over the top, frantically trying to pull away from the dragon's grasp.

"That's nice." Samara lowered her bow and frowned. "But how are we going to make the owl stay? He looks like he's ready to fly away."

I'll make him stay, of course, the dragon snapped. *It can't be that hard. Surely you didn't expect a meek little bird that was so dumb that it didn't want to fly away.*

When he noticed that Kaine was still asleep, he jumped down to her level. The owl flapped, squawked, and snapped at anything near its mouth. *Here, grab hold of his claws.* He shoved the owl in her direction.

Samara's heart ached for the owl. The magnificent creature didn't like how it was being handled, and she couldn't blame it. She felt terrible but needed to keep up the pretense that the owl was her familiar. "Sorry, little boy, but I must do this." She clasped one of the owl's talons between her fingers. The owl flapped profusely, managed to get one foot loose, and grabbed onto a branch. Tentatively, she grabbed the foot and pulled the owl down from the tree. He continued to flap and squawk, determined to get away. She clenched her teeth, certain their plan wouldn't work.

Suddenly, Ulrieg turned invisible, and seconds later, she heard Kaine's voice behind her. "Is that your familiar?"

She spun around in shock then huffed a laugh. "Yeah, he's a little bit feisty." Embarrassment wracked her. As she suspected, the wild owl wasn't settling like a familiar was expected to do.

"It's beautiful. Does it have a name?"

"Yeah, sure." A whirlwind of names spun through her head. His face was a beautiful pure-white circle, and gray-flecked feathers covered his back. "Er, Gray. Gray's his name." She noticed how well his feathers blended into the tree trunks and held the owl against one. "This is why you couldn't see him before. He blends in so well, and they sleep all day."

"I can see that. Why is he flapping so much?"

Warmth rushed to her cheeks as she cooed softly to the owl, trying desperately to calm it. "I guess you could call it teething problems. He's not used to being around beings like us, and it makes him nervous, I guess. We haven't had a smooth start like the others at the coterie. But we're bonded." She held out her right hand, showing off the mark, which could easily be mistaken for a bird claw. "And I've got the tattoo to prove it." Her voice was higher-pitched than she would've liked.

"I guess a pet is out of the question, then?" he asked. "I have always wanted to pet an owl."

Samara nodded too enthusiastically. "Right now, I'd have to say it's too soon. Even I struggle to pet him without being bitten. He doesn't like being touched."

She turned to the owl. "Now, Gray. There's no reason to be so upset. You can just sit and relax. Neither of us will hurt you," she said soothingly.

Suddenly, something fell from the tree and landed at her feet. She looked down and saw a dead rat. Disgusted, she said, "Lovely! Look. Some of its catches have fallen down." She glanced upward, looking for the dragon, but had no luck.

See if food stops him from flapping so much. Maybe if you feed the owl, he'll settle down.

Samara fought not to respond. Sometimes it seemed as though Ulrieg liked to intimidate her when she couldn't reply.

Gritting her teeth, she forced a smile and bent down to pick up the rat by its tail. No matter how much she tried to keep a straight face, her nose screwed up in distaste. "Perhaps this is what he's getting upset over. He hasn't managed to eat yet." When she spotted a flat rock, she laid the rat on top and lifted it to the owl's height. "I'll just hold it up here for him."

Gray paused and eyed the rat with interest.

She released one of his claws, and the owl picked up the rat and tore at its flesh with his beak.

Grimacing, Samara turned away. "Oh, lovely! That's a first. I haven't seen meat eaten like that before." She slumped to the ground with the owl still on one hand, the rat clasped in his claws. Blood and small pieces of ripped flesh covered her hand and turned her stomach. Yet she had to pretend she loved everything the owl did because he was her familiar.

As soon as Gray finished destroying the rat, he reattempted to escape, flapping and pulling against Samara's restraint. She worried her bottom lip. Having the owl act like that wouldn't do. Other than feeding him, she didn't know how to make him stop. Maybe she should magically sedate the owl and hope he would act like her pet while docile.

Kaine's laughing cut through her thoughts.

Her brow furrowed. "What's so funny?"

"I've never seen a familiar act like that before. But everyone is different. Who knows? Mine will probably want to run away from me too. Maybe that's why you didn't get one straightaway." He chuckled.

Wow. He is as dumb as he looks, Ulrieg said from above, which put Samara in a better mood after Kaine's mild taunting.

She smiled sweetly at Kaine. "I imagine your familiar is still running. That's why you haven't found one yet." She tilted her head to one side as if to study him. "You're quite scary, always pretending to be so charming."

Stifled laughter came from above. *Wow, just knock him down with one big swing. That's my girl!*

Samara barely resisted gazing at the spot where she knew he lay invisible. Although it was a good distraction from the owl tearing apart more rat flesh that he had missed earlier.

"Way to hurt a guy!" Kaine's eyes dulled, but he didn't seem upset. "I guess I deserve that. When the owl's finished, you'll have quite a mess to clean up." He nodded toward the blood all over Samara's hand. "I would've made the owl eat somewhere else."

She eyed the bird. "If letting him eat while on my hand helps him bond with me, I'll put up with it. I'm sure I'll deal with worse things later."

Gray seemed to be settling down the more he ate near her. He seemed to realize that Samara didn't want to hurt him. Although since he jerked his leg every so often, he must not be keen on her hanging onto his claws. She didn't blame him.

When the bird had finally finished eating, he settled on Samara's hand and cleaned himself without trying to pull away.

Samara breathed a silent sigh of relief. The dragon had been right. A bit of food, and the owl had settled, which held hope for the future of showing him off to the people at the coterie. It would be easier to pretend he was her familiar. She would have to work on a different kind of bond with the owl to pull it off.

By the time the owl had finished, the sun had disappeared from the sky. "I think it's time we left. Have you gained any more energy?" Samara pulled a cloth from the back of her quiver and rubbed at the blood on her hand. She would have to wash it as soon as she saw a creek.

Kaine slowly rose to his feet, pushing against the trunk. He wobbled slightly but braced himself against the tree. Samara moved to help him, but he shook her off and waited to regain his balance. After a few moments, he pushed off the tree. "I'm fine now. My head just spun a bit. I got up too quickly."

With the owl in one hand, she placed the other under his elbow to brace him as he moved. "We'll take it slowly. If you feel bad, just let me know. I aim to cover enough ground that we can hopefully be at the Sacred Flame coterie by morning."

When he had steadied and walked fine by himself for a bit, she dropped her hand. Then she picked up her bow and threaded it over her head and lay it across her chest. The newly made arrows rattled in her quiver. While she was distracted, the owl broke free from her grasp and flew to the branches. She watched him to see what he did. Amused, she watched it struggle with an invisible force.

The struggle caught Kaine's attention, and he stared at the owl. "What's going on with him? I'm starting to think you found yourself a crazy familiar."

"It looks like I have." She smirked, trying not to laugh at the preposterous struggle between the owl and Ulrieg before turning to Kaine. "Well, that's going to make life interesting." She tilted her head to one side as she watched the owl's attempts to free himself. "It's time to go. The owl should follow, I hope." Fingers crossed, she glanced over her shoulder at the owl as she walked away.

It's over to your right. Not that way. Ulrieg sounded flustered, making Samara's smirk grow.

She paused for a moment and took stock of what was around her, catching sight of the slightly diminished full moon, before she called to Kaine, who was scuffling past her. "Wait! I just need to get my bearings." Pretending to think about it, she studied the different trees and their markings before pointing to the right. "I'm pretty sure it's this way." She turned, and without questioning, Kaine followed her.

"You were the only one awake when they took us." He shrugged. "I've got no idea. I don't know if they walked north, south, east, or west. So I'll follow you. Fingers crossed it's the right direction."

CHAPTER THIRTY-SIX

Before they left the trees' cover, a soft breeze brushed Samara's hair, and she smiled, certain Ulrieg was letting her know he was still close.

Turning, she spotted that Kaine had fallen back. "We'll take a break. You look like you need a rest." The sound of a bird struggling came from the bushes nearby. "I'm going to see if I can get Gray down and bond with him a little more."

Kaine nodded as he sat against a tree trunk and rested his arms on his knees.

She pulled a pouch of berries from her quiver and left him several walnuts with a couple of stones before heading in the direction of the flapping bird.

Out of earshot, Ulrieg jumped to the ground, the owl wrapped in his wings. *Such a brilliant idea of yours to pretend to have an owl for a familiar,* he said, his teeth exposed in a grimace.

Samara raised an eyebrow. "Do I need to remind you that it was *your* idea to rope an owl into this? I mean, the poor thing just wanted to live his life only to suddenly be caught by a dragon and forced to like a being who's half-elf and half-human."

Sounds like someone else I know, he grumbled.

Samara threw up her hands. "Hey, I didn't force you to bond with me. I wasn't even trying to bond with you. I didn't know what a dragon was, let alone whether it was a creature to be bonded with." She crossed her arms across her chest. "It's not like you're pleasant anyway. You're always saying some-thing sarcastic, and you love to comment on how stupid I am. If you don't want to be with me that much, then I'll ask around to see if there's a way to break the bond."

Emotions that looked like hurt passed over Ulrieg's face. *I thought you liked me.* He hugged the owl tighter.

She huffed. "I do. But sometimes you don't make it easy. So I'm not going to force you to be my familiar if you don't want to be. You've made it clear how much you hate people from my coterie. I'll see if I can get the bond broken."

Ulrieg looked at the ground. *Nah. You've grown on*

me. And since we're bonded, I could be a bit nicer to you. I do kind of like you. He bashfully scraped a talon over the forest floor before looking her directly in the eyes, the red in his burning.

Samara held her hand over her heart. "Wow! You actually like someone!" She squatted down to his level and touched the side of his jaw. "I know you like me. I was just letting you know that I'm not going to force you to be my familiar if you don't want to be. I don't want you to feel like you're being forced into something you never signed up for."

His red eyes burned with mischief. *Don't get too comfortable. I will still tell you if you're stupid and do something stupid. And don't expect me to like your friends.* He stood tall. *Especially since they're from the coterie.*

Shaking her head, Samara chuckled. "I wouldn't dream of it."

Gray peered over the dragon's wings, his eyes wide.

"Hey, little guy. I don't want to force you, but we have a long way to go, and I need you to relax and trust us." Holding her hand just out of reach of being nipped, she said, *"Childora."* The owl instantly relaxed and stopped fighting Ulrieg, even when Samara held her hand close then stroked his head. "There you go. I promise we'll look after you."

Ulrieg relaxed his wings, opening them to expose the owl, and Samara scooped him up. Gray didn't struggle or nip her, and she placed him on her shoulder, feeling his weight.

"That's it." She looked at the owl from the corner of her eye, pleased to see him relaxed. "I'll feed you more when we get to the coterie."

Finally! Ulrieg's shoulder sagged with relief. *It's been extremely difficult clasping on to him with my talons while trying to fly. He put up a good fight for someone his size.*

"How are we doing for direction so far?" she asked.

Pretty good. You need to head a little more to the right. He indicated with his wing. *I'll be able to concentrate more now that I don't have to fight with the owl the whole way. I'll give you more directions from the sky.*

"Great!" Samara rose to her feet. "I should go back and see how Kaine is doing."

Ulrieg spotted a rabbit hopping in the opposite direction. *Sure. I'll be in the sky as soon as I have a snack. You two are slow compared to flying anyway.* He pushed into the air, and his black form zigzagged through the trees, following the rabbit until he disappeared.

When Samara returned to Kaine, she ignited a

small flame above her palm. The color had returned to his cheeks.

"I'm ready to go when you are," he said cheerily.

When she offered him the hand without the flame, he grabbed it and used her weight to pull himself up.

His eyes traveled to Gray. "I see you managed to get your owl to come down."

Samara nodded. "It took a bit, but he's here for now." She took the empty pouch from him and placed it in her quiver.

They traveled over plains and valleys and passed through more forests. Samara remembered some of the landmarks along the way. Under the moonlight, they looked different from how they'd looked during her trip with the trolls but still recognizable. Besides the landmarks, she followed the markings of the moss to lead them south.

Ulrieg's directions had them cutting a straight path to the coterie whenever they could while he kept invisible or above the trees, out of sight. Their tiny steps made the trip seem much farther and longer that the trolls' giant ones had.

Even with the dragon's guidance, it took until the sun rose in the morning before they reached the pine forest. Branches shook, the noise shifting closer, and Samara glanced at the treetops.

It's just me. I can't see the building. Maybe I should be on your back when you cross the threshold.

She nodded and spoke to the owl. "I'll get you to hop onto my hand." She placed her hand under his chest, and he instinctively stepped on. Wariness had grown in his eyes, and Samara wrapped her fingers around one of his legs, just in case the spell had a time limit. She had never spelled anyone to relax before. She was just in time. The owl flapped wildly, displeased with her hold. His claws dug into the flesh on the back of her hand and drew blood. She clenched her teeth. She would have to find some gloves and probably something to cover her arms to protect her skin when she wore her favorite sleeveless tunic.

The commotion caught Kaine's eye, and he shook his head. "You do have a strange one there."

The strange one is the guy who accepts that the owl was suddenly happy to stay on your shoulder all this time. I can't believe he fell for that, Ulrieg retorted.

Samara was glad that neither Kaine nor any other being could hear what Ulrieg said about them.

Incoming!

Samara braced just in time to balance Ulrieg's weight on her back. His front talons dug into her leather tunic, and his back ones clasped the leather of her quiver. He seemed to grab her as though she were a tree trunk. He wriggled, and she felt the prick of his talons piercing through the leather on her shoulder, and she clamped her teeth.

Here. Let me grab Gray. Ulrieg's weight shifted on her back as he grabbed the owl and secured him to her shoulder. The owl flapped and cried out in frustration.

"I hope when I get my familiar, it won't be as feisty as yours." Red and black rings circled Kaine's eyes from tiredness and the infection, but they shone with fascination over the owl's behavior.

Gently grabbing his arm, she pulled him after her. "Come on. Let's find you a healer as soon as possible."

By the time they reached the coterie, the sun had risen above the horizon. A fresh display of clouds was clustered in the east, illuminated by the golden colors of the morning. The large stone building that housed the coterie apprentices was bathed in golden light, which made it seem almost heavenly, especially after the ordeal they had been through.

"Now there's a sight for sore eyes." The sun shone across Kaine's face, illuminating his blue irises. "I hope they'll accept me again. I certainly didn't find a familiar on our way back."

Samara squeezed his arm. "You'll be fine. You deserve to stay and have a second chance. By

310

escaping the trolls, we proved that we deserve to be in this coterie under Callista's leadership. Surely Callista will see that."

A shadow passed over his eyes. "But you're the reason that we escaped, not me. It was you who found the familiar and you who regained your magic."

She rubbed his arm, doing her best to ignore the protesting owl and the weight of Ulrieg on her back. "You'll be fine. I promise. Come on. Let's go in."

Together, they approached the stairs.

I don't see anything. Ulrieg's talons dug farther into her leather tunic, dangerously close to piercing the skin.

The stairs spread before them, turning sharply to the left halfway up and directing their path to the building. The straggly trees framed the sides, some branches towering over the balustrades. They started to ascend the stairs, the additional weight of the dragon and owl overworking Samara's thighs.

The owl flapped in an attempt to escape, only to be secured in Ulrieg's grasp. When Samara hit the third step, a voice entered her head.

Ah. Now I see it. I was worried I'd be knocked off your back by a magic force as you disappeared.

They reached the top of the stairs, and Samara pushed the main doors open, her magic opening it easily. As soon as they entered, a squeal rang through the room.

"You made it!" Devi ran toward them from the far corner, and Zion followed close behind. The wolf eyed Gray, his eyes narrowing, and Samara protectively raised a hand. The owl nipped her fingers.

"Ow!" Samara pulled her fingers away.

Devi wrapped her arms around her, and somehow, Ulrieg seemed to pull away from the embrace. When the teacher didn't cry out in pain or alarm, Samara relaxed, making a mental note that she would have to ask him how he'd managed to avoid it later.

"You're both back." She ran to Kaine and embraced him as well. He grimaced in pain from the contact. "I'm so glad to see you both." She released him. "So, did you defeat them with your magic?"

Seeing a teacher excited to see them back made Samara relax. Even though Callista had said they could return if they escaped, it still felt like they'd failed. "No."

"What?" Devi was shocked. "But you're both strong in your defensive magic."

"We were stripped of our magic as soon as we entered the field where we were to go against the trolls," Kaine said, surprisingly sounding upbeat. He smirked. "It was our great fighting skills with our weapons that did it."

Her eyes wide, Devi asked, "Really?"

Dragon Moon! Even the teacher lacks brains. Well, I assume she's a teacher because of her age. Is everyone in this coterie that dumb? Is she seriously trying to claim that her magic teaching is what saved you?

Samara reached back and shoved a finger at him, pretending to play with her hair. Her finger hit something that felt like his neck.

Huh. That was pointy.

Unable to say anything to him, she just focused her attention on Devi, casting Kaine a side glance. "Unfortunately, it wasn't our weapon skills either. We were captured and imprisoned. But somehow, Gray here managed to find his way into the dungeon and bond with me. My magic returned, and with Kaine's help, we escaped."

"That's fantastic!" Devi said then frowned. "It's rather odd that your magic was stripped away. I thought the whole point was that you had to prove your worth by fighting the opponent with your magic. The weapons were supposed to be extra in case your magic failed."

Both Samara and Kaine shrugged, the owl writhing after the sudden movement.

Kaine said, "We were shocked as well, but we managed to get through it together."

"I'm so glad you're back. Let me take you to Callista. She'll be ecstatic that you've made it back." Devi turned and led them away. Realizing that they hadn't moved, she spun to face them. "Come on! She told me she'd be in her office this morning."

Hesitantly, they fell into step behind her as she led them up the stairs to the top level and through the extensive corridor that veered to the right. When they reached Callista's office door, she knocked loudly, and the door opened with magic.

"Callista, look who has returned!" Devi excitedly led them into the room. Zion waited outside the door.

Callista was behind her desk. The large crystals sat on their pillars in the corners of the room. Their vibrations hummed as though magic was being drawn from them.

Mystique sat in the back corner, her tail whipping from side to side. A chill ran down Samara's spine as soon as she met Mystique's yellow eyes. They were the last thing she'd seen as they battled the trolls. Help could've been only several feet away, but the cat had only sat watching them being slaughtered. She wondered if she should tell Callista about that.

The black jaguar lifted her nose and sniffed, her slitted eyes narrowing on the owl. Her actions made Samara wonder if the cat could smell Ulrieg, and the thought made her more nervous.

Ah. So that's what the high-and-mighty head sorceress looks like. Not that impressive, if you ask me.

Callista rose to her feet, and the crystals ceased their humming. Her face expressionless, the head sorceress moved from behind the desk. With a closer look, she seemed to have a slight pleasantness added to her expression. "Welcome back!" She opened her arms in a welcoming gesture that lacked the warmth Devi had greeted them with. "I was worried for you. Mystique said you failed."

Everything seemed to fall into place. Samara glanced back at Mystique. She had only been watching to see the outcome.

As though reading Samara's thoughts, Callista said, "Mystique couldn't enter the fight, but she watched to see what would happen to report back to me. I couldn't bear to watch."

Instantly, Samara eyed the jaguar in a different light. The cat still made her feel on edge, but she forgave the cat for doing what had seemed like a heartless thing.

Uh-uh! Nope! There is no way I believe that. Don't

you dare tell me you accept that. That's the stupidest excuse I've heard.

Samara struggled to block out Ulrieg's pessimism. She had expected it, but it wasn't helping her concentrate.

"So, how are you here?" Callista asked. "Although it's good to see you, of course."

"We were taken captive, and Kaine was quite hurt. But I managed to bond with this owl. So I have—"

"So you have a familiar now." Callista cut Samara short.

"Yes, I do." Samara held out her hand, showing off her mark.

Callista wrapped her cold hands around Samara's wrist as she studied the mark. "How lovely. Congratulations! That's fantastic!"

She turned to Kaine. "How about you, Kaine? Were you able to find one?"

Kaine's eyes filled with sadness, and he shook his head, the disappointment accentuating his fatigue. "No. I didn't."

Samara felt terrible for him. "But with his help, we escaped from the trolls and their dungeon. Kaine played a large part in our escape. I met the owl in the dungeon, and he reinstated the magic stripped from me before the fight."

"I'm sorry about that," Callista said. "It was the terms placed on you by the higher magic force. The almighty wanted to see how you proved yourself."

If you ask me, it all sounds rather fishy. Ulrieg's weight on her back suddenly seemed to get heavier. Not only was he half her size, but it was probably also because of his negativity toward her coterie and Callista. He was doing a good job of holding the owl in place, but she hoped he didn't have to be there every time she wanted to prove the owl was her familiar.

When Samara's back stiffened, Ulrieg seemed to notice. *You'd better not be falling for this. If you are, I'll have to start believing you've lost a few brain cells.*

Samara made a mental note to talk to him about his attitude later.

"That makes sense," Kaine said. "I was worried we had done something wrong. And that you'd stripped us of our magic."

Is he serious right now? I mean, look at him. He's about to collapse. Can't she see that? It really makes me wonder where her loyalties lie.

Samara flicked her fingers behind her head and connected with the dragon.

Ouch! That got me on the nose.

"I know." Callista sat on the edge of her table and brushed her long lilac hair over her shoulder.

"Remember, I gave you the crystals to enhance your magic to help you succeed. But they would do nothing if you had no magic at all."

Samara wanted to rub that information in Ulrieg's pointed face. She fingered the crystals in the hidden pocket in her tunic remembering that she had found Kaine's crystals next to him in the dungeon and pocketed them.

The sorceress went around the other side of her table. Her long dress, covered with the black outlined leaf pattern, swished around her ankles and touched the ground when she sat. "Tell me some more. How did you escape?"

After a glance at Kaine, Samara saw he was still unstable on his feet. "After I bonded with the owl that happened to be down in the dungeon, my magic returned, allowing me to open the locks. After I unlocked Kaine's cell, he had a large part in helping us escape. He was vital in spotting any danger or an approaching troll as we made our way out of the building and through the forest. He's also very acquainted with where our coterie is, as he had traveled far when he practiced his weaponry. So I followed his guidance."

Lies, lies, and more lies. Surely the great and mighty sorceress isn't dumb enough to fall for this.

Samara glared threateningly over her shoulder.

She didn't know where his face was but hoped he would get the message.

Callista faced Kaine. "That's very knowledgeable of you. Well done!" Her piercing blue eyes turned to Samara. "Naturally, Samara is welcome back into the coterie, and her family will be provided for again." She steepled her fingers and considered her words. To Kaine, she said, "You're welcome back for a while, but you still need to find your familiar. I hope you will find your one before the next lot of students start to connect with theirs."

Despite Kaine's smile, apprehension passed over his eyes.

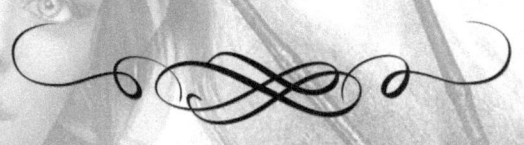

CHAPTER THIRTY-SEVEN

When Callista dismissed Kaine and Samara, she sent them to wash up and head to their rooms to get some much-needed sleep. Artemise concocted healing potions for Kaine's infections, and Eliphas patched him with healing poultices from different plants.

Though Samara wanted to catch up with all the other apprentices, Devi had Forgrac make up some delicious meals especially for her and Kaine, and the dwarf delivered hers with a smile.

"I was worried for you." He entered, and the plate, loaded with roast fowl and vegetables, clacked on the study bench in front of the window.

Samara breathed in deeply. "That smells so good. Thank you."

"I took the extra time for my favorite apprentice

at the coterie." The dwarf placed a friendly hand on her shoulder. "Your male companion should be grateful I made a little extra."

"Don't you like him?" Samara sat in front of the food and picked up the metal fork and knife.

"Oh. It's not only him. You're the only one who has given me any attention all the time I've been here. The others can jump in a lake, as far as I'm concerned."

Samara studied him. He seemed to be telling the truth, but she struggled to believe him. "Surely not."

I'd believe it, Ulrieg cut in.

Samara almost groaned at the dragon's hate for the place. She still hadn't had a chance to talk to him about keeping his constant negativity to himself. "Kaine and my other friends talked to you the other day on the steps."

"Only because you instigated it." Forgrac shrugged. "It is what it is. My time here will be over soon." He indicated her food with a stubby finger. "Eat up. I'd hate for it to go cold. Then get some rest. I'm sure you've earned it. I'll get your plate later." He made his way to the door, his short legs making him appear to waddle. Walking past Gray's stand, he called, "Beautiful bird. A familiar you can be proud of. He's even better because you get to stay at the coterie."

Samara forked a large piece of fowl and smiled as the dwarf let himself out. She had made Gray's stand out of a couple of sticks Ulrieg collected from the forest. The dragon had caught him a rat from inside the building. Samara had to face the other way to eat her meal as the owl tore into its flesh. After being given more food, the owl seemed to settle. Each time Samara provided him with food, he showed a little more trust in her. She put aside a little of the meat from her plate to save for him to have later. She wanted the owl to be calm when they were in public and knew she would have to nurture a relationship with the wild owl. It would make it a lot easier to pretend he was her familiar if he sat placidly by her side. When Gray had finished his rat, she fed him the pieces of meat from her hand. Despite being held captive in her room, he seemed to be warming to her.

She finished setting up the stand, attaching a metal bowl for water, and placed an old cloth under the stand to catch the owl's mess.

Ulrieg watched her from the corner, visible since they were alone. *I chose well,* he said, watching how the owl settled in quite well for a wild bird. *This owl actually seems to like you.*

"Normally, I'm quite likable." Samara cast the dragon a sly look. "And I do like animals. He's probably picking up on that." She handed the owl another strip of meat, and he took it, tearing off smaller pieces to swallow. "It's daytime anyway. Gray's probably ready for a nap. It's been a long night for all of us."

The dragon climbed down the wall and sat on the end of her bed. *It's quite a dubious setup they've got here, hiding a building of this size in plain sight. No wonder nobody could find it. I'm impressed. I couldn't see it when I flew over it, and I didn't see it until I was on your back and you had mounted a few stairs. It's as though the magic wouldn't let me in until you carried me across the threshold.* His beady red eyes focused on her with intent. *Although I'm still not convinced this is an innocent coterie. Why would they have to hide the building if they were here to teach you how to protect the kingdoms? Innocent undertakings shouldn't need hiding.*

Samara shrugged, plunked down on the bed, and kicked off her house shoes. She felt so much better cleaning herself up and eating. All she needed was sleep.

"I think the protection spell protects Callista more than the building. She can't be alert all the time and would need rest from beings wanting to harm her. People need to rest."

She's an elf, Ulrieg said.

Samara shrugged. "I'm half-elf, half-human. What does it matter?"

An elf's magic is stronger, Ulrieg argued. *Everyone knows that.*

Shaking her head, Samara said, "Actually, there are humans in this coterie whose magic is quite strong. And their magic is highlighted when they have a familiar, just as much as an elf's is."

Ulrieg spread his wings and lifted his shoulders in what looked like a shrug. *If you say so.*

"Anyway. What I was saying is that Callista needs some downtime too. She needs to be able to rest and not worry about evil finding her. Here, if the danger does get past the illusion, teachers and her apprentices surround her, ready to protect her." She lay on her bed, her pillow feeling like heaven after sleeping on a solid rock bed with only a little straw. She hooked her hands behind her head and crossed her ankles. "I think it's quite smart to keep this building hidden. It protects all of us working to save the kingdoms. We can hide from the evil that lurks outside."

Ulrieg plodded up her bed and sat next to her hip. He was careful not to hurt her with any of his horns. *I still think I'll wait and see before I agree with you. Or if I agree with you. You'll have to prove to me all this innocence you claim this coterie is holding. So far, I'm not convinced.* He tucked his tail around himself and curled up next to Samara.

"Which reminds me. Can you keep your very vocal opinions to yourself until you see more of the coterie? It's rather distracting."

His glowing red eyes focused on her. *But they're true.*

"That may be what you believe, but knowing how much bias you already hold, I'm not going to believe you until you've seen more of the coterie with an open mind."

Ulrieg huffed. *I guess.* He curled tighter, his hot breath coating her hip.

She didn't mind his closeness, despite his angry disposition. He had started to show her some affection.

He opened one eye and peered at her. *I just want to make clear, now that we're in private, that I don't believe for one second about the overall magic being demanding that your magic be stripped before you had to fight those trolls.*

When she opened her mouth to protest, he raised a talon and shook his head. *But I'll let you try to prove me wrong. I'll give you that much. I promised I'd let you prove your side. And that's what I'll do.* He frowned. *But I'm still skeptical. I mean, look at how unemotional Callista's face is. It's like she's hiding something.*

Samara chortled. "No. She's just like that because she has so much on her shoulders. If she restrains her emotions, she can cope better."

We'll see. He snuggled in by her side. *But when I'm done, and I'm pretty confident I'll be right, I'll explain to you more about our side.*

Samara left the topic alone, giving it time to develop. "It's bizarre not being able to share you as my familiar. Are you sure they don't like dragons?"

Like we promised each other, give me a little while to prove it to you. I think you're in for a big surprise.

"I hope you're wrong. My world is about to be ripped apart if you're not." Samara placed a hand over his front claw.

I won't take pride in proving you've been taught rubbish. His glowing red eyes seemed to fill with compassion. *From what I've seen, it will rip out your heart and put your family at risk. And I don't want to cause you pain like that.*

Samara yawned, and her eyes drooped. Though she still thought he was the one in the wrong, she wouldn't continue arguing. She had time to prove it to him. He would be living by her side and eating at the coterie.

She gasped. "I'm so sorry! I didn't get you any food from the hall. I was only thinking about feeding Gray to try to win him over."

Ulrieg lifted his head and tilted it to one side. *I noticed.* His eyes glinted. *But I knew what you were doing. Besides, there are lots of rats around here that I can catch. I'll find plenty of food I can catch on my own. Fresh is always better anyway.*

"But you'd have to get outside to be able to do that," she said.

The dragon muttered what sounded suspiciously like an insult under his breath. Instead of voicing it, he nudged her with his nose. *You've got a window, don't you?*

As soon as he said the words, she felt embarrassed. "Of course. Would you like me to open it now so that you can get out to catch a meal?"

Keep it closed for now. Open it later when you wake up. That way, the owl won't try to escape while we sleep.

He laid his chin on her leg, and Samara gently placed her hand on his side between the many horns that protected his scales. He'd proved that his personality was prickly like his horns, but deep within, he had a soft center. He honestly cared, and she was already falling in love with that side of him. She just wanted to prove him wrong about the coterie and how Callista was training them to protect the realms instead of what he feared they were being trained for.

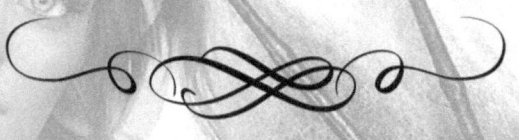

CHAPTER THIRTY-EIGHT

Revitalized, Samara woke with daylight cracking through the curtains. She didn't know how long she'd been asleep but hoped all the lessons were finished so that she could catch up with the other apprentices. Raising her arms above her head, she stretched the entire bed length, and Ulrieg stirred next to her.

Gray perched on his stand, his white face hidden within his gray wings as he slept. She rose to her feet and studied his soft form. It would be interesting to go through a whole day pretending the wild bird was her familiar. He was slowly relaxing around her, but he still had a long way to go.

Ulrieg watched her from the bed. *Why don't you charm him again with a spell that will make him placid?*

Samara turned to face him. "That's a good idea,

to a point. I don't want to make him too docile or control him so much that he'll hate me. Although I should be able to give him a calming spell, at least. Perhaps that'll make him want to stay with me for the long term, plus being enticed by the food I give him." She chuckled. "Would you look at that! Thanks to your advice, I'm already feeling wiser."

Ulrieg rolled his eyes. *Please don't do that. It makes it really, really hard not to say you're stupid if you do things like that.* His serious expression was overtaken by a grin exposing his vast array of teeth.

Samara waggled a finger at him. "I know you're all prickles on the outside, but deep within, you're a big softy."

How did you get that from everything I've done for you? I've always shown my tough side, not my soft side. He crossed his wings over his chest as if protecting himself from anything she said.

Smiling, she went to him. "You've shown me enough of your soft side to let me know that you're not all prickles and horns." She touched the tip of one and quickly pulled the finger away. "Ow! They're actually quite sharp."

He tilted his head to one side, and a strange expression crossed his little face. *Really? That's what you're going to say to me?*

Baffled, she asked, "What?"

He spun and shook his head, grumbling. *Maybe it will be harder than I thought to be nice to you. When you say things like that, it makes it so difficult.*

Samara chuckled. "We've already covered this. You're all prickles on the outside and soft and cuddly on the inside. Not threatening to me at all."

I'll work on it. I'm hungry, and I want to leave by the window. Can you make the little owl docile so that he won't fly away? He gestured at the owl with his wings.

Samara padded to the owl, picked up the leftover piece of meat from her plate, and handed it to the half-sleeping owl. Instantly, Gray took it and ripped away shreds before swallowing them. While he was distracted, she whispered, *"Childora."* After waiting a moment, she stroked the tips of his furled wing to test the spell's result. Gray ignored her touch, only concentrating on his food. "Are you nice and calm?"

His only response was a passive blink, and he didn't flinch or protest when she stroked his back. She moved her fingers gently over his head and down his neck. The owl remained unfazed, and he didn't try to bite her. Samara reveled in the softness of his feathers. They were thick and luscious, unlike the dragon's hardened scales and horns. If their interaction continued like that, she could easily pretend the owl was her familiar. He was such a majestic bird. Her eyes traveled to Ulrieg, who was watching her intently. Trust her to find something odd to be her familiar—so strange that the familiar didn't even want to be known to her coterie.

Confident that the owl was settled, she walked to the window. "Are you ready? I won't leave the window open in case the spell is only light, but I'll let you out."

Am I ready? I'm famished. He jumped to his feet. *I don't want to live off just rats forever.*

"Fair enough." She pushed the window open wide enough for the dragon to get out then closed it quickly after he exited and turned invisible.

Gray didn't attempt to escape. He merely glanced at the open window briefly before returning to his meat.

The sun was in the far west, filling the sky with brilliant hues as it set to disappear after another day. She went to her cupboard, grabbed a clean pair of loose-fitting leather pants, pulled them on, then slipped on a comfortable jerkin.

She held her hand up to the owl's chest and prompted it to hop on. "Are you coming with me, Gray? I would love your company. They all think you're my familiar. So I hope you don't mind."

The owl stared at her.

"They won't hurt you. You'll be looked after well because they think you're my familiar." She brushed the soft feathers of his chest. "You're so incredibly soft. I could bury my hand in those beautiful feathers and rest my head against your body. But I'm certain that would scare you. If you hop on and come with me, I can give you food straight from the food hall when I eat my dinner." She tapped her shoulder. "You could just catch a ride down." Giving it one last try, she pressed two fingers against the owl's chest. Slowly, Gray lifted a leg and stepped onto her hand.

Samara smiled, and she secured the owl with a thumb over his claws and descended the stairs in her soft moccasins. Her stomach roared with hunger. As she hooked a hank of hair over her ear, she was reminded to inject her hair with magic to bring out her magical hair color more. Grabbing a clump of hair, she focused, inserting the magic, and watched its brilliant pink turn brighter than before. She twirled a strand in her fingers in amusement. It must be a result of her having a familiar.

She hurried through the empty corridor and moved toward the smell of the food wafting through the passageways. The hum of the students' chatter filled the air, and when she entered the dining hall, the students all clapped.

Not expecting a greeting like that, she froze. Then she smiled and went farther into the hall. She held Gray high, showing him off, and received many gasps of awe at the magnificent creature.

"It looks like you and I must keep our familiars apart," someone said from behind her.

She turned to see Paxton quickly tucking Jojo securely under his jerkin.

"Owls tend to eat frogs."

"I certainly hope Gray knows the difference between a frog and a familiar," Samara said. "But it's best to be on the safe side. Congratulations, though," Paxton said, eyeing Gray. "You have picked a familiar to be proud of. It may be late coming, but he's a beautiful creature." He held his hand closer to the owl, and Gray snapped at it. He yanked his hand away and stepped back.

"I'm having a few teething problems. Gray isn't quite tame for me, either. Although he's getting better the more time we spend together. Don't be surprised if you see him flapping profusely, looking like he sometimes wants to get away." She chortled when Paxton looked at her strangely. "Oh, don't worry. It's going to change. He's already getting tamer and less likely to take off."

"I've never heard of a familiar wanting to flee."

"Well, there are familiars of all shapes and sizes. Nothing would surprise me," Samara said. "After all, they're still wild animals."

KATRINA COPE

"I can see you're quite busy with him. I'll go and grab you some food. Why don't you take a seat?"

"Is Kaine in here?"

Paxton shook his head. "I think he's still asleep. Either that, or he's gone out to look for a familiar again."

A pang of guilt wracked Samara. "I hope he finds one soon."

CHAPTER THIRTY-NINE

A loud knock woke Samara. Blinking, she gazed at the window. Light peeked through the gap in the curtains, showing the new day had begun. Samara stretched and startled when the loud knock sounded again.

"Coming!" she called, quickly taking stock of her room. Ulrieg was nowhere to be seen. He was either still out hunting or invisible.

She wrapped her dressing gown around her and plodded to the door, the stones cold under her bare feet.

Thoughts of the previous night's meal went through her head. They had only been back about a week, and Gray had behaved exceptionally well. He had sat on her shoulder, and it gave her hope that maybe their plan might work. Perhaps she could be bonded with the dragon, and he could remain a secret, and the owl could pretend to be her familiar. Maybe one day, she wouldn't even have to sedate him with a spell.

Gray sat on his perch with his beak tucked under his feathers. He hadn't made a ruckus all night, which was fantastic. She was worried that he might stay awake at night but had given him a few pieces of fresh meat she got from Forgrac.

She swung back the door to find Mist standing in the corridor, Okak perched on her broad shoulder. Her white hair looked almost ghostly, and she was dressed as though ready for battle in her leather jerkin and black pants. Her arms were bare, and a sword, her weapon of choice, swung from her hip. She relished in weapons training and had the muscles to prove it. She could quickly put many of the males in the coterie to shame. Although Samara and Mist were similar in age, they didn't have much in common.

"Mist! What's wrong?"

Mist shook her head. "Nothing. This is a wake-up call. Come on. Get ready. You have your familiar-welcoming ceremony."

Samara's face must have betrayed her nerves.

"There's nothing to be worried about. You saw my ceremony. It's very laid-back."

Samara nodded. She wanted to scream, *Yeah, but my familiar isn't really my familiar.* But she held her tongue.

Mist smiled reassuringly, and it was a strange look on the she-warrior's face. "I'll let you get ready. But hurry. Callista has a lot on her plate today. That's why she wants to get it done before breakfast." She closed the door behind her.

Samara grabbed some loose-fitting pants and a tunic and got dressed. After sedating Gray with the spell, she lured him onto her shoulder and hurried downstairs, heading straight to the common room.

Many of the students had already gathered. Mist was there, and Okak sat on the beams above, preening. Gray fluttered briefly because of all the ruckus of the room. Samara could imagine having so many people around would be quite intimidating for a wild creature. He calmed quickly when Samara slipped him a small piece of meat. It pleased her that he was rapidly settling in. She hadn't seen any sign of Ulrieg all night but assumed he had spent the night hunting. She didn't own him, and if he genuinely was her familiar, he would return when he was ready. It wasn't as though he was a frog that Artemise would want to add to a potion. Although he hadn't shown her any sign of aggression, a creature with teeth and horns like his would have a good chance to protect himself. He probably enjoyed the freedom of the night, and it wasn't as though she could show him off to the other apprentices.

Mystique sat in the corner, eyeing her as she entered. As soon as those yellow-slitted eyes met hers, a shiver ran down her spine. Even though Callista had explained why the jaguar was watching their battle with the trolls, the memory still unsettled her. Each time she looked at the cat, she saw a replay of that terrifying moment when they were being defeated. Under the scrutinizing gaze of the large cat, Gray grew restless. Samara moved quickly away and took a seat at the front of the room.

Paxton sat beside her, his frog tucked safely away in his jerkin, and his gaze wandered around the room. Leaning close to Samara, he whispered, "I don't know if I'm reading things wrong, but Mystique seems to have some kind of infatuation with you."

Samara spun to find that the black jaguar's eyes were still fixed on her and Gray. She whispered, "Yes, she gives me the shivers. The cat watched us being defeated by the trolls and didn't help. Although from what Callista said, she was only doing that to report the outcome to her. Still, it was eerie."

Paxton's face paled, and his jaw dropped. "That

would be eerie, especially if you were being defeated."

Despite Samara's calming spell and the pieces of meat, Mystique's constant surveillance made Gray restless.

Callista sat at the front, facing the room on her throne-like chair. A different set of flowers adorned the weaved branches on the backrest, all magically selected by Callista. The head sorceress sat straight-backed and slightly forward so that she didn't squash them. She wore what appeared to be her favorite beige gown covered in leaves, and her lilac hair was pulled back, exposing her pointed elf ears. She tossed crystals lightly in one hand as she waited for the last of the students to join.

Peadar, Rehan, and Luna rushed through the door and took their seats.

Callista nodded in acknowledgment and stood. "Welcome, apprentices. We have much to celebrate today." She spread her arms wide. "We have the return of Samara and Kaine." She indicated Samara before scanning the room for Kaine.

Mutters passed through the room. Kaine was nowhere to be found.

With a wave of her hands, Callista said, "I believe Kaine will join us later. He was quite injured when he returned and is possibly still recovering from his ordeal." She faced Samara. "But we are gathered here this morning to celebrate not only because both apprentices returned after fighting many trolls, being caught, then escaping but also because one of them connected with a familiar in the process." She extended an open palm to Samara and beckoned her forward.

With Gray still on her shoulder, Samara stood and steadily paced forward, careful not to startle the owl. Mystique didn't move from her spot in the corner at the front of the stage yet her fixed gaze had Gray on edge. Samara stood next to Callista, ensuring she stood on the other side of the large cat.

Callista placed a hand on Samara's shoulder, observing the owl. "Such a healthy familiar at that. We have much to celebrate."

Just then, Samara felt something climbing up her back, and she held back a wince as she tried not to let the additional weight pull her down. Instinctively, she peered over her shoulder, even though she suspected she wouldn't be able to see anything.

It's just me. Since I'm your familiar, I thought I should be here.

Samara had suspected it was Ulrieg, although she was glad for the confirmation. Gray flapped suddenly as though startled, and his sharp talons pierced through Samara's leather jacket and into her skin. Quickly, Ulrieg grabbed the owl, prohibiting him from flying off but also causing him to act crazy.

Settle down. Settle down, Gray. It's just me. Stop panicking.

But Gray became more unsettled and ready to take off. She couldn't blame him.

That cat over there is giving him the heebie-jeebies. Besides, it's not like you can redo your calming spell in front of everyone.

Callista eyed Gray curiously as the owl flapped and squawked, kicking up a fuss. Undoubtedly he would've looked weird, acting like he wanted to fly off.

Samara shifted and held her tongue. She wished she could communicate with the dragon without having to speak. He was hurting her with his talons as he climbed up her back, especially since she wasn't wearing her quiver to buffer the damage.

"You have quite a live one there," Callista said. "Never mind. Sometimes the feistiest ones are the best and most loyal in the end." She looked pointedly at Mystique. The jaguar yawned and licked her paws with her long tongue.

After a little while, Gray settled in Ulrieg's grasp, only fluttering every so often. Samara braced her core, working hard to stand up straight under the extra weight.

Callista waved her hands in front of Gray in a blessing. "We welcome you, familiar, to this coterie. May you have a long and lasting relationship with your bonded and together grow in wisdom and strength."

"What about mine?" came a voice from the back of the room, and all turned to find Kaine entering the hall, wearing a broad smile. The dark rings of exhaustion under his eyes betrayed their ecstatic gleam. "What about welcoming my familiar?" Trailing behind him, prancing elegantly, was a beautiful bright-orange fox. White fur looked like socks on each of her feet as she moved silently on the stone floor. "I've finally found her, and she's beautiful!"

Chatters of excitement passed through the room as they made their way to the front and stood by Samara.

Kaine wiped his brow with the back of his hand. "I'm so tired, but it was worth it. I stayed up all night in the forest, and this lovely little lady bonded with me."

"Welcome, Kaine." Callista inclined her head in acknowledgment. "We're so pleased about this news. Of course, we'll welcome your familiar also."

Callista waved the fox forward. "Welcome, new familiar. It pleases me that Kaine has finally found you. May you have a long and lasting relationship with your bonded and together grow in wisdom and strength. We need all the apprentices we can get to help save our kingdoms, and you familiars have given your bonded, stronger magic needed for this battle."

Ulrieg shifted, drawing Samara's full attention to the talons on her back. *Huh! A fox. That's saying a lot about his character. I'm so glad you kept me a secret from him.*

Samara wanted to protest that she was keeping his existence a secret from *everyone*. Instead, she ignored him, reached for Kaine's hand, and squeezed it. She leaned in slightly and whispered, "I'm so glad you finally found one. I was starting to feel guilty that you hadn't and I had."

Kaine squeezed her hand back and held it steady, causing a rush of warmth to flood Samara's arm. "There was no reason for you to feel guilty. It wasn't your fault that I couldn't find my familiar straight-away or when you did. After all, you're the one who saved us from the trolls." His hot breath tickled her ear and made her body tingle. When he pulled back, he winked at her and smiled. Her cheeks warmed.

CHAPTER FORTY

After a quick breakfast, Samara went upstairs. They had a day off from lessons, and because her body was still exhausted after their ordeal, she decided to get some more rest. She also wanted to talk to Ulrieg to see what he'd been doing all night. As she walked through the halls, plants fell over, and Samara cringed.

It's just me. Wingless flight! That's the stupidest place to put things. Pieces of pottery scattered as the dragon clawed over the mess. A light tap of his talons sounded on the stone floor, leaving a faint trail of dirt.

A puff of breeze brushed strands of Samara's hair into her eye, and she assumed the invisible dragon had taken flight up to her room. When she got there, the hinges squeaked as she opened the door, and his talons tapped into her room before she closed it behind her. She relished the room's silence, glad to be rid of the other students. Though they were only being friendly and welcoming, the constant attention while trying to hide a dragon and pretend a wild bird was her familiar had been more draining than she'd imagined.

Her mind spun. She was still recovering from the battle and being captured by the trolls. Since she'd returned to safety, the trauma was catching up to her. She struggled to push it out of her mind and enjoy the quiet time set aside with Ulrieg and Gray. Their presence seemed to speak to her soul, which was particularly helpful.

She placed Gray on his perch then flopped onto her bed and let her back sink into the soft mattress, which was a far cry from the stone bed in the dungeon, firmly reminding her that she was safe.

Ulrieg turned visible and sat on the end of her bed. She still hadn't grown used to his glowing red eyes, and even though she knew he was her friend, they still made him look evil. She rubbed the claw mark on her hand.

That's some kind of weird ceremony you just had. Ulrieg wrapped his pointed tail around his body. *Does this place value having a familiar that much?*

Samara nodded. "Yes. Having a familiar is highly

regarded because it enhances your magic. I have felt it, even in the short time of being bonded to you. And I've also seen it happen to the other witches and wizards." She crossed her ankles. "The ceremony is just a way of formally acknowledging and approving the new familiar bond."

If you ask me, it almost seems like they're sussing out the familiar. It seems rather suspicious. I bet if they disapproved of the animal, then they would force you to break the bond. I wouldn't be surprised that if you'd stood up front with me, you wouldn't have received approval.

Samara sighed. "Do you question everything wherever you go?"

Ulrieg's eyes filled with shock. *I guess I do, but I can assure you that I'm more suspicious of this place than any other I have been. I've already told you the reasons behind it before we arrived. My opinion hasn't changed after what I've seen.*

The soft pillow squished under Samara's head, and she slid her hands under it.

"Which reminds me. Where have you been all this time? I've been dying to ask you, but I can't when we're out in public because I look like I'm talking to myself. We should try to fix that. Is there a way?"

I just thought that would be part of the bonding-with-a-familiar experience. Ulrieg shifted up the bed, closer to Samara. *Do other people talk to their familiars out loud, or do they talk using their minds? I haven't seen any of the people with familiars here speak out loud to them until they are addressing them openly in front of everyone. It would be stupid if they had to talk to their familiar out loud all the time. Why would you have a familiar if everyone could hear your conversations with them?*

"Good point, now that I think of it. Most don't seem to talk out loud to their familiars, not in front of people. They'll only do it when they want people around them to hear. Surely they can't postpone all their conversations until they're in private. We'll have to work on that." She tilted her chin to look down the bed at him, her mind lost in thought. "Maybe we can start by touching each other and see if we can communicate while we're touching. Maybe you can put your front foot in my hand, and we'll see how we go."

The dragon shuffled even farther up the bed stretching his wings wide for balance when he walked on uneven patches. When he reached Samara's hand, he held out his talons, and Samara clasped them.

A knock sounded at the door, startling Samara, and she sat upright, pushing Ulrieg's foot away as he turned invisible. Samara got up and opened the door to find Kaine and his fox standing outside. All words evaporated from Samara's brain, and her jaw dropped.

With an endearing grin, Kaine asked, "May I come in?"

Still speechless, Samara shook her head, and Kaine's smile dropped.

"Oh, okay. I was hoping we could talk."

"No. I mean yes. Come in. I was just shocked to see you at my door." Still feeling shy, she hesitantly pushed back the door and stood aside. "Come in. I'm not sure how your fox and my owl will get along, though." The fox was the nicest-looking she had ever seen. Just like Kaine, she thought, and instantly felt bashful, even though she hadn't said it out loud. She studied the fox's beautiful bright-orange coat and white chest. "Her white socks are adorable. What's her name?"

"Ginger." His eyes softened when he looked at the fox.

"Does she mind if I pet her head?" Samara knelt, ready to stroke the fox, and Ginger bared her teeth. Quickly, she pulled her hand away and stood.

Kaine chuckled nervously. "I guess familiars don't like being handled by somebody else." He eyed the owl on the perch. "He should be safe up there."

Samara raised an eyebrow. "As long as Ginger

doesn't jump up to get him. Foxes are good jumpers."

Kaine turned to the fox and said, "Stay by the door."

After flashing him a disapproving look, Ginger curled up and lay down by the door.

Kaine sat on the edge of her bed, and feeling nervous, Samara sat a bit away from him, constantly scanning the room to check that Ulrieg had remained invisible.

Ginger's eyes focused on Gray, making Samara nervous in a different way. She didn't want to take her eyes off the fox in case she decided to try to eat the owl.

Her legs swung as she rested her hands behind her on the mattress and leaned back as awkward silence filled the room. It felt weird having Kaine there. "What do you want to talk about?"

Kaine cleared his throat. "I just never got to thank you for saving me back there. I know I had all that time going home, but I was so out of it and didn't think to tell you how much I appreciated your efforts. On top of that, you also protected me when we were in battle against the trolls. You could have just fought for yourself and forgotten about me."

Samara shrugged. "That's what we do. We train to fight for each other and the kingdoms."

"I think that's just your theory. It's what you do. Not many of the other apprentices would have done that for me." Kaine held her gaze. "And that's what makes you special." He shifted closer and grasped her hand softly.

Butterflies flitted in Samara's stomach. Coyly, she met his eyes and forced disbelief into her voice. "You say that to all the girls."

Earnestly, he said, "But I don't. Only to you."

Samara scoffed, pulling her hand free. "I've seen the way you act with all the other females. You're like the most charming one in the coterie. You have every female wrapped around your finger, and you make them all feel special." Her nerves got the better of her, and she waved her hands expressively. "They all swoon over you, and I'm no different." She let her hands fall to her lap.

Kaine raised his eyebrows, grinning. "You swoon over me too?"

Samara shot him an incredulous look.

He shook his head. "Forget I said that." He captured her hand. "You're different. Trust me. You've always been different. But now you have also saved me. And you helped me when I needed it the most." He pulled her hand gently to his lap.

The fox shifted to look at them before placing her head back down, and Ulrieg's words flashed through Samara's mind about how the fox familiar must say something about Kaine's personality. She pushed the negative thought away. He was skeptical of everyone in the coterie.

Kaine shifted closer to Samara, and she froze, not knowing what to do. She didn't want to fall for lies. As she gazed at the floor, Kaine shifted closer still. With his body pressed against her side, warmth seeped through her clothes.

His strong hand tilted her chin so that he could look straight into her eyes, and when she dared to look back, his were awash with genuineness. "I'm telling you the truth, Samara. I know I plaster on the charm for all the females and anyone I think I can manipulate to get my way. But you *are* different. I promise you, and you have proven to me that you deserve my special treatment and that my heart is correct to desire you."

Her cheeks heating, Samara struggled to believe what she was hearing.

Kaine smiled softly and ran his thumb across her cheek before he shifted closer, brushing his lips against hers. His tenderness and the expression in his eyes melted Samara's heart. She relented, enjoying the softness of his lips as they meshed with hers and tasting the slight traces of maple syrup that remained on his lips after breakfast. The smell of soap filled her nose, and the edges of his hair were still damp from bathing after his long night in the forest.

A loud clang exploded from the corner of the room, startling them. Kaine pulled away, searching the corner. Lines creased his forehead when a strange scratching sound followed.

Oh, dragon moon. Thank goodness that's over. Yuck! That was getting rather disgusting! Are you seriously meshing lips with this guy? Pfft! Don't answer that. I know what I saw. I'm disappointed in you. Have you forgotten what I said about having a fox for a familiar and what that must mean about his personality? Even you said he's charming to other females. That should mean he's disloyal.

Samara tried to ignore Kaine's confused expression and act normal, but it proved difficult while her dragon ranted at her.

Can't you get that through your thick head? I'm going to be sick. He gagged.

"What was that noise?" Kaine asked, luring her attention back to him.

Samara followed his gaze and spotted Gray sitting near the path to the noisy corner and where they sat. "Uh, that was probably Gray. I don't know. Maybe he's jealous because of what you just did. Or maybe he's on edge because your familiar keeps eyeing him like he's her dinner."

Kaine laughed. "That's funny. But I don't think that's the case." He hooked a strand of her hair behind her ear, his full attention returning to her. "I meant what I said, and I hope we can pick this up again later." He gazed deep into her eyes. "But honestly, I'm so tired and need some sleep. Perhaps I'm imagining noises."

"I understand." Samara's nerves settled. "I'm still tired from our ordeal, and I wasn't badly injured or up all night, looking for my familiar. Congratulations on your fox. I'm so glad you get to stay in the coterie. It's nice to know our families will be looked after again. Yours will continue to have prestige, and mine will be able to live a decent life."

Nodding, Kaine got up to leave, and Samara saw him out.

As soon as the door clicked shut, Ulrieg's voice echoed through her head again, and he turned visible, his red eyes narrowing on her. *Oh, thank the moon! I thought he was never going to leave. I still can't believe you kissed him like that. That's disgusting.* He gagged.

At first, Samara found his efforts comical, but then it became annoying. The most handsome guy in the coterie had taken what seemed like a genuine interest in her. "You're lucky I couldn't speak to you. Otherwise, I would have been yelling at you. That was rather rude," she snapped.

The dragon waggled a talon at her. *I was trying to get rid of him before you made a mistake. Who knows what a guy and a female would do in a room by themselves at your age?* He flew down and landed on her bed, close to her. *I must tell you things, and I can't have him in the room to do it. What I must say to you is crucial. You'd be surprised what I found out last night.*

CHAPTER FORTY-ONE

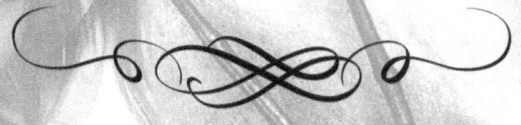

"What do you have to tell me?" Samara had her hands on her hips, still annoyed with Ulrieg for interrupting her time with Kaine. "I thought you were just going out for food over the last few nights."

It doesn't take me that long to hunt, trust me. I'm very quick at catching my meals. The invisibility helps a lot. He sat up straight on the bed. His front legs were tucked between his back legs, and his wings were furled by his sides. *Since you brought me here, and I now know where this coterie building is, I'm going to do some investigating. Other dragons I have lived with and come across have warned me about this coterie base. They said it is filled with great evil.*

Samara scoffed. "We've had this conversation. The coterie building isn't filled with evil. Callista

355

and the teachers are here to help us learn to protect the realms. Under Callista's guidance, the apprentices are growing stronger. One day, I hope, I'll be helping her too."

Yeah, and I think they're blinding you. They're telling you a whole heap of hogwash, and you're believing it because you've all come from little villages that haven't seen the rest of the kingdoms.

"There you go again, making us out to be stupid. I'm not stupid." Samara resisted the urge to stomp her foot like a spoiled toddler. "I have a passion for helping people and making the realm stronger, and I have the right kind of magic, which is growing under their training. You can't just keep calling me stupid because you have a different opinion."

Ulrieg scratched his head with a hook on his wing rib then spread his wings in exasperation. *I wasn't calling you stupid. I was calling you and every other student here naive. Being gullible and being stupid are completely different.* He stopped to think. *Though sometimes they coincide. In this case, I believe you're only naive.* He huffed, and steam shot out of his nostrils. *I can see your heart is in the right place. I know you have a passion for helping people. And I believe that Callista has seen that, and she is milking it for all it's worth. And guiding you and all these apprentices along the wrong path without your knowing. Although I get the vibe that some people will be quite happy to follow even when they find out the truth.*

Samara crossed her arms. "You still have a long way to go to prove it to me. So far, it's all criticism, and I haven't seen one thing to prove it. You say the dragons are good and that evil is destroying the lands and has blocked off your realm. Now you're trying to tell me that Callista is this evil sorceress."

I didn't say that Callista was the evil magician. I'm merely using her name because she's the current great sorceress and a figurehead. It could be someone else, but from what the dragons say, this coterie is vital to that evil.

"So prove it. What did you see last night that you think is so important to tell me about?"

I saw this wonderful Callista of yours disappear into some catacombs. I got a feeling from those tunnels.

Samara raised an eyebrow. "So you're going by a feeling and because she visited the underground of a building she runs?"

There was a presence within the tunnels. It gave me an eerie feeling.

Samara leaned on one leg. "Callista converses with a higher magic power. So that sounds about right. I believe she accesses the higher magic power in the catacombs."

Under the building?

Samara frowned. "I think that's where she visits it."

The dragon's eyes burned brightly. *Uh-huh. Have you ever been inside these catacombs?*

"We're told not to go down to the lower levels. They're out of bounds because the power is too strong, and we wouldn't be able to handle it. Callista keeps us away from it to protect us." Samara shrugged. "That's all it is. It probably feels eerie to you because you're feeling the strength of its power, warning you that you can't handle it."

And what if I told you strange noises were coming from those catacombs? The power isn't what's eerie. The noises disturbed my soul.

"What kind of noises?" Samara asked.

Like something was being hurt or in pain. The sadness in his eyes pulled at Samara's heartstrings. *Does she sacrifice things to this higher power? Like animals or beings?*

Samara pulled back. "Ew. That's gross. I should hope not. Surely Callista wouldn't do anything like that."

You'd be surprised what some people do for power, Ulrieg muttered. *Another thing I've noticed is that she always has those crystals with her. And the person who destroyed the dragon realm used crystals to enhance their power.* He threw up his front talons in resignation when he saw the disapproval on Samara's face. *That is what the myth says.*

"That's where she gets her main magic. She's a crystal witch. Her strength is from crystals, which is why she always has them close. I don't see how that makes her evil."

Ulrieg took a deep breath and twirled around on her bed before settling down and curling his tail around his body. *I can sense you're quite loyal to her. And the only way you will believe me is for you to physically see what is going on. When we have some spare time, we should do some discovering of our own. If you trust me as your familiar, and if I'm to help you be wise, I hope you will listen. I'm not like these other familiars I have seen. They are locals and young animals that don't live long. They don't know the sort of information that I know.* He yawned and rested his head on his front talons. *I understand your loyalty to someone who has protected and helped your family.*

His comment played with Samara's emotions. She was supposed to listen to her familiar, but she argued with him most of the time instead. She lowered her defensiveness slightly. "I have trusted your guidance so far. If you show me what you think you know, I will make my own decisions. I know you're a skeptic, especially regarding this coterie and Callista. Now I need your proof of the contrary. I'm not automatically going to accuse someone who has shown nothing but good faith and kindness to my family and me since I met her. You will need to show me solid proof."

Eyeing Samara's distraught face, Ulrieg shrugged. *The person who imprisoned Dragoria could be someone else. Remember, I'm mainly pinpointing Callista because she is the head of this coterie and the strongest sorceress of the lands.*

"Then who do you suggest the suspect is?" Samara asked.

I don't know. I'm only going by what I've heard. And I've heard that the person came from this coterie and that the coterie base is suspiciously difficult to find. Ulrieg rested his chin on Samara's thigh.

"Then perhaps we have a rogue teacher. It could even be a student from the past or present. We should find out and tell Callista about it. I'm sure she would be most upset. She has done nothing but serve this realm and help protect the other realms."

Ulrieg yawned. *All right. I'll take that. Tonight, when it's dark, and the moon has risen, we shall go and search the grounds, and I will show you what I've found. I think we should check out this place and find out what the noises are.*

"Agreed."

CHAPTER FORTY-TWO

That night, after the sun had gone down, and they had eaten their meal, Ulrieg climbed onto Samara's back as she grabbed Gray and placed him on her shoulder. Ulrieg secured Gray by his ankles, and they made their way downstairs. At that moment, Samara was particularly glad the apprentices were free to come and go from the building as they pleased. She wasn't good at lying, and making something up if asked would most likely give her away. The only reason they were taking Gray was so he could be their cover if someone asked. After all, it was night, and the owl needed to hunt.

A dark shadow in the corner of the foyer moved, and Samara jumped. Her heart raced when she spotted the yellow eyes of Mystique cutting through the darkness. The cat seemed to appear everywhere at the worst times.

"Mystique!" Samara placed a hand over her heart. "I didn't see you there."

The jaguar sauntered toward her, her lean muscles rippling under her dark spotted coat, and surveyed her suspiciously.

Ulrieg dug his talons into Samara's back, and she tried not to flinch, although she was certainly grimacing on the inside.

When the jaguar had finished her rounds, she returned to the corner, her eyes remaining on Samara as though expecting an answer. The cat's actions immediately squashed Samara's thoughts about the coterie allowing apprentices to come and go as they pleased. Mystique always made her feel as though she was under scrutiny.

Samara fiddled with the hem of her leather top then tugged at the long black glove, making sure it was halfway up her upper arm. The glove protected her from both the dragon's claws and Gray's. On her other side, she had a black leather band around the upper arm and a strong leather glove with exposed fingertips. Those were more spots for Ulrieg to put his talons so that they wouldn't dig into her bare skin. They were perfect additions to her sleeveless tunic, which she wore because of the humidity.

Under the cat's scrutiny, Samara felt nervous, and despite her efforts to appear composed, she stumbled over her words. "I-I'm just going outside for a walk. I need to give my owl some fresh air and let him hunt." She pointed awkwardly at the large double doors that led outside, as if the jaguar didn't know what they were.

Mystique yawned widely, her tongue lacing over her jagged teeth, before she licked her paw.

Samara took that as an answer, allowing her to exit the castle, even though she usually didn't have to ask for permission. It was probably because she knew she would be up to something that night that she felt so nervous. However, having the cat watch them as they fought a losing battle and not doing anything to help still rankled.

Ulrieg whispered in her ear, *Let's go!* Although he didn't need to whisper because he spoke directly into her mind, she was glad he did because a normal-volume voice would probably have made her jump.

Without wasting a second, she prompted her feet to move to the door, which she pushed open and exited the building, away from Mystique's scrutiny. Her heart pounded as she rushed down the stone steps avoiding the branches reaching over the balustrade.

"Where are we going?" she whispered.

Just wait and see. Keep following the building to the right. First, can we let this owl go so that he can catch some food for the night?

Samara moved toward the right, and as soon as they reached the side of the building, she said, "I'm happy for him to have some freedom, but I still need him. What am I going to do if he doesn't come back?"

Can't you put a spell on him to return to you at the end of the night?

"I don't know. I've never had to make something come back before." Samara eyed the owl's white face. She would miss him if he didn't come back. He was a beautiful bird.

Haven't you trained him to like you a bit?

"I have trained him to be somewhat of a pet, but he still has a long way to go. It's only been a short while. It takes time to build a strong bond, especially since we don't speak the same language."

Ulrieg exhaled loudly. *If he doesn't come back, I'll go and search for him.*

"And if you don't find him?"

Then I'll find you another owl, and we'll start again. What we have to do is more important than keeping Gray, even if you are making progress with him.

"Not if I have to explain to the apprentices and

the instructors why I don't have my familiar anymore."

Trust me. Though he was still invisible, she could tell he was grinning. *I will find your replacement if he doesn't return. However, this may go a lot easier if you place a charm on him.* He grunted as Gray flapped wildly. *But I can't hang on to him all night. I need to have my talons free. And he's rather distracting when he wants to fight the restraint I have on him.*

Samara grabbed the owl's foot with her finger and thumb and let the other foot rest on her hand. Gray's claws dug into her glove and scraped lightly against her skin. The dragon was right. The owl was a distraction. She whispered an incantation and allowed a moment for the magic to work before she opened her fingers to release the owl's foot. "Go find some food. Hunt through the night, but return to me when you see me come back."

She lifted her hand into the air before quickly dropping it, urging the owl into flight. He headed straight for the forest, his beautiful wings gracefully flapping.

"I hope he returns. I've grown rather fond of him, even if he's not my familiar." Samara caught sight of the dragon's red eyes, though the rest of him was still invisible.

The owl landed on the nearest branch and rested

there, his head turning one hundred eighty degrees as he searched for prey.

"Which way?" she asked Ulrieg.

Under cover of darkness, Ulrieg turned visible and pointed his wing. *Just keep following the building around to the right. But try to dodge any windows, especially ones with lights on. I still don't want to be seen.* He balanced his weight evenly on her back and hooked his tail under her arm.

"Don't worry. I'll stick to the shadows. It's bad enough knowing I'm sneaking around my home, spying. I still feel like I'll look suspicious, even if you're invisible. And I'm a terrible liar."

Every few yards, Samara had to crawl slowly over the ground, under the ledge of a window. She crept through the grass and shrubs around the castle, often using them to hide. Determined not to get caught doing something she couldn't explain, she put up with the sticks and branches scraping her arms and the stones digging into her knees. She could always blame Gray if someone asked her about the scratches. Ulrieg had jumped off her back and crawled along the ground with her. His black body easily blended into the shadows.

She was thankful that the moon was only half full, but their progress seemed slow under the faint light.

Stop! It was around here. You'll have to dig around a bit to find it, though. It was well hidden.

Samara searched the ground with her hands but was unsuccessful, and her impatience got the better of her. "Where?"

The dragon scurried around a bush and called from behind it. *Down here. You'll have to push aside this bush.*

The bush was small, and Samara wondered if someone her size could fit behind it. She pushed it aside to find a large hole that led underneath the building.

She gasped. "That was well hidden."

Yes. Suspicion filled Ulrieg's eyes. *I found it by accident when I sensed something underneath and followed it. I first sensed its power when I arrived here, as my full moon senses hadn't dulled yet. Then I pinpointed the estimated spot and made a note to investigate when I had a chance. My senses have dulled now, but I've spent the last few nights scouring the area to find it.* He stuck his head into the hole for a quick look before facing Samara again. *I think the noises helped guide me as well. I went down to investigate but couldn't pass through the door. I was hoping that perhaps you could work your magic on it or something.*

After a quick check around them to ensure no one could see them, they descended the stone steps together. They were damp and slippery, and Samara braced herself against the wall, feeling the coolness seep into her skin. Only one sconce burned, casting very little light and making it hard to see the next step. The place had a similar feel and smell to the troll dungeon, only it wasn't as dank.

She had to tiptoe to keep from making noise on the stones until they reached the bottom and followed a corridor to the right. If Samara had her bearings right, they were under the building. When she spotted a torch hanging on the wall, she almost squealed with delight. She grabbed it from its holder and held it in front of her.

Ulrieg led the way through the corridor, which was barely wide enough for one or possibly two thin people to walk down side by side. Several shut doors lined both sides of the passage.

"Was it any of these?" Samara whispered, hoping they wouldn't have to go much farther. The area felt ominous, unsettling her nerves and tainting Samara's image of a clean coterie.

The dragon shook his head.

"What's behind those doors?"

He shrugged while spreading his wings. *Nothing behind them called to me, so I haven't investigated. After we deal with what is calling to me, I'll explore them. Although the call grows fainter as the moon diminishes.*

Besides, the noises I heard behind the door were disturbing and are etched deep into my mind.

They pressed forward, passing several more doors until, eventually, Ulrieg stopped in front of a door that looked and felt no different from the others.

But Samara trusted the dragon's judgment. She twisted the brass doorknob, but the door didn't move. Pressing a palm against it, close to the invisible latch, she muttered an incantation. *"Aperti."* She tugged at the door handle but was again unsuccessful. She frowned. The spell usually worked. She tried again. *"Aperti."* Then she turned the handle again. Nothing happened.

She met the dragon's eyes. "Are you sure it was this door?"

He nodded. *I can still feel it, even if it is fainter.*

Pursing her lips, she frowned at the lock. "I feel nothing, and my spell didn't work. I'll try it again." She waved her hand in front of the lock before flicking her fingers at the handle. *"Aperti."* When she turned the handle, again, nothing happened.

CHAPTER FORTY-THREE

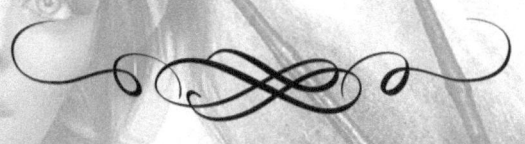

With each attempt, Samara's annoyance rose. It took effort to keep her struggle quiet. No matter how many times she tried, the door wouldn't budge.

Halfway through another attempt, a strange noise bellowed from inside the room, and she froze.

"What was that?" All feeling left Samara's arms. If that was someone from the coterie, she wouldn't be able to explain her actions if caught.

Ulrieg placed his head on the ground as though trying to peek under the door. *That was the strange noise I told you about.* He stood up straight, his eyes burning with annoyance. *I can't see anything in there. I wish I knew what it was. It's really bugging me.*

The noise came again, sending chills down Samara's spine. "It sounds like something is in pain."

His face grave, Ulrieg nodded. *Exactly!*

Saddened, Samara hoped their assumption was wrong. "Maybe it's the wind."

Ulrieg gave her an incredulous look.

Samara's shoulders sagged. "Well, I don't know how to open the door. I'll have to do some research and see if I can learn any other opening spells. The one I have isn't working."

Ulrieg pointed a talon at a strange emblem at the height of the handle. *Or keep an eye out for something that will fit into that. Maybe it's a keyhole.*

Samara nodded, disappointed. She inspected the emblem, which was a triangle with softened corners and a five-pointed star in the middle. "I'm sorry I couldn't open it for you." The strange noise reached them again. "That noise makes me want to find out what's in there also."

Obviously frustrated, Ulrieg turned and started to head back. *We'll have to make it our top priority. The sound is giving me nightmares.*

Samara placed the torch back on the wall, and they headed toward the outside. Their trip back up was silent.

The night's fresh air was a welcome respite, and Samara was relieved when Gray came to her when she called. After her magic had failed on the lock, it was a pleasant feeling when the owl landed on her hand then hopped onto her shoulder as though it was something that came naturally to him. She was growing quite fond of the owl.

Just after Gray landed on her shoulder, a movement caught her eye, and she turned. Ginger padded out of the shadows and stood in front of them.

Don't you dare tell Kaine what we've been doing, Ulrieg warned Samara.

She grunted, wanting to argue that she wouldn't because they didn't even know what was going on yet, but they hadn't worked out whether they could mind talk to each other yet. Instead, she froze. Ginger hadn't been friendly earlier, and she didn't know if she would attack her. Trying to sound confident and friendly, Samara called, "Ginger, what are you doing out here?"

Gray flapped profusely, and Ulrieg's grip on his leg tightened.

The fox stood and stared, her eyes often shifting to Gray.

Samara placed her hand up to block the owl. "Now, Ginger, Gray isn't food for you."

Another shadow moved, and Kaine worked his way around a bush, his pale face barely visible in the dull light. "There you are, Ginger. I've been looking for you." He followed her line of sight, spotted Samara and Gray, and grinned. "Oh. Hey, gorgeous. I wasn't expecting anyone to be out here. I can see how I lost Ginger's attention." He moved in closer and looked like he was going to hug or kiss Samara but stopped short when Gray flapped his wings. Samara wondered if Ulrieg was behind the owl's behavior, but it probably wasn't the best time for Kaine to get close. She didn't need him accidentally rubbing his hand over the invisible Ulrieg.

"Ginger wanted to go hunting, and I lost her a little while ago." He eyed Gray, who was still flapping. "I guess you're out here doing the same."

Samara nodded, giving her throat time to warm up to the lie. "He's only just returned to me after hunting." It wasn't a complete lie. She didn't think the owl had been hunting, as she had fed him a lot of food over the day, but she was confident that the wild animal would have enjoyed his short-lived freedom. "We were about to head inside when we ran into Ginger."

Ginger eyed Samara and Gray. Samara hoped she was reading too much into the fox's expressions and that Ginger hadn't been spying on them and was telling Kaine they were lying.

Kaine chuckled. "Come on, Ginger. Let them past." He gazed earnestly at Samara. "Although you could stay out with us for a while if you want to. The animals can hunt, and we can spend some time together in the dark."

Gag! Oh please!

Annoyed with Ulrieg, Samara struggled to keep a straight face. "It sounds tempting, but I need to get back. Gray is still settling down, and I'd hate for him to be put off me because of a fox." To prove her point, Ulrieg caused Gray to flap some more. "As you can see, he's still quite feisty."

"Yes, he is. I'll let you go *this time*," he said playfully.

Samara smiled coyly, starting to entertain the idea that perhaps Kaine was interested in her more than the other females. Only time would tell.

Can we leave now? Please?! Ulrieg's grumpy voice cut through her thoughts.

Samara moved past Kaine and, hoping he wouldn't hear, said softly through clenched teeth, "I'm not making you stay."

"What was that?" Kaine asked.

Her face heated, and she turned back to face him, glad for the darkness. "I just said we'll have to meet like this when our animals are settled." She made a show of looking through the dark forest. "It's so quiet out here at this time of night, and both our animals hunt well at night."

No! What are you doing?

Samara flicked her fingers at Ulrieg's head and was confident she'd hit his nose.

Ow! For one, it's gross, and two, we don't want him hanging around at night, waiting for you, when we want to sneak around undetected.

Kaine smiled broadly, and his straight white teeth glistened softly in the dull light. "We'll have to do that."

Samara nodded quickly, knowing that Ulrieg was right about not needing him waiting for her when they wanted to go unseen. Having a fox would also give him an advantage in finding her easily. "I need to go inside. See you tomorrow."

Kaine straightened his shoulders. "Absolutely!"

CHAPTER FORTY-FOUR

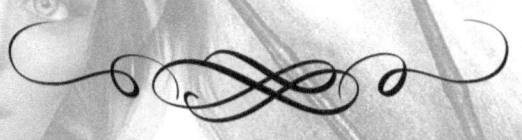

The next day, Samara struggled to concentrate. Not only was she exhausted from not getting any sleep the night before, but her mind was also wandering as she tried to piece together what they had come across.

She pulled on her boot with Ulrieg sitting on the chair back, watching over Gray and her, before his attention traveled to the trees. Sometimes, Samara thought Ulrieg would like to be on his own. From the start, he had made it clear that he wasn't keen on people. Yet he still communicated and worked with Samara. She could only put it down to their bond.

Sliding on the other long boot, she said, "You know, there is a possibility that the noise we heard was simply wind passing through the catacombs."

Ulrieg scratched behind his ear with the hook on

his wing rib. He looked deep in thought but also skeptical. *Maybe. The wind has been known to make those noises. Still, I'd rather know for sure, especially because I lack trust in people from the coterie. The sound just makes the place seem eviler than I expected. And you know I'm probably right.*

Samara laughed. "Oh, you have it bad. But I understand you would want to check it out properly. And I know we won't get close to agreeing about this coterie until we investigate."

You got that right! He grabbed the back of the chair with all four claws and shook his body.

"Do you think the emblem is why I couldn't open the lock?" Samara tapped her boot softly on the floor.

No idea. That's your department. Do you have a teacher you could ask?

"Callista should know."

Besides her.

Samara smiled. "You make it so easy. I was only playing with you. Of course I wouldn't ask Callista first, although she should know."

I imagine she would, he deadpanned.

"Even if she did, she's away at the moment." Samara finished tying on her tunic and plopped onto the bed. "I just remembered. I have a little extra time before I have to go downstairs. We should use it to see if we can communicate silently."

What do you suggest we do?

She patted the mattress next to her. "Come sit here, and I'll try to speak to you with my mind."

Ulrieg jumped, making the chair knock into the desk. He landed next to Samara with a thump.

Samara placed her hands on his front talons and focused hard on projecting her words from her mind. *Say something!*

The dragon jumped. *Dragon Moon! You don't need to yell.*

"I didn't realize I was. I was trying to make sure you heard the words." She grinned. "I guess you did."

Oh, I did, all right. This time, try to speak softly.

Samara concentrated and tried for something simple. *Hello!* She imagined saying it only slightly louder than average.

Much better. You could even say it softer. Since the words go straight to our brains, there's no interference from other noises. So it's easier to be heard than if you had to speak out loud. Now, why don't you try to talk to me without touching me? If ordinary animals can do it with their bonded, then surely we can.

Samara pulled her hand onto her lap and thought about speaking directly into Ulrieg's mind. She remembered to keep her voice quiet so he wouldn't startle. *Can you hear me?*

The dragon sat still, his eyes trained on the window. After a few moments, he looked at Samara. *Whenever you're ready.*

Samara frowned. "I already said the words. Didn't you hear them?"

Ulrieg shook his head. *Nope. I didn't hear you say anything.*

What about this? she asked.

He didn't react.

"Didn't you hear me that time either?"

The dragon shook his head.

Samara sighed loudly and grabbed his claw again. *What about this?*

Yes. I heard you that time.

"Then why can't you hear me when I'm not touching you? I need to be able to communicate with you when we're not touching." She kicked the sole of her shoe along the stone floor.

The horns on Ulrieg's forehead bunched together when he frowned. *Why don't you try yelling when you're not touching me like your first effort? See if that works.*

Samara frowned in concentration. *Hello! Can you hear me?*

Ulrieg jumped. *I did hear that. It was a little louder than your normal voice.*

Great! Samara said a little softer.

That's better. Ulrieg got up and jumped onto the back of the chair. *Try it again.*

Samara did, and he grinned, showing off his vast array of pointy teeth. He looked violent, and she was glad he was her friend. She couldn't fathom how scary the large dragons must look and understood how someone could mistake them for being dangerous, evil creatures.

You did it. Now you need to practice while we're out in public.

Samara smiled. *That's great! I knew it must be possible.*

What lesson do you have now?

Potions. But I still have a little more time, and I want to go to the library to see if I can find something about that symbol.

Ulrieg jumped from the chair, and Gray untucked his head and blinked at the dragon before puffing out his feathers and snuggling in for a longer rest.

When she reached the door, Gray didn't move. "I think I'll leave him here to sleep. I don't need to take him everywhere." She turned the handle and stepped into the corridor.

CHAPTER FORTY-FIVE

The library's walls were filled with books that spanned over two levels. Some areas in both the upper and lower levels consisted of multiple rows of wooden bookshelves. Many reading desks lined the floor on the lower level, surrounded by the towering upper balcony filled with books.

Samara didn't know where to start. She climbed the stairs at the back and started perusing the books. The library wasn't her preferred place, and it never ceased to amaze her how quiet it was. She preferred to spend her time outdoors.

She pulled out several books and flicked through their pages before placing them back on the shelf and moving on to the next one. After she'd pulled out the sixth book, it was starting to feel like it would take her much longer than she'd thought to find the emblem.

Books toppled from the top shelf and onto the floor a few paces behind her.

She looked up, not noticing anything unusual. *Is that you, Ulrieg?*

Yes. Sorry. I'm not used to places as stuffy as this.

Samara backtracked and picked up the spilled books before placing them back on the shelf. *It's all right. But be more careful. Someone else may be in the library, and I'm not usually that clumsy. You may raise suspicions.*

A voice came from behind her as she reached up to place the last book on the top shelf. "Are you all right?"

She spun, her heart thumping. "Paxton. I didn't know you were in the library."

He gave a small smile. "Where am I usually when I'm not in class?"

"True. I'm hardly ever in here, so I didn't connect the dots."

"Do you need help with something? We don't have a librarian, and I've taken it upon myself to know most of these books."

Samara's eyebrows rose. "Really? All of them?"

He huffed a laugh. "Yeah, I know that's not how normal people act." He pulled at the hem of his jerkin. "But that's what I've done. I haven't memorized all of them, but I have a better idea than anyone else in the coterie."

Lost in thought, Samara gazed at the top shelf where Ulrieg had knocked off the books.

The dragon took it as an unasked question. *I can't see how it would hurt if you're discreet. I like this member. I hope he's not a backstabber. Be cautious, though, just in case.*

Samara eyed Paxton for a moment. His shoulders were relatively thin for a flail swinger or a baton user, and she never saw him out practicing with his weapons. His pale complexion also gave away his lack of time spent outdoors. "Actually, maybe you can help. I'm running out of time before our next class. I'm looking for the meaning of an emblem. Do you know much about them?"

Paxton's brow furrowed. "I don't know them off by heart, but I have a good idea where to look. What does it look like?"

"It's a triangle with softened corners and a five-pointed star in the middle."

"Where did you see it?"

Samara paused, not knowing what to say. She couldn't tell him it was under the building, somewhere they shouldn't have been.

Tell him you saw it on a tree in the middle of the forest. He doesn't look like he goes out there very often.

"I saw it out in the forest somewhere."

Paxton didn't seem convinced but said, "I'll have a good look. Class is about to start. Why don't you head there, and I'll come later."

"But you're supposed to be there too." Samara didn't want him to get into trouble because he was researching something for her.

He shrugged. "She's not exactly my favorite teacher after what she did to Jojo. So I don't mind disappointing her. I'll tell her I lost track of time because my nose was stuck in a book."

Samara's jaw dropped, though she didn't blame him for not liking her. What she'd done to Jojo was unforgivable.

"Go on. Go!" He shooed her away with his hand. Jojo peeked out from under his shirt at his collar.

"All right. Thanks. But don't be too late. I'd hate for you to get in trouble."

CHAPTER FORTY-SIX

Artemise Snow stood over her cauldron, stirring the contents with a long stick. She squinted as Samara entered the room then shook her poofy orange hair. "Cutting it a bit fine, aren't you, lovey?"

Samara nodded. "Sorry, Potions Master. I was doing some research and got distracted." She felt Ulrieg climb off her back and assumed he was heading to the rafters. She hoped he wouldn't knock down any of the drying herbs or hanging dried pieces of animals.

Artemise's face scrunched with disapproval, and her many wrinkles deepened. "Where's your familiar?" The potions master seemed to drag out the word *familiar*, making Samara's blood boil.

"He's resting. He's not used to being up all day, so

I let him sleep." She wanted to add that no one trusted the potions master with their familiars after what she'd tried to do with Paxton's frog, but she held her tongue. Samara's eyes flicked to the bench behind the potions master to see her cat peering up at the rafters. Samara hoped Tabatha couldn't sense Ulrieg. Tabatha yawned and rested her chin on her front paws.

Samara made her way to the front of the class to the two empty seats. She caught sight of Kaine sitting next to Luna, and felt a pang of jealousy, making it hard not to glare at the beautiful elf. To add to her distress, Kaine looked overly confident since he had his familiar, who was curled on his lap. He smirked at her, and she pushed aside her worries, telling herself she was being stupid. She returned his smile before taking a seat.

Artemise stirred her pot some more before grabbing a hen's heart from the shelf and throwing it in. She added some herbs and spices before pinching some fur from Tabatha's back. The cat yowled and gave Artemise an angry look then licked the spot absent of a few strands of fur.

The back door squeaked, and Paxton pushed through, earning himself a glare from Artemise. "Where have you been? This is the second time since you've gotten a familiar that you've been late. Do you think having a familiar pardons you from turning up on time?"

Paxton scowled back at her as he hurried along the short aisle and sat next to Samara. "No. I recall the first time I was late. I was looking for my familiar, which you had in your possession, ready to add to your potion. This time, I admit it was my fault. I was in the library and lost track of time."

Artemise grunted. "Always with your nose in a book. You should be so clever. Tell me, what am I brewing?"

Paxton took a few steps to the front, ensuring his arms covered Jojo. He sniffed the potion and took in the color and texture. "You're making a simple healing potion that restores the cells."

"Hmm. Very good. You have been studying. What were you studying this time that made you late for my class?" She stirred the cauldron more.

Paxton returned to his chair. "I was studying emblems."

Artemise's face distorted, once again deepening her wrinkles. "What kind of emblems?"

"It's a triangle with softened corners and a five-pointed star in the middle."

"Really?" The potions master cocked an eyebrow.

He nodded. "I can't find it in the books in the library. Do you know what it is?"

Artemise dropped the stirring stick and left it in the cauldron, giving her full attention to Paxton. "And where did you see this emblem before searching for it?"

Samara froze. She didn't know what kind of emblem it was or if it was supposed to be secret.

As though Paxton could see her tensing, he grinned sheepishly and said, "I honestly can't remember. It could've even been in a dream. Why's that?"

The potions master waved a hand dismissively. "Oh. No matter. Although I do know what the emblem means. It's not a very commonly used one."

Paxton remained calm and shrugged. "All right. What does it mean, then?"

Artemise paced the floor, her long gown billowing around her feet. "It represents the inner circle of the Sacred Flame coterie. Only people magically approved and ordained into this circle can use this symbol or enter areas marked by it. If it is marked next to a lock, only an approved witch or wizard may open that lock with their magic or sacred skeleton key."

Paxton frowned. "Does that mean that we can go into these areas?"

The potions master shook her head dramatically. "Oh, no. You're not accepted into the inner circle."

He tilted his head to one side. "I thought we were accepted into the Sacred Flame's inner circle when we joined the coterie and were double-approved when we bonded with our familiars."

The teacher scoffed. "You are only apprentices. You are not part of the sacred circle."

Paxton crossed his arms.

Artemise grinned and added, "Perhaps if you saw it in a dream, it is part of a prophecy of your future." She turned back and went to the other side of the cauldron.

Did I ever tell you I like this guy? He is seriously much better than the heartbreaker. Ulrieg's voice settled Samara's nerves.

Samara grunted. *I believe you have told me a couple of times. Paxton is undoubtedly a great guy and has proved it further today. I didn't know he could be so sly.*

I think you mean observant and can act on his feet. Sly is the one with the fox.

Oh, so now I'm getting an English lesson, Samara grumbled.

Ha! Listen to you. You're starting to sound like me. You make me proud.

Samara resisted the urge to roll her eyes. *No. I'm merely having a temporary lapse in judgment and letting my annoyance with you shine through. Sometimes I wish you would keep your judgment to yourself. You haven't proven you're right about the coterie, and Kaine is being sweet, and maybe he honestly likes me and wants to be with me. After all, we did just go through a serious ordeal together.*

All right, all right. Don't get your tail all twisted. I was just having fun.

You call that fun?

In my way. You should know by now I have a twisted sense of humor.

You have humor?

Ouch! Now you're really acting like me.

Grrr!

Ha-ha. That was a joke.

"Are you all right?"

Samara startled and turned. Paxton was staring at her, concern etched on his face. "Yes. Of course. Sorry. I was lost in thought. A lot has happened over the last couple of weeks."

"Who's talking in my class?" Artemise squawked.

"Sorry, Potions Master. It was me," Paxton said.

Samara's jaw dropped. "What are you doing?" she whispered.

Paxton gave her a comforting look.

"Well, stop it. You're supposed to be learning, not talking to your classmates." Artemise scowled.

"Of course. Sorry."

Samara squeezed Paxton's upper arm and smiled. He was being sweet, and she appreciated it.

After acknowledging Samara's thanks with a nod, Paxton turned his attention back to what Artemise was doing.

Samara knew she should be paying attention, but her brain was whirling. *How are we going to get into that room if only the inner circle has access?*

I don't know. But how strange is it that only the inner circle of the Sacred Flame coterie can get past those signs?

Samara crossed her arms. *And here you go again—writing them off before anything has been proven. To be honest, I wouldn't class it as unusual for a strong collection of magic wielders to have a hierarchy where only a select few can access certain information. I would class that as smart. You don't need the whole world to know your business. It may give away your next move to squash the enemy.*

All right. Point taken.

I wonder if some teachers have a key to the door or anywhere the symbol is posted. Samara returned her attention to what was happening in the room and realized Paxton was watching her with concern. She uncrossed her arms and gave him a small smile.

CHAPTER FORTY-SEVEN

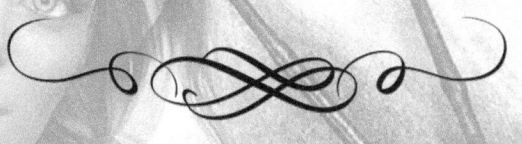

A couple of nights later, Samara finally had a chance to get a good night's sleep and had gone to bed early. She had lost a lot of sleep after spending the last couple of days worrying about the symbol and how they would get past it. Ulrieg had gone out hunting, and Samara had loaded Gray's plate with a selection of fresh meat for him to rip apart.

Her dreams were filled with images of her family being happy and well taken care of. She had returned to her home for a quick visit to see them clothed and well-fed, with each sibling having their own room. They looked healthy, no longer skin and bone. Her heart warmed.

Oy! Sleepyhead!

Samara's body rocked violently, breaking her

peaceful sleep. Groaning, she cracked open an eye, only to meet Ulrieg's fiery red ones. "What is it? I was finally getting some deep sleep, and it even came with a good dream."

Ulrieg's face distorted. *Please don't tell me it involved a particular charming blue-haired male with a fox familiar.*

She pulled her pillow from under her head and whacked the dragon with it. "Don't be ridiculous. Not all my happy thoughts are about Kaine." She yanked her pillow back, only to hear the fibers ripping on his horns. She sighed. "I guess I didn't think that through." His horns were covered with feathers. "I'll have to find a new one or fix it somehow." She squinted at the dragon. "What time is it anyway?"

Ulrieg shrugged. *I don't read time, but judging by the moon, I'm pretty sure it's the middle of the night.*

Samara groaned. "That's nowhere near enough sleep." She flopped back onto her pillow, releasing a shower of white feathers. "So why did you wake me?"

I found this. Between his talons was a small ornament attached to a string.

Samara frowned. "That's nice. But it still doesn't warrant you waking me."

The dragon let out a puff of steam. *Have a closer look. I think you're missing the importance.*

Sighing, Samara grabbed it and held it under the torch burning on the wall. She turned it until she spotted an embossed symbol. She moved it closer to her eyes and sat up, pulling the torch from the sconce. The ornament was a cylinder shape, and on the end, opposite the attached string, was a raised triangle with soft corners and a five-pointed star in the center.

Her back straightened. "Is this what I think it is?"

He grinned. *I don't know. I think so. We'd have to see if it works.*

"How did you get it?"

I've been thinking about who would be in the inner circle of the Sacred Flame coterie and have a key or emblem to get into the restricted areas. I think all the teachers here would be part of the inner circle, especially Callista. But out of all of them, I thought it would be the hardest to get into her office.

"That's understandable. Plus, she's away at the moment. So where did you get it?"

I thought I'd follow the lovely potions master. She seems like such a lovely elderly lady who would be willing to share, he said sardonically. *I saw the strange-looking trinket sitting next to her cat during the other day's lesson. So while I was invisible, I followed her around yesterday afternoon and watched where she put it. Then when she fell asleep tonight, I snuck in and pinched it.*

Samara crossed her legs, twirling the trinket in her fingers. "That's excellent thinking, Ulrieg."

So come on. We have to get down there before she notices it's missing. I hope because it's the middle of the night, none of the students will be awake and outside, letting their familiars feed. The dragon shifted off her bed and landed on the floor, looking expectantly at her.

Samara swung her legs over the side of the bed then changed out of her pajamas and into her leather pants and tunic before sliding on her long leather boots. She grabbed Gray from his perch for an added explanation as to why they were outside at that time of night, and quietly, she shut the bedroom door behind them.

They snuck down the stairs and through the common room to the foyer. Samara checked every shadow, looking for the slitted eyes of Mystique. It had almost become standard practice for her. Having not yet seen the cat, she could feel the tension growing. It felt like she had missed something, and the thought of Mystique spotting them and following them without her knowing was eating her up inside. *Ulrieg, have you seen Mystique?*

Ulrieg was invisible in case they encountered anyone. *No. I haven't. She'd be away with Callista.*

Of course. Usually, Jet takes her place. I can't see him anywhere either. He doesn't normally hide in the shadows and act like a stalker like Mystique.

I'll keep an eye out.

Thanks. It's making me worried. Maybe we've been lucky, and Jet is curled up in a ball, hibernating for the night.

I wouldn't count on it. But that would be nice for us.

Before scanning the room behind her, Samara checked the shadowed corners near the exit. There was no sign of Jet. *I still can't see him. Are you ready to exit the building?*

I'm right above you.

Samara slowly opened the door, trying not to let the hinges squeal. As soon as it was open, a gust of breeze ruffled her hair as Ulrieg flew past. She stepped through the doorway and carefully closed it behind her. When she spun around to face the forest, she couldn't see anything. *It's so dark.*

Of course. It's a new moon.

I get that, but I can hardly see anything.

Don't worry. I'll be your eyes. It'll also stop others from seeing us if they look out their window. Why don't you encourage Gray to go hunting?

Samara stroked the feathers on the owl's chest,

and Gray climbed onto her fingers, his claws clasping tightly. "That's a good boy. I honestly love having you with me as well. I hope I'll see you soon." She raised her hand into the air then pulled it down rapidly. The owl flew off and headed toward the forest.

After hurrying down the stone steps, she worked her way around the right of the large building. She could still see hardly anything, even after her eyes had adjusted to the lack of light. She had to feel most of her way around the sides of the building and the plants. A puff of breeze passed over her as Ulrieg scanned the area.

I can't see any sign of Jet or anyone else. I think we're in the clear.

Can you see where I'm going?

You're doing great. Just watch that rock...

Samara tripped on the rock and stumbled a few paces. *Thanks. That was a little too late.*

Hehe. My bad. He turned visible, though it was still almost impossible to see him in the moonless night. *We're almost there. I can see the bush just ahead. Your path looks clear of rocks.*

Great! Samara continued, finding it hard not to stumble, as the ground wasn't even.

Ulrieg landed not far ahead of her on the path, making a *thump* and a *whoosh*. *We're here!*

Samara stumbled a few more paces.

Stop! You're just about to walk into me.

She dropped to the ground, feeling around for the small bush.

The hole's just there. Ulrieg breathed a tiny wisp of fire, enough for Samara to catch a glimpse of the spot. She pushed the bush away and felt her way down the hole. Ulrieg followed her and ignited the torch sitting on the wall with his flame.

"Thank you! I was missing being able to see." She grabbed the torch and carried it with her as they made their way through the catacombs, passing several doors to find their way to the one they'd tried to open the other night. A light pulsed underneath the door, and nerves made it difficult for Samara to breathe. She pulled the chain attached to the trinket over her head, removing it from her neck. "Are you ready?"

Ulrieg nodded. *As ready as I'll ever be.*

Samara lifted the trinket to the engraved spot on the door, holding it in line with the lock. She pulled strength from her core and pushed it into the area, jumping when a click sounded from the door. Cautiously, she reached for the doorknob, unsure whether it would be hot from whatever was shining on the other side, and she twisted. The latch clicked open.

CHAPTER FORTY-EIGHT

As Samara slowly pushed the door open, she poked her head through. A bright light filled the room. After the darkness of the passageway, she had to squint against the glow. The light was so bright that she couldn't tell if anyone was in the room. After putting the torch in the sconce outside the door and blinking a few times, she peeked around the door again. She still had to squint, but her eyes had adjusted enough to see.

In the center of the room was a large chasm in the floor. Inside, a large glowing orb pulsated, spinning on its axis. Bright-yellow-and-orange light filled the expansive room, which looked like it used to be the base of a cave before the building was constructed on top.

Samara couldn't see any beings inside and

pushed open the door, Ulrieg following. Cautiously, they neared the large orb, constantly checking for any movement.

What is this place? Ulrieg walked on all fours, his large eyes wide as he surveyed the room.

My guess would be that this is the greater power, the one that Callista answers to. Samara threaded the trinket's necklace over her head. *I had heard it was hidden somewhere close, probably under the building. So this must be it.*

They stood only a few feet away from the orb. Samara started to move closer, only to be stopped abruptly.

Is it behind a barrier?

It appears that way. Samara pushed her palm cautiously forward. The barrier thrummed under her touch. *Oh. That's right! I remember now. It is said that the great evil that ruled the lands captured this power and enclosed it behind an unbreakable barrier. Not even Callista can free it from its enclosure. Although I believe she is trying. She comes down here regularly to converse with it.* She glanced at the trinket hanging from her neck. *I guess all the exclusive members have access to this power, if they all have these gadgets that work like keys.*

Slowly, they circled the orb, confident that no one was in the large room.

Ulrieg sat in front of the orb and tilted his head

to one side. *This explains the light under the door and the strange feeling I was getting from this room, but it doesn't explain the weird noises we heard the other night, unless it makes sounds occasionally. To me, it looks like it would be almost silent.*

Samara pursed her lips. *I don't know whether Callista converses with it with words, she is sent images, or she senses what it wants.* She pulled her eyes away from the overpowering orb and observed the walls, noticing several doorways lining the sides. *Have you seen all those?* She indicated with her head.

Ulrieg glanced up, his jaw slackening as he surveyed the entrances. *Do you suppose they're all access doors to this room, or are they rooms coming off this one?*

Rubbing her arm, Samara said, *I don't know. We should have a look while we're here.*

They studied the strange pulsating orb once more then headed to the doors on the left side of the room. Samara peeked through the first door to find an empty gurney in the middle of the room. Benches with medical utensils lined the walls. Her brow furrowed. She hadn't heard of a medical ward below the building. She looked at Ulrieg, only to find a puzzled expression. He scurried along to the next door and peeked in, and Samara hurried to the next one along to find an exact replica of what she'd spotted in the first room.

When she caught up to Ulrieg, they peeked into the room together. The room was precisely the same. *This is weird. These look like medical rooms, yet I've never heard of them, nor are there any patients in them. Maybe the orb has healing qualities that surpass those of the senior sorceresses and sorcerers.*

Ulrieg spread his wings wide. *I have no idea. It's your coterie. There's still something about this place that gives me the creeps.*

We'd better check them all just to be sure. Samara rubbed at her arm nervously.

They pressed on to the next doorway and peeked around the corner. It was the same.

How many rooms are there?

Samara counted the rooms quickly. *There are twenty.* She frowned. *Precisely the same number as the current student population.*

Curious! His horns bunching together made him look angrier.

They were about to peek into the next one when a groan sounded from the opposite side of the room. They glanced at each other, their eyes wide with concern.

Is that the sound we heard the other night? Samara asked.

I believe so. We should go have a look.

Together, they followed the noise, bypassing the other openings. When they reached the other side of the room, Ulrieg turned invisible, and Samara put her back to the wall and peered around the edge.

The small cave was dark. Only the light from the orb shone into the room. An extinguished torch hung on the wall over a bench top laden with surgical tools. In the center, once again, was a gurney, but something lay on it. The thing shifted and groaned, and its four legs were tied to the gurney. It took a while for Samara's eyes to adjust to the lack of light.

Wingless flight! No! Ulrieg had never sounded so distraught. *No!*

What's wrong? Samara moved farther into the room.

It's Byzarid. My cousin. What have they done to you? Ulrieg turned visible and approached the table.

Samara quickened her footsteps and met him at the bench, and he climbed up her back. She peered down at the figure lying on the table, her eyes slowly adjusting to the minimal light. Before them was a dragon not much bigger than Ulrieg. His scales looked brown, and on several locations on his body were deep open cuts that looked infected.

What have they done to him? He looks terrible! We were wondering where he'd gone.

The pain in Ulrieg's voice almost broke Samara's heart. She set to work injecting healing magic into Byzarid, although she still hadn't mastered healing infected wounds. She didn't know if she could help much. He looked half-dead.

Is this what these rooms are for? To torture and sacrifice dragons to this magical orb? Ulrieg pulled his eyes away from his cousin long enough to peer out at the other rooms. *I told you this coterie was evil.*

Samara was shocked. Not only was a dragon underneath the coterie's building, but he had been defiled.

I bet it's exactly as I've been telling you. Callista has to be behind this. Ulrieg gritted his teeth.

I know you're upset, and you have every right to be, but Callista is away, remember? This could be the work of anyone with access to the inner circle.

Or it could be all of them.

Samara thought of Devi and how open and friendly she always was and shook her head. *I don't think all of them would be involved. Maybe the inner circle has an even tighter inner circle. Or perhaps it's just one person who wants to torture dragons or possibly any other magical being. Maybe Callista doesn't know about this. She can't be everywhere at the same time. As powerful as she is, she can't know everything that's going on around her.*

I'm still not convinced.

Samara injected more healing power into Byzarid and grunted. *This doesn't seem to be working. I don't know what else to do.*

Can we unchain him and carry him out of here? Maybe we can take him back to where the other dragons are, and they will know what to do.

I don't know if I'll be able to leave the coterie for an unauthorized field trip. It's not like I can say I'm just going to help my dragon. Samara studied the chains securing Byzarid's legs. They were made of solid metal. *I guess the first step is to get him out of here to see if we can give him a chance to survive. Maybe if he is looked after and fed well, he might be able to fight the infections.*

All right. Let's do that. Get the chains off him, and I'll help you get him out of here. Ulrieg jumped to the end of the gurney to give Samara freedom to move and work on the locks.

A door clicked shut somewhere nearby.

Someone's here. We have to go. Ulrieg turned invisible. *Come on.*

But what about your cousin? Samara had trouble pulling her eyes away from the injured dragon. *We can't just leave him here.*

I don't want to. Trust me! But we can't be caught down here. If we are, I'll end up like Byzarid, and you'll be kicked out of the coterie. Then we wouldn't be any use to him or any other dragon or creature that might be captured down here. Ulrieg's talons clicked on the stone floor. *Come on! At least I'm invisible, but you need to hide.*

Samara injected a quick bolt of healing magic into Byzarid. *We'll be back. Hang on,* she said before bolting out of the small cave's entry and hurrying to the back door, making sure the walls mostly hid her.

She pulled the door behind her until only a sliver of the main room could be seen. *Are you here, Ulrieg?*

Yes. I'm right underneath you.

Samara peeked through the opening and into the large cave. A cloaked figure walked in, their footsteps quick and purposeful. Samara squinted, trying to see the face under the large hood as the person crossed the room, heading straight for the small cave containing Byzarid. The room brightened as though the torch on the wall had been lit, and within a few moments, cries of pain came from the dragon.

They must be torturing him again, Ulrieg growled.

Another cry of pain echoed.

I can't listen to this. There's only one of them. I'm not letting a dragon or any creature be harmed this way. Samara pushed the door wider, ready to rescue Byzarid.

Wait! Ulrieg cried. He grabbed Samara's arm and yanked her back, pulling the door mostly shut behind her.

What? I can't leave him there.

And I understand. I want him rescued also, but more footsteps are coming down the passage from the building.

Samara peeked through the gap in the doorway. Just as Ulrieg had said, another figure entered, cloaked from head to toe, making it impossible to see their face as they joined the other hooded figure in Byzarid's room.

I hate to say this, but we'll have to come back another day. You might have a chance against one person in your coterie, but you won't against two possible senior members. We're going to have to get to the bottom of this. After we rescue Byzarid, we'll have to investigate and see if it's all your coterie or just a couple of extremists working on their own. Ulrieg slowly pulled the door closed, and Samara turned the handle to prevent it from betraying them with a click.

Silently and with heavy hearts, they returned to their room.

ACKNOWLEDGMENTS

I'm touched by the enormous support I have received from my immediate family. My husband has been a helpful first reader and, at times, been an excellent motivator, with hints of ideas to help me through the blanks. The support from my three sons has also been overwhelming. They have spent years putting up with my head in the clouds, thinking about the next plot twist or story, along with many hours spent working on my books and keeping in touch with my readers.

A huge thank you to my editor, Susie D., for her editing and writing tips, and my proofreader, Caroline E., for picking up the things we missed.

Thank you to all of my readers who have loved my work, and continue to read my stories.

BOOKS BY KATRINA COPE

Pre-Teen Books

The Sanctum Series

JAYDEN'S CYBERMOUNTAIN

SCARLET'S ESCAPE

TAYLOR'S PLIGHT

ERIC & THE BLACK AXES

ADRIANNA'S SURGE

~~~~~

Young Adult Urban Fantasy

Afterlife Series

FLEDGLING

THE TAKING

ANGELIC RETRIBUTION

DIVIDED PATHS

TRUTH HUNTER

Afterlife Novelette

THE GATEKEEPER

~~~~~

Young Adult Urban Paranormal Fantasy

Supernatural Evolvement Series

(Associated with the Afterlife Series)

WITCH'S LEGACY (Prequel)

AALIYAH

~~~~~

Young Adult Norse Mythology Fantasy

Valkyrie Academy Dragon Alliance

MARKED (Prequel)

CHOSEN

VANISHED

SCORNED

INFLICTED

EMPOWERED

AMBUSHED

WARNED

ABDUCTED

BESIEGED

DECEIVED

Thor's Dragon Rider

SAFEGUARD

PURSUIT

ENTRAPMENT

HOODWINKED

RELINQUISHED

SHROUDED

ASSIGNED

ACCOSTED

DESTRUCTION

~~~~~

Young Adult Epic Fantasy

Dragoria: the Lost Dragon Realm

DRAGON MOON

DRAGON HEART

Get updates & notifications of giveaways

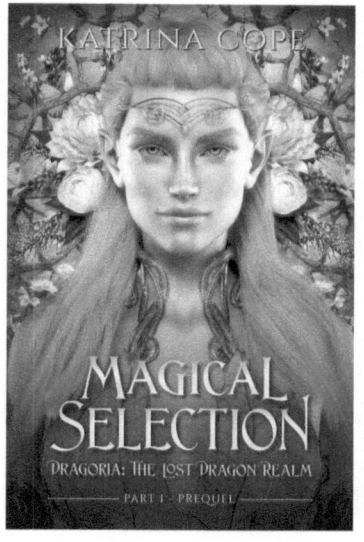

Would you like a FREE ebook?

Click here to get started: FREE copy of Magical Selection

Through this link you can sign up for my newsletter and receive a FREE copy of Magical Selection plus updates about my fantasy books, sales and notification of giveaways.

ABOUT THE AUTHOR

Katrina is an author of several books in epic fantasy, young-adult fantasy, and a middle-grade sci-fi thriller series.

Her series include:

Dragoria: The Lost Dragon Realm - Coming of Age Epic fantasy

Valkyrie Academy Dragon Alliance - YA High fantasy

Thor's Dragon Rider - YA High fantasy (Spin-off of Valkyrie Academy Dragon Alliance but can be read separately)

The Afterlife - YA fantasy (contemporary)

The Sanctum Series - Middle-grade Sci-fi thriller

She often talks to creatures of all kinds and has a passion for animals, nature, and travel. She lives in Queensland, Australia, with her husband and has survived teaching her three children how to drive.

Katrina's online home is at www.katrinacopebooks.com

You can connect with Katrina on:

tiktok.com/@katrinacopebooks

facebook.com/Author.Katrina.Cope

instagram.com/katrina_cope_author

bookbub.com/profile/katrina-cope

twitter.com/Katrina_R_Cope

pinterest.com/katrinacope56